Call of the Owl Woman

Call of the Owl Woman

A Novel of Ancient Peru

k. m. huber

SPARKPRESS

Copyright © 2025 k.m. huber

All rights reserved. No part of this publication may be reproduced, distributed, or transmitted in any form or by any means, including photocopying, recording, digital scanning, or other electronic or mechanical methods, without the prior written permission of the publisher, except in the case of brief quotations embodied in critical reviews and certain other noncommercial uses permitted by copyright law. For permission requests, please address SparkPress.

Published by SparkPress, a BookSparks imprint,
A division of SparkPoint Studio, LLC
Phoenix, Arizona, USA, 85007
www.gosparkpress.com

Published 2025
Printed in the United States of America
Print ISBN: 978-1-68463-304-3
E-ISBN: 978-1-68463-305-0
Library of Congress Control Number: 2025901882

Interior design and typeset by Katherine Lloyd, The DESK
Cover art and map by Cristina Stanojevich

All company and/or product names may be trade names, logos, trademarks, and/or registered trademarks and are the property of their respective owners.

This is a work of fiction. Names, characters, places, and incidents either are the product of the author's imagination or are used fictitiously. Any resemblance to actual persons, living or dead, is entirely coincidental.

NO AI TRAINING: Without in any way limiting the author's [and publisher's] exclusive rights under copyright, any use of this publication to "train" generative artificial intelligence (AI) technologies to generate text is expressly prohibited. The author reserves all rights to license uses of this work for generative AI training and development of machine learning language models.

for Milo
my heart's companion
with whom life
is always an adventure

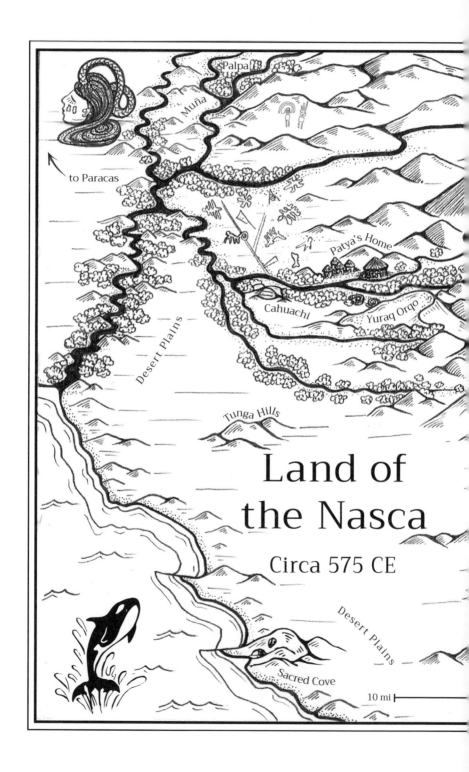

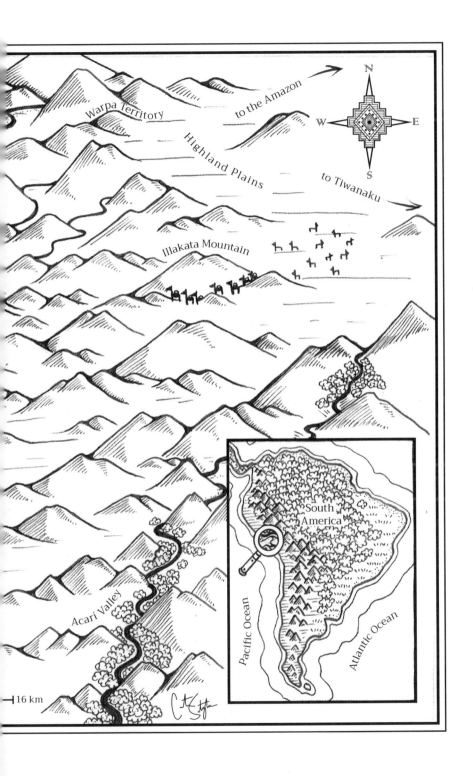

Intro

The desert coast of South America is veined with rivers that carry fresh water from the inland Andes mountains westward into the Pacific Ocean. For almost a millennium, the Nasca people flourished in the narrow coastal valleys of what is now southern Peru by tapping deep underground waters and engineering tunnels and canals to feed their farmlands. The Nasca also used the arid plains as a giant canvas to create art and ritual in the vast, empty landscapes. The adobe ceremonial complex of Cahuachi rivaled the Egyptian pyramids, and they produced textiles and ceramics still enviable today. The Nasca overcame drought after drought, earthquake after earthquake, ever resilient and resourceful, until the end of the sixth century, when their world began to come apart. Patya's story begins in the midst of the worst drought the Nasca have ever faced.

Cast of Characters

Patya's Family

Patya: fifteen-year-old Nasca girl

Tachico: Patya's seven-year-old brother

Ecco: Patya's older brother (17), a ceramicist

Otocco: Patya's oldest brother (19), assistant to Yakuwayri

Yakuwayri: Patya's father, water-guardian

Keyka: Patya's mother, healer, wife of Yakuwayri

Kuyllay: a healer, Patya's grandmother (paya), Keyka's mother

Chochi: Kuyllay's pet monkey

Weq'o: Patya's uncle, Yakuwayri's brother

Uchu: Patya's cousin

Aru: Uchu's son, hurt in an earthquake

Hukato: Keyka's cousin

Umasapa: Patya's cousin (literally "big head")

Faruka's Family

Faruka: Patya's best friend, Ecco's wife-to-be

Farina: Faruka's younger sister

Pillku: Faruka's paternal uncle; daughters Quri and Nikta are Keyka's apprentices

Yantu: Faruka's cousin, drummer from Palpa

Temple-Keepers, Shamans, and Sorcerers

Achiq: Cahuachi priest

Tikati: temple priest, an old friend of Paya Kuyllay's

Mishka: the Oracle at Cahuachi

Amaruyu: the oldest healer/shaman near Cahuachi; "he who speaks with Amaru"

Waqar: Amaruyu's assistant, "given" to the temple-keepers by her husband

Ceetu: Palpa's main shaman

Others

Terzhic: Nasca farmer, influential elder in the ayllu

Nuqta: Terzhic's wife

Chanki: Terzhic's second son

Pikaq: peddler, collector from Acari

Jorat: caravanner from Condor's Perch

Waru: Warpa hunter/settler from mountains of Huamanga/ Ayacucho, brother of Kantu

Kantu: brother of Waru, unable to stop the hunters from assaulting Patya

Mochico: Moche warrior/sailor from the northern coast

Unay: the community's keeper of seeds

Takiri: a choreographer for ceremonial dances in Patya's community

Tawo: a drummer

Wiksa: Patya's favorite dog

chapter 1

LOSS

Late sixth century, Nasca Valley, Atacama Desert, western coast of South America

Even from here, I can see Achiq striding up our valley. The torches cast shadows off his staff with its feathers and foxtails swaying. Light glistens across his golden mask as drums begin to echo up and down the valley, letting everyone know the priests are coming. Coming to claim my grandmother's head.

Leaving the outside lamps dark, I slip back into the house and place an extra lamp next to my mother. "They are in the valley," I say. She doesn't look up, just continues preparing my grandmother, my *paya* Kuyllay, for burial. She nods to the basket of bracelets.

I pick out Kuyllay's favorites and arrange them on her arm. I linger over the orca tattoo on her wrist. It's identical to mine, except that Kuyllay's orca is as dry and lifeless as our riverbeds, while mine glistens with sweat and quivers with anger. The shaking travels to my lips and unclenches my jaw. "How can you let them do this?" I blurt out. "She belongs here!"

Mother still says nothing.

CALL OF THE OWL WOMAN

"Kuyllay died last night," I remind her. "It's a full day's walk to the temple, yet their runner was here before midday. How did they find out so fast?"

Mother brushes a line of red cinnabar powder across Kuyllay's forehead. When she finally speaks, all she says is, "I don't know, Patya. I don't know."

The drums begin a slow dirge. Each beat deepens the hole in my heart. *Kuyllay is gone. Kuyllay is gone. Kuyllay is gone.* The great heart at the center of my days is gone. I have lost the hands that healed me when I was hurt, fixed me when I was broken, soothed me when I was sad. My teacher has left me before I have learned all she had to teach. My Kuyllay, my paya, more mother to me than Keyka who bore me. It was Kuyllay who marked me from birth, who forbade them from binding my head. Who promised I would be glad of it one day. But that day has not come, and Kuyllay is gone.

"We haven't much time," my mother says, her voice strangely vacant.

I don't like her eerie calm. I want to shake her. Wake her. Make her see.

"Our ancestor Tuku Warmi's *umanqa* has been with our family for more generations than we can count," I say, pointing to the altar behind her. Smoke rises from a bowl there, filling the room with the heavy, otherworldly sweetness of *wanqor* wood. The tattoos on Tuku Warmi's leathered skin are still vivid. Her long hair coils around her head, propping it up as if to watch us. I don't want to think about how she became an umanqa, about how Kuyllay's head, too, will become an umanqa. How they will remove Kuyllay's skin to clean the skull and how they will pull it tight again over the empty bone and stuff in bits of cotton to round out her cheeks. I flinch at the thought of the long thorns piercing her eyelids and mouth to hold them shut. I have always revered Tuku Warmi's umanqa and thought her beautiful, but I

Loss

never knew her living, breathing face. It is another thing to see my beloved paya now and know what they plan to do. I turn back to my mother.

"If Paya Kuyllay's head is to become an umanqa, it should stay here with her family, not the priests!" I continue. "Do you really believe it is the will of the gods that her head go to the temple?"

Mother won't look at me. I can't stop myself. "It's more like the will of Achiq!"

Her lips tighten. She smooths another red streak across each of Kuyllay's cheeks then finally looks up, her face blank, her voice full of sadness. "We've already talked about this, Patya. Kuyllay does not belong to us alone. She may be my mother, she may be grandmother to you and your brothers, but she is beloved all along our coast and far beyond the mountains. If she can still help the priests do medicine work even in death, she would want that." She sighs as she arranges Kuyllay's hair. "I just never thought this time would come so soon."

"And I did not think the priests would come so soon. Achiq," I snap back, spitting his name out like the poison he is. "You know he feeds on power. Now he wants hers too."

"Patya!" Mother holds up her hand. "Enough! Do not say things that the winds could carry to the wrong ears. It cannot be changed."

I glare at her. Why does she refuse to see evil that is so obvious to me? She locks eyes with me, but she has blocked me out. The silence between us fills with the ominous pulse of drums, ever closer. They throb inside me. *Kuyllay is gone. Kuyllay is gone. Kuyllay is gone.*

Mother gentles her voice. "This has always been a possibility, Patya—a way to bring hope to our people after her death. Like great healers before her, like our ancestor Tuku Warmi. She accepted the will of the elders, as you must. For the good of our people, Patya. No questions, no complaints. We must pray

CALL OF THE OWL WOMAN

that Kuyllay's voice from the beyond can sing our rivers back to us."

I bow my head, but I'm not giving up. Yes, I will pray to bring the waters back, but I know Achiq is not the one who can do that, even with Kuyllay's help. Yes, I will pray. If I can't stop Achiq from taking Kuyllay's head, then I will pray to find a way to get it back.

The drums ebb and flow as the procession zigzags its way up the steep hill to our home. Even in the blur of cleansings and floral waters, incense, and prayers, I haven't stopped searching for an explanation. How could she die with no warning? How could her spirit leave so suddenly? My mind can't stop hunting for clues while I rub oils into Kuyllay's skin, braid her hair, choose the ceremonial cloths, gather offerings for her tomb. I review our morning together collecting medicinal plants, Tachico tagging along, full of his usual mischief, and Chochi, the equally mischievous monkey, riding on his shoulder. The afternoon hanging herbs to dry. Patients stopping by for salves and tonics. The evening meal. The usual night routine.

Kuyllay was on her sleeping mat, me on the floor next to her, painting a pot, and Chochi was curled up between us. Kuyllay complimented each creature that took shape under my brush. Her voice grew soft as she drifted into sleep: " . . . don't forget the shape-shifter." There was a late-night chill when I finally finished painting her favorite shape-shifter with Orca's fins, Jaguar's face, and Great Owl's wings. I remember stepping out to greet the moon, full and glorious, before going back in to cover her with an extra blanket.

I remember the impossibly cold skin when I bent to kiss her cheek.

I don't remember crying out, but that's when Mother leapt to her side. Even Mother, trained by Kuyllay herself, could not bring back the breath that had left my paya's body.

I begged her spirit to return. But the wind carried Kuyllay's

Loss

voice farther and farther away until only echoes remained. Echoes of the lists she had drilled into my memory. *Golden jaguar headdress, three bowls of purple maize, sandals for the rocky paths, knives to cut through haze* . . . That's when I realized that my paya Kuyllay had been preparing me for this since I was small.

She used to joke that preparing for the afterlife was like furnishing a new home. She made me guess what she wanted in her tomb and gave me a treat for each item I guessed right. Her tricks worked. My mind automatically ticked off the list. *Two crocks of hearty chicha beer, three double-spouted jugs, a pot adorned with seabirds, a thick alpaca rug.* She also wanted the usual llama to make her burdens easy to carry and a baby alpaca so wool would be ample. I remember the gleam in her eyes when I would recite, *Two plump and tasty quwis, two black ones for divining, the platter with the monkey in a tree reclining* . . . How could I forget that one? Kuyllay made me promise not to let anyone bury her pet monkey with her. "The platter will be enough reminder," she said. "Chochi is meant to finish out his life here." But I haven't seen Chochi since last night.

Wind laps at the drape that covers the doorway. A gust of air slithers across my neck. Voices begin to mingle with the wind. My father and brothers are back. Otocco, bossy and impatient as usual, is directing Tachico where to put things. He's the oldest and thinks the rest of us should jump at his command. Tachico doesn't mind the way I do—he just loves to be included by his older brothers. It sounds like Ecco is soothing a nervous llama. Maybe it senses its imminent sacrifice. Ecco's always been good with animals. And with people. He's a couple of years older than me, but he doesn't have Otocco's mean streak.

I am reluctant to leave Kuyllay's side, but I go to greet my father. He looks haggard as he lays his hand on my shoulder, gives me a reassuring squeeze, and then goes inside to talk to Mother. The lamps outside are lit now. All that much easier for the priests

CALL OF THE OWL WOMAN

to find their way. I lean over the low wall that circles our terrace and corral. The procession is halfway up the hill. Tachico joins me, watching the flames of their torches dance with the shadows. "Are they really going to take her head?" he whispers.

I put my arm around my sweet little brother. Somehow, he makes it easier to breathe. "Come on," I tell him, "let's say goodbye before they get here." Ecco joins us as we go back inside and kneel next to our grandmother. Her face is calm, as if she's merely asleep.

"May you be at peace, Paya Kuyllay," Ecco says softly. "May you visit us in our dreams and live in our hearts. May our footsteps on the earth feel the echoes of your passage before us, and wherever we walk, may we honor you by living your teachings and sharing your memory."

"Let it be so," I say.

Otocco is whispering with our parents in the corner. The only words I catch are "they shouldn't watch." And then drums are on top of us. Father goes out to meet the priests, but Mother stands next to our paya, straight and proud.

Achiq's form fills the doorway completely. He overwhelms our house the moment he steps in, wearing his full regalia—a fox skull headdress adorned with an excess of foxtails, a cloak of fine furs, and three umanqas on his belt. With his arms spread wide and his staff bumping the roof, I have to squeeze against my paya to let him go by. As he parades past me, I recognize one of the umanqas on his belt—the head of the priest in charge before Achiq. The one who died mysteriously.

My father follows behind Achiq, then takes his place beside Mother. Otocco and Ecco bow and retreat outside to watch from the door. Otocco gestures for me to leave also, but I ignore him and pull Tachico close to me. The other priests stay outside, waiting to be summoned. Their torches light a circle within the low stone walls.

Achiq's voice booms, "As the solstice approaches and Tayta

Loss

Inti pauses his journey through the sky, it is auspicious that our revered healer, Kuyllay, shall be honored in the custom of our ancient traditions. From the other side of death she shall continue to serve the sacred and to serve our people. We bear witness to this sacred ritual that consecrates the head of Kuyllay of Nasca, Clan of the Orca, Lineage of Paracas Medicine Women. Tonight her mortal flesh and bone shall be transformed into an everlasting umanqa." He pauses for effect. Another priest enters with a tray that he places beneath Kuyllay's neck. I almost don't recognize the haggard face, but when I notice the sadness in his eyes, I realize it is Tikati, an old friend of Paya Kuyllay's.

Achiq raises the ceremonial knife.

I can't help myself. I lunge toward Achiq, but something yanks me backward out into the corral. Otocco has a hold of my arm. "Don't be crazy," he says into my ear. "You'll get us all into trouble." I shake him off and try to go back in, but he drags me to the end of the corral.

"You don't care, do you?" I cry.

Otocco looks at me like I'm a kid having a tantrum. "You have to think about others, Patya. It's not just about you."

I hate it when he acts superior. How could he have any idea? He's never spent time with Kuyllay the way I have. His life won't be that different because she's not here. He doesn't mind the idea of Achiq using her umanqa to impress people. Might even like the status it gives him.

"It's about keeping the peace," he says. "And giving people hope."

"Go ahead, tell yourself that," I reply. *Our parents might believe that*, I want to say, *but all you really care about is your reputation.* I look to Ecco for support, but he disappoints me.

"He's right, you know," Ecco says.

Tachico is also regarding me somberly, his eyes glistening with tears. There is no sign of the impish little brother I'm used to. "You're not the only one who loves her," he says.

Call of the Owl Woman

It's like a punch in the stomach. Tachico, the one who always looks up to me, is looking at me like I've done something wrong. I realize I haven't even noticed him since last night. The boy has only seen seven sun cycles, but today he seems more grown-up than me with my fifteen. He's in as much pain as I am, but I am the one who is sinking into a dark cloud. It swallows me. I don't want to see what they are doing. I don't want to feel it.

It takes two days to get to the ancestral burial grounds of Muña. I do what I am told. Carry what I am told to carry. Recite the prayers. My body goes through the motions, but it's all such a blur that I can't even tell if I am crying. I don't speak to anyone, not even faithful Tachico, who's always beside me.

We fill the tomb with everything Kuyllay wanted and more, including the beautiful ceramic head jar that Ecco made for her mummy bundle. Another reminder that her head is now an umanqa in the hands of Achiq. People come from all over with offerings for Kuyllay's tomb. The rest of my family is proud of all the honors given to Kuyllay. Not me. I can't stand the way Achiq parades her umanqa around everywhere as if she had given him a special blessing. I can't stand all his talk about making sacrifices so that the rains will come back. He wants blood.

I try to shut it all out, and look to the moon for comfort. But even Mama K'illa shrinks away from me, night by night, little by little, until her final sliver disappears, so I wrap myself in the tapestry of stars to wait for her return.

When we finally return to the familiar outline of Yuraq Orqo, I begin to feel present in my body again. In the shadow of that mountain, I am home. The razor's edge of sadness begins to soften and merge into the haunting, mournful drumbeat that pulses in my soul.

chapter 2
Pachamama Speaks

Almost three moons have passed since I last worked in the drying shed. I haven't been back here since bringing the last batch of plants I collected with Paya Kuyllay. The shed is bright with afternoon sun. Flowers and vines hang everywhere—dry, withered, and waiting to be stored. My nose wrinkles as I pull down a batch of pungent leaves and stuff them into a clay jar. I fill another pot with clusters of *muña*, savoring the earthy scent even though it makes my longing worse. I find myself wondering if the burial grounds were named Muña because the plant once grew there in abundance or because of its properties—useful for preserving things, helpful for breathing in thin mountain air, good for digestive problems. So useful that I left several pouchfuls in Kuyllay's burial chamber. She will not lack remedies in the afterlife.

Ay, my beloved paya! How can she be stuck in a desert tomb three valleys away, wrapped in radiant layers of ceremonial cloth, while her umanqa is hostage to fanatics in the temple? *I must find a way to bring her home*, I tell myself, repeating it vigorously as I wrestle a thick root apart and break it roughly into pieces.

Mother's voice interrupts from the door. "Patya, don't bruise them."

Mother is busier than ever now that Kuyllay is gone. More patients. Always in a hurry. She deposits a basket of herbs beside me and places a hand on my shoulder. "Be careful not to let your feelings bleed into the plants," she says. "You don't want to damage their potency." As she leaves, she glances back. "I'll send Tachico up to help."

I hide my smile. She knows I would rather be painting pots than filling them with herbs. I hate trying to keep up with the medicine plants, but at least Tachico will make it fun. Watching after my little brother and keeping him out of trouble is still my favorite chore. His company will be welcome in this dusty shed.

I am finishing with the fever bark when the ground begins to tremble. Herbs start swinging; ceramics clatter. I freeze, waiting to see if another tremor will follow. The floor shudders slightly, then stops. I let my breath out and continue working. I have gotten used to the earth's stirrings and try not to worry unless it gets worse. Pachamama may be awakening, but it's probably just a sleepy stretch.

My mother suddenly rushes in, her face flushed. She grabs me and tugs. "Get out!" Tachico is standing outside at a distance, pale and nervous, his wide eyes half hidden behind his disheveled hair. The herbs are still swaying.

"But Mother, it's over." I shrug her off to finish putting the last of the bark in its pot.

"If we are lucky!" she says.

"You used to tell us it was just Pachamama waking from a nap," I protest as she tries to pull me out the door. "Or shaking her skirts. Remember?"

Once we are outside, she takes my shoulders and holds me, her eyes sharp and demanding as she looks into mine. "Some-times it is. But that doesn't mean we shouldn't be careful. When

Pachamama Speaks

Pachamama shook those skirts once, they buried my brother. If a beam falls down, Patya, I don't want you under it." She cups my face in her hand. "Promise me you won't wait next time." Tachico is peering up from behind her, his worried face fixed on mine. "Promise me!" she demands.

"Yes, Mother," I reply.

Tachico wraps himself around my legs in relief.

As we approach the house, we hear canal-keepers climbing the hill, with urgency in their voices as they call out for our father, "Yakuwayri, Water-Guardian!" Father stands tall and calm with Otocco beside him. They welcome one after another and listen to their reports. Old channels, already repaired many times, have broken open again. With water so scarce, even the smallest leak can be devastating. The tremor had not been as benign as I thought.

Tachico lets go of my hand and runs to Father. "Can I help, please? Can I help?"

Father nods at me as he pats Tachico's head and then pushes him back toward me. I recognize the look. *Keep Tachico from getting underfoot. We have work to do.*

So Tachico and I climb the rocky slope behind our house until we find our favorite boulder to sit on. We watch dusk fall as people continue to gather below. We've watched such scenes before. Tension fills the air—worry that a bigger quake might be coming. I distract Tachico by telling stories about Mama K'illa the Moon, how she fell in love with Tayta Inti the Sun, how the sky keeps them apart but they speak to each other through dreams, how I once witnessed the flash of their kiss during an eclipse. We sing songs to the moon until we are ready to slide our way back down the hill toward bed. Before we go in, Tachico announces, with all the confidence of his seven years, "I will ask Mama K'illa for a dream tonight. She will show me where to find more water."

CALL OF THE OWL WOMAN

⬧ ✦ ⬧

The next morning, Tachico wakes me up, all excited. "I dreamed about the old well near Uncle Weq'o's farm!" he tells me. "I saw a snake go into the opening. It slithered in as dry as the desert, but it came back out all wet and muddy."

"I remember that well. It stopped flowing before you were even born," I say.

"I know! Father said an earthquake opened a crack underground that swallowed all its waters."

"I was about your age then. I remember them digging for weeks and never finding another access."

"Well, I think this tremor shifted things again." Tachico smiles, eager to get going.

Tachico has a gift. He has found water before. Nothing big, but in times like these, even a trickle means a lot. Like last year, when the spring dried up by where the caravans usually camp. Tachico found a branch to his liking, made himself a divining rod, wandered around a bit, sort of trancelike, and then moved some rocks and found another spring! No one had suspected it was there just beneath the surface. I don't know how he does it. It's like the water calls him. But it's unpredictable. Water has its own spirit and its own time, but when it does call him, it is usually around a full moon.

While the work groups go off to take care of repairs up the valley, Tachico and I gather our supplies and set out in the opposite direction, toward the lower valley. He is in great spirits, scampering down the hill with sure steps. We reach the dusty riverbed and then work our way down the valley. "Remember the old digging song?" he asks, but doesn't wait for my answer. He just starts singing, "*In the rocks below, in the hills above / seek cracks and veins / to find earth's blood. / Some will close, some open wide. / The best of them / are deep inside.*" He grins at me. "We just need to find the right crack."

Pachamama Speaks

I laugh. "Some look for silver and gold. We look for cracks."

"And we will surely find a good one!" he says, then stops and turns to me, suddenly serious. "Patya, you do know that water is more useful than silver or gold."

"Of course, Tachico. Anyone who has ever been thirsty knows that very well."

We have stopped right where we need to turn. We follow the scraggly line of *guarango* trees toward the valley walls that border the once-productive cotton field. Now the area is nothing but packed earth littered with rocks. Not only has the water disappeared, but the rich soil that once produced plentiful harvests was washed away in a *huaico* from the highlands. The deadly combination of flash flood, rocks, and mudslide swept away the harvest and left the field useless, but we still come here every year to gather guarango pods from the trees that survived.

The well here is one of the first *puquios* our ancestors engineered to reach the underground waters. Close to the steep hillside at the end of the field, the stone-lined path that spirals into the earth is narrower and steeper than most. I pick my way carefully, testing the ground with each step, but Tachico dances his way down, intoning a water song to the beat of his feet. He continues the song while he waits for me at the bottom. "*Yakuta mañamuy, yakuta mañamuy, taquiricuspa mañamuy, taquiricuspa mañamuy.*" Asking we come, asking for water, asking we sing, singing we ask. The words vibrate in the empty well.

When I get to the bottom, I add my own prayer to Pachamama. "Have mercy on our people and our thirsty fields. You have seen us through hard times before, shown us the way to your waters, and once blessed us with abundant crops and generous game. Now these lands have grown so dry that the deer have gone, the guanaco are scarce, and even the fox cries for mercy. Please guide us, your children. Show us the way—"

"Amen!" Tachico interjects, eager to get going.

CALL OF THE OWL WOMAN

"Let me finish." I shush him and continue, "We ask permission for Tachico's journey into your womb, we ask your blessing, that you may show him where to find your life-giving waters."

He waits for my nod, then touches the wall of the puquio and says, "Amen. May it be so."

I get the safety rope ready while Tachico peers into the tunnel opening. Suddenly, I am not so sure that this is such a good idea. I wish I felt as confident as he does. He waits impatiently for me to tie the rope around his waist, then climbs down the stone wall to the level of the tunnel. I stand at the end of the path, my feet level with the top of the tunnel, Tachico's head level with my knees. I light a small torch from my coal pot and pass it to him. He ducks down and crawls into the opening. I let the rope out slowly, feeling more nervous with each length that unwinds. How did I ever agree to do this? Mother would be furious.

Tachico has no fear. He is short enough to walk upright through some of the bigger tunnels, thin enough to squeeze through narrow sections, and young enough to ignore the dangers. Each moment he is underground, my heart clenches a little more. I won't feel right until he is out of there and back aboveground. But it isn't just Tachico that worries me. I glance around to make sure we are still alone, but we are below ground level, so I can't see the land around us. The poison darts hidden under my tunic give me some comfort, but I am still uneasy. I do not want anyone to take me by surprise, not ever again.

As the rope uncoils into the darkness of the tunnel, I watch a pair of birds peck at the ground nearby. At least that's usually a good sign that the ground will not be shaking soon. After a bit, the rope goes slack. He has stopped advancing. I lean my head down and shout into the opening. My voice echoes back. "Tachico!" I tug at the line but get no response. I tug again. "Tachico!" Nothing. I take a deep breath. Try to tame my fear for Tachico so deep under the earth. Tame the worry for myself. I

14

touch my darts, just to make sure they are there, and force myself to breathe the way Kuyllay taught me. I inhale the fear, taste it, and exhale it, cleansed of its poison. I inhale the dark images that rise from the shadowed places of my mind. I let them rest in my breath, conjuring her presence, her compassion, her love, and exhale those images, knowing that no arms are holding me down now. It is only the shadow of memory. Shadows that cannot hurt me.

Something else tugs at my attention. I tell myself again to breathe. A garbled sound comes from deep within the earth. Another tug. My mind clears when I realize it is a triple tug on the rope—Tachico's code for more line.

I yank back with a firm "no." I do not want Tachico going any farther.

He tugs again, three quick, insistent tugs. A pause. Then three more. Reluctantly, I relent, let out a little more line, then wait. And worry some more. I give the rope another sharp tug. It jerks in reply, then goes slack. Thank the moon he is on his way back! I tie a piece of red yarn to the rope to mark the distance and then begin reeling it in, thanking Pachamama for tolerating our intrusion, grateful that Tachico is coming closer with each loop around my forearm. "If we have offended you, please forgive us," I pray, "and let the waters flow again."

Tachico's head emerges first, his dark eyes gleaming and toothy grin shining through the dirt on his face. "I know where it's blocked!" I put the rope aside and lie on my stomach to reach down to take the torch from him. He passes it to me, then stretches his hand for me to help him climb back up.

Suddenly, the ground jolts. Just as I grab hold of Tachico's hand, the lintel above the opening gives way. The air fills with dust. Terrified, I pull with all my strength. Rocks clatter and tumble. I lose sight of him but tighten my grip on his hand. I manage to get my other hand around his wrist. While the earth caves in

CALL OF THE OWL WOMAN

around us, I pull hard and pray. Everything stops—breath, sound, time—as I struggle to keep my grip in the rubble. My arms tremble, my muscles straining in desperation. I summon a last burst of energy and twist myself backward, dragging his weight with me. In a sudden lurch, Tachico lands at my side.

Gasping for breath, my heart racing, I rub the dirt from my eyes and try to see Tachico through the dusty haze. The ground becomes still again. As the dust begins to settle, I can make out his scratched face and a muddy red stream flowing down his shoulder. "You're bleeding!"

Tachico glances down, but he barely flinches. "Blood," he says matter-of-factly, "a gift for Pachamama. I owe it to her. Don't worry, I'm okay."

Once we get back to the surface, I fuss at his wound. "You'll survive," I say, "but hold still so I can get the gravel out from under this flap of skin." He winces, then lets me check the other side. "Oh, Tachico, look at the rest of you! You'll be so purple tomorrow." I am already dreading Mother's reaction.

"It was worth it," he says. "I told you there was something here!" He pats the ground. "I reached a bend blocked by rocks, but Patya, I could smell water. I just kept pulling the rocks away. Then I found it, a break in the earth! I could hear the water below. It's deep, but I know we can get to it. Pachamama wants us to have it."

I just stare at him, not sure whether to laugh or cry. I finally nod and pour some water from my pouch onto the ground with as much ceremony as I can muster. "Beloved Pachamama, thank you for your protection. We celebrate the water in your veins. May its abundance bless us." I cup my palms together, blow my prayers into them, and then blow my thanks to the earth. Tachico repeats my motions with water from his own pouch and then drinks thirstily. We gather our things and start for home.

Pachamama Speaks

"Before the blockage, there was a horrible smell," Tachico says. "Something rotting. I almost vomited . . . There were bones cracking under my knees."

"I'm just glad it didn't end up being *your* bones in there."

"Stinky flesh falling apart . . ."

"Please, no more details." I walk faster.

"Something oozing . . ." Tachico taunts.

"I'm not listening."

"Bugs crawling . . ."

"Tachico, stop!"

By the time we get home, the sky is rolling pink across the hilltops. Our parents receive Tachico's report solemnly. Mother glares at me, but I keep my eyes on the ground.

"Patya," she starts, but I interrupt.

"I know it was dangerous. But Tachico—"

"Is seven years old," she snaps.

"I'm sorry."

Father places his hand on Mother's shoulder. "Keyka, if the gods have honored our son by guiding him, we must be grateful. A few cuts and bruises are little to pay for such a gift. This is a good day. The canal upriver should hold up with our repairs, and Tachico has given us a new task. We will begin tomorrow and pray that we can reach the water he speaks of."

I pray that Tachico is right.

While Mother tends to Tachico, I linger on the terrace, looking out over the valley. I used to sit here with Paya Kuyllay and listen to her stories. She liked to tell how our ancestors chose this place to build their home, above a fold of rock where the Aja River from the north meets the Uchumarca River from the east. "It is auspicious to live near such a place," she would say, "a *tinkuy* where two energies merge. We are also high enough to be safe when heavy rains in the mountains send huaicos crashing through our valley." I find it hard to imagine so much water ever passing through here again, though. Not even a minor flood has threatened since the last river walls were rebuilt.

When I would complain about having to carry water up the hill, Kuyllay would remind me that there was no view as beautiful as ours. From here, high above the riverbanks, we would watch Mama K'illa's nightly journeys across the sky, watch her grow daily from a silver sliver to a bursting fullness, and watch her shrink again until she disappeared. Each morning we would welcome Tayta Inti's golden rays as he rose from behind the white slopes of Yuraq Orqo. We measured our days by his travels across the sky until he reached the sea and dove in, taking the light with him.

A plume of smoke rises from a house on the far hillside, and a condor glides past like the Lord of Winds, spreading his wings to greet the night and disappearing over Yuraq Orqo. I long to be there, at the top. My solo pilgrimage to Yuraq Orqo was supposed to be on the solstice but was postponed after Kuyllay's death. Now I will have to wait until after Ecco's wedding. Kuyllay won't be here to help prepare me, but I am impatient to complete the ritual, not just to take my place in our community but because Yuraq Orqo is more beloved to me than all those distant highland peaks. Next to those great Apus, our sacred mountain may be small, but she is a beautiful mystery surrounded by legends, the manifestation of a goddess. I love the way the sun turns her golden, the way the moon bathes her in silver, the way they are her companions as she is ours, constant and true. I can't help but wonder about something, though . . . Kuyllay called Yuraq Orqo the Giver of Waters and told of how she showed compassion for our ancestors by sending them water when they suffered. Why does she not do so now?

"What are you thinking about?" Mother asks from behind me. She envelopes me in a hug, so she must have forgiven me for my adventure with Tachico. Her hands fold over mine. She sighs and says, "Your hands are long, like your grandmother's."

Mother never seems to tire of pointing that out. I don't know why it bothers me now; it didn't use to. Now it's just another reminder that Kuyllay is gone. I pull away and turn on her, suddenly impatient and irritated. Heat rises to my cheeks. "It's bad enough that Grandmother's body is in Muña," I say, "but how could you let them take her umanqa to Cahuachi? She belongs with us!"

Mother looks disturbed. "I thought we were past that," she says. "The decision was made by the elders. I know you want it to be different, but what we want . . ."

"Is not always what we get," I retort. "I know. I hear it enough. But why do people do things just because it's been done that way before? What if something needs changing?"

"Patya-cha," she says, "you will understand better when you are older."

"Older?" The affectionate "Patya-cha" only annoys me even more. "I am not a little girl. I am old enough to understand that a boy can find water where men do not, that some people are evil and should never be trusted, that there are men who do things for no reason but to pleasure themselves with power. That the worst of them use the gods as an excuse. And you allow it! I am old enough to know that Paya Kuyllay would have preferred to be buried here. Here!"

My words echo against Mother's silence. After a while, so softly that I can barely hear her, she says, "I miss her too, Patya, more than you know." She turns and goes back inside. I want to rage at my mother, but my anger is losing its edge. Of course I've noticed how she will catch herself mid-sentence, about to call to Kuyllay for something. The way she lingers at Kuyllay's sleeping mat, stroking the shawl that still hangs next to it. The way the bed is still there, unchanged. I stare out over the valley. Kuyllay is gone. Anger will not bring her back.

I take a deep breath, close my eyes, and put my hand to my heart. "Mama K'illa," I whisper, "light my way through this darkness." I open my palm to the wind and blow my prayer to the heavens.

When I turn to go back inside, Mother is standing in the doorway with a small lamp. She gestures for me to follow her. Our shadows dance across the wall as she leads me to the back room. "Kuyllay left something for you," she says. She has me sit, then reaches under a pile of furs and fabrics. The bundle she pulls out is wrapped in fine blue cloth. "Go ahead. Open it."

I untie the cord carefully, unfold the delicate layers, and lift out a robe of white feathers. Beneath it is a silver mask with the face of an owl. Something in the air changes. A trembling, a sudden hiss from the lamp, a feeling I can't name. Light ripples across the surface of the mask. It seems to breathe. I am entranced by the shimmering details in the owl's face, the impeccable stitchwork on the robe, the sheen across the feathers that stir at my slightest breath. "It's stunning," I whisper. "I can't imagine anything better for Ecco's wedding." With a costume like this, I can create a dance truly worthy of the ceremony that will unite my brother with my best—and only—friend, Faruka.

Mother places her hand over mine solemnly. "No, Patya. When the caravan gets here, we will get all the feathers you need to make a cape for the wedding dance. What you are holding now is consecrated for high ceremony, for stepping into the spirit world through a sacred, secret dance . . ."

The shadows lean a little closer. Feathers flutter and settle while I take in what Mother is saying. I watch her fingers flutter toward the mask, tracing the lines that shape the eyes, the beak, the embossed texture of feathers. It is a stunning mask. I can't remember seeing anything so beautiful.

"The legacy of our ancestor Tuku Warmi, the Owl Woman," she says in a reverent whisper, "is more than a legend. When the time is right, you will discover the purpose and the power of this gift." She glances up at me. "Kuyllay said that the most difficult part for you will be the wait."

I fold the tunic carefully, place the mask on top, and then arrange the cape, careful not to damage the long shoulder feathers. I rewrap them together in the blue cloth, tie the bundle, and hold it to my pulsing heart. It is heavier than it looks. I close my eyes and breathe in the smell of time, the hint of Kuyllay's ceremonial flower water, the tickle of dust in my nostrils. The moment settles deep into my chest with the next breath. When I open my eyes, Mother's soft brown eyes are watching mine, her forehead smooth and untroubled for the first time in weeks. I bow my head and say, "I can wait."

chapter 3

Caravan

When I get up the next morning, the llamas are already loaded with tools and provisions. Tachico runs back and forth between them, thrilled to be part of the team going to salvage the old puquio. I wave goodbye to him as they leave and finish loading the llama that Mother and I are taking with us to visit her patients. We set out with saddlebags full of herb mixes, ointments, and elixirs. We quickly finish with the nearby families and are halfway across the riverbed when we notice a small group of men coming toward us from the other side. As they get closer, Achiq's strut is unmistakable.

When they are near enough to recognize us, he stops, lifting his chin and planting his staff firmly on the ground as if expecting us to pay him homage. I want to vomit, but Mother nods respectfully. I am glad that at least she does not bow. I try to focus on the ground in front of me, but my eyes travel up Achiq's wooden staff. A carved serpent winds from the bottom upward, its head merging with the top of the cane. Then I see his belt. Two umanqas hang at his side. One of them is Kuyllay's. I want to reach out to her, touch her, but the sudden loudness of his voice startles me into taking a step back.

Caravan

He addresses my mother in a voice that booms as if there were an audience behind us. "I have had reports, Keyka," he says, "that your son has affronted the Great Mother by entering a tunnel without her permission."

Mother bristles. "You are mistaken, Achiq. He entered in answer to her invitation."

He pounds his staff, raising a cloud of dust. "The tremor we all felt was a sign of her displeasure! And you, young woman?" He leans toward me. "Did your grandmother teach you nothing? Pachamama is a jealous mother. Any female entering into the womb of the earth brings bad luck. You have angered her, and all of us shall pay for your mistake until you make it right."

"There is nothing to make right, Achiq," Keyka replies. "No wrong has been done."

I stand as tall as I can, not wanting to give him the satisfaction of intimidating me. "I stayed outside the tunnel," I say, "offering prayers to Pachamama. I never went under the surface."

Achiq's eyes still accuse me. "Pachamama does not tremble for no reason."

Mother places herself in front of me, locking eyes with Achiq. "How dare you accuse my children when you should be giving thanks that they have led us to water!"

Achiq glowers at her and stiffens.

Before he can say anything, I add, "Tachico was very respectful. He gave his blood as an offering."

A low buzz of approval passes through Achiq's companions until Achiq raises his hand to silence them. He gestures for Mother to move aside and tries to step forward, but she stays where she is. "What brings you here now, Achiq?"

He sidesteps my mother and sweeps past her. As he passes me, he hisses, "Do not interfere with the will of the gods, child, or they will demand sacrifices far, far greater." He raises his voice again. "We must obey the will of the gods!"

CALL OF THE OWL WOMAN

His admonished entourage follows, intoning in a single voice, "Obey the will of the gods . . ."

I have to clench my jaw to keep from retorting with something I might regret.

A few days later, I am cheered by the sight of campfires on the horizon. The llama caravan is finally here. I am almost as eager as Tachico to see what the traders have brought this time. I even agreed to go with him to meet the caravan in the hills so he can walk with them the rest of the way, but that means we'll have to leave before dawn. Thankfully, Ecco volunteered to come along as well. It feels safer.

I don't sleep well that night. I'm still wrestling with an intense dream when Tachico starts poking at me to wake up. I fumble to get ready in the dark, making sure that my leather pouch is well secured against my thigh. The darts Kuyllay made for me help make me less nervous. It's not the caravanners I worry about but the stray Warpa hunters that come down from the mountains unexpectedly. I kiss my thumb and touch it to the pouch with a quick blessing, then smooth my tunic over my leg and step outside. "May Mama K'illa keep us safe and Kuyllay be with us," I whisper, raising my eyes to the moon. I unwind my headcloth, then twist my hair into a high knot at the back of my skull, and rewrap the fabric to make my head look long and tapered like other Nasca girls. It's always easier if the roundness of my head is not too obvious.

Tachico paces impatiently. "We'll never get there before sunrise." Ecco hushes Tachico, puts an arm around his shoulder, and pulls him toward the path.

When I sling the water bag over my shoulder, my fingers linger at the side of my neck. My first tattoo. My first orca. I flinch a little, remembering the sharpness of the needles as Paya Kuyllay

Caravan

marked my skin to honor my first sighting, but I am proud to have it. It marks my first experience with our clan's most sacred being, one that still gives me shivers whenever I think about it—seeing her so close, the way she held my eyes. Her immensity did not surprise me as much as what I saw in her eyes. It was like seeing into an ancient soul. The sea is distant now, but as I inhale, I taste a hint of its salty air. I nod to Tachico and start down the hill. "Finally!" he blurts out, trotting beside me. "I bet there are a hundred llamas in this caravan! And jungle fruit, Chochi!" he adds, patting the small head peeking out of his bag. "Aren't you excited?"

"If they even have any," I mumble, wishing I could have slept a little longer. Tachico's merciless enthusiasm can be hard to take so early. The dream he yanked me out of still tugs at me with strange images—sand pouring through the valley like a river racing to the sea. There was a cloaked figure riding the current, standing impossibly calm, astride what looked like a great sea beast—part orca, part jaguar, part bird.

Tachico suddenly races ahead to catch up with Ecco. Chochi chatters as if to hurry me. I'm glad the little monkey is back to his irritating self. "I'm right behind you," I retort.

The bright moon makes it easy to follow the trail. We cross the dry riverbed of the Aja River and walk beside it to where it meets the Uchumarca River. A narrow ribbon of water still meanders at the Uchumarca's center, so thin that even Tachico barely notices stepping over it. We turn east to the steep shortcut up to the ridge. As we gain height, I glance back at the few scattered homes that dot the rocky edges of cracked earth that used to be farmland. There won't be much to trade this year. The wind picks up, so I loosen the gauzy tail of my turban and pull it over my face to keep the sand out of my nose. I chew my special mix of leaves to quiet the ache in my hip and catch up to Ecco and Tachico. We don't slow down until we reach the ridge.

CALL OF THE OWL WOMAN

We scramble up over the last rocky outcropping just as the sun clears the top of Yuraq Orqo. The gently curving dune that covers the mountain's peak glows in the golden blaze of sunrise. I raise my arms to Father Sun, our Tayta Inti, and to begin the morning I chant, "We greet you and thank you for your glorious light." Tachico fidgets and starts kicking rocks off the edge. I offer him my conch shell. "Want to blow my *pututu* to salute the sunrise?" He accepts the shell eagerly and takes a deep breath. He gives it a blast so hearty that Chochi tries to bury himself in my turban.

"They'll hear that as far as Palpa!" I laugh. I'm still trying to peel Chochi off my neck when a frenzy of barking erupts. Two snarling dogs race toward us, and Chochi dives back into Tachico's bag. I push Tachico behind me, grip my walking staff tightly, and hold it in front of me, ready to fend them off, but Ecco is two steps ahead of me.

A shrill whistle stops the dogs as a dusty caravanner appears. He is as tall as Father but has broader shoulders. "They won't hurt you!" he calls to us. "Just doing their job."

The caravan comes into view behind him, beginning the descent toward the valley. As soon as Tachico spots the leader, he hurries toward him and begins pelting him with questions. "Where did you start? Where have you been? Did you bring obsidian? Any trouble with raiders?"

Ecco seems amused. "I'll make sure he doesn't annoy them too much," he says, then trots after Tachico.

The weathered caravanner pats Tachico's back. "Slow down, little friend. Give me time to answer!" is the last thing I can make out as they zigzag their way down the hill beside the llamas, deep in conversation.

I am happy to lag behind, grateful to the wind for dissipating the thick smell of llama fleece and human sweat. My thoughts turn back to my dream, hoping I can conjure some more details.

Caravan

But the man who called off the dogs falls into step beside me. I stiffen. He seems to notice and leaves more space between us while keeping pace with me. He appears to be a gentle, fatherly type, just trying to make conversation. "Is it true your rivers are lower than ever before?"

I nod.

"Strange times," he says, his voice as deep as the valley. "We came through some bad weather in the mountains. No rain but hail as big as stones."

In my whole life, I have never seen rain, let alone hail. Nothing more than a bit of mist ever reaches Nasca. People who have seen hail, snow, and lightning say it is like seeing the hand of Creation itself. Wiracocha can turn the world to ice with a sudden flourish or blanket it with white dust that turns into water at the touch of a hand. Spears of fire can fly across whole valleys and set trees ablaze. From all the stories I have heard, it seems a fearsome thing to approach the highest Apus, the great spirits that animate the mountains. I once went within sight of the great Illakata, wary of all the legends of Illakata filled with thunder and rage. But behind Illakata were even greater peaks beyond: stark, white, and jagged. I find the courage to ask, "Was there any fire from the sky?"

"Lightning? Oh, yes," he says. "Like I've never seen before." He grows pensive as we walk. "There was a bad storm by Illakata. The earth rumbled as if it would open wide. Dark clouds streaked with light. Two local men were struck. Died instantly. A boy was badly burned. Lost his sight." He grimaces. "The Apus must be angry."

I am startled to hear words come out of my mouth. "Or trying to be heard," I blurt out. It is something Kuyllay might have said. My tongue betrays my thoughts. "What did their shaman say?"

"He was one of those who died. He had no apprentice." The path curves suddenly, and he pauses to appreciate the view of distant hills glazed by the morning sun, then turns back to me. "The

CALL OF THE OWL WOMAN

boy's mother asked us to contact a healer in Nasca called Kuyllay. You must know of her. Is she as remarkable as they say?"

Of course she is, I want to say, but even as I think it, the word changes to *was.* She was the best. Everyone knows that. But my voice catches. My chest tightens. I have to squeeze the words out. "She left us three moons ago." I can't say the word "died." My throat closes and the rest comes out like a whisper. "Kuyllay was my grandmother." The moment feels interminable.

To my relief, a boy runs up to us, babbling about a sick llama. My walking companion bows to me apologetically. "I regret that I have work to do," he says. "I am deeply sorry about your grandmother. And for my rudeness. My name is Jorat. From the salt flats of Condor's Perch. What might I call you, young woman?"

"Patya," I answer, with a slight bow of my own, "of Two Rivers."

"Tonight, Patya of Two Rivers," Jorat says with a smile, "we will be singing songs and telling tales. I hope you and your family will join us."

"I would like that," I reply, surprising myself again.

After Jorat continues on his way, I slow my pace and imagine Kuyllay next to me telling me stories the way she used to when we made our way to caravanner campfires. Such gatherings usually made me nervous, but her stories would distract me, and I would be fine. Until someone commented on the shape of my head.

I keep to the inside of the path but have to press in against the hillside whenever clusters of llamas crowd past, their saddle-bags full, their rainbow-colored ear tassels swinging brightly. The valley spreads out below, flattening into wide coastal plains that stretch between these hills and the sea. Images from my dreams flicker across my vision—invading waves of sand, Kuyllay laughing. Sometimes she visits my dreams and just sits with me quietly. Sometimes she sends visions. I still half expect Kuyllay to appear in person. To return as if she had merely gone off with another caravan to relive the world of her youth—the one that had begun

Caravan

when her mother died and her father traded his only daughter for a pair of llamas.

Paya Kuyllay used to say that even the worst pain could turn into a blessing. The caravanners had been kinder to her than her own father and taught her more than she had imagined possible. "My mother shared everything she knew about medicine plants, but the earth has so much more to teach us!" Kuyllay collected healing plants and traditions along the way—from the highlands, from the jungle, from coastal peoples north and south. She shared in their work, listened to their stories, and absorbed everything. "I never regretted leaving home," she told me, "but I was glad to return. Thankful that your mother was born here. Happy that you came along."

I just want her back.

My mother Keyka is almost as famous as Kuyllay for her cures, and since I am Keyka's only daughter, everyone expects me to follow the same path. But painting pots is a lot more fun than preparing remedies and sorting plants. And looking after Tachico is fun. He may be half my height, but he has twice my energy, as well as a special gift for sensing hidden waters. He also has a passion for exploring and a talent for trouble. My own passion is to dance, to let the rhythms flow through my body. It's as if I can tap into the pulse of life through movement, feel the heartbeat of the earth beneath my feet, the pull and reach of heavenly transcendence, the twists and turns of the world we live in. I love it when the fire circles of visiting caravans are transformed into throbbing choruses of drums, flutes, and panpipes—where I can lose myself in the darkness and the music.

Another scene from last night's dream comes back to me— the silhouette of a drummer on a hillside. The figure reminds me of Yantu, Faruka's cousin from Palpa. But what would Yantu be doing in my dream? I was in a daze during the burial ceremonies, but I do remember the music he played, the soulful dirge that enveloped our procession. It resonated through my whole being and left its rhythms still echoing there. But I don't want to think about him. About the way his brows furrow when he plays. The way his lower lip sticks out ever so slightly. The way . . . No. I can't think about Yantu.

The shadows are growing long by the time the caravan stops to make camp. I can't wait until they are ready for trading, but first they have to set up their camp. The old well has gone dry, so I show them where to find another, smaller spring to replenish their water and then set off to find Tachico and Ecco. Ecco could not have picked a better bride than my best friend. My only friend. Soon she will also be my sister! I will need a good selection of feathers if I am to make Faruka the most beautiful wedding shawl ever. I stop to appreciate a dazzling pattern of light on the ground under a sprawling guarango tree. The play of sunlight through its branches gives me an idea for the shawl's design, so I grab a stick and start sketching my idea in the dirt. I am so immersed in drawing that I barely notice the low whistle coming from across the clearing, but soon I find myself humming along. I look up to see where it is coming from.

An oddly dressed man is setting up a tent. Hunched over in the late afternoon shadows, he seems only half human. A pair of clawed feet dangle from each side of the pelt on his back. Strings of feathers hang from his neck. His ears are weighted by large round plugs in the lobes. The strange-looking merchant suddenly turns his head to stare straight at me. When he locks his narrow eyes onto mine, it's all I can do to keep myself from flinching and turning to flee. I look away, pretending I had not been watching him but merely scanning the landscape. I spot Tachico and Ecco

Caravan

unloading a llama and I wave to them, but they do not notice. Chochi does.

The monkey bounds toward me but suddenly turns and veers straight into the merchant's campsite and disappears into a whirl of fabric and fur. The merchant reaches into the center of the commotion. One hand comes out holding Chochi by the scruff of his neck. In the other hand squirms a smaller monkey with fur the same copper color as Chochi's, with the same white markings around the eyes and a tiny green jewel in one ear. The man looks at me and holds Chochi out toward me, clearly waiting for me to come retrieve the wayward creature.

Reluctantly, I go to retrieve Chochi, but I hate the way the man seems to be studying me. The pelts overwhelm his slight body, and his nose pokes out, thin and angular. His hair is partially covered by a turban, but loose strands, strung with beads, hang down to his chest. His eyes dart from my feet to my turban to my throat. His breath smells of long-chewed coca leaves. "You must be Kuyllay's granddaughter," he says.

My skin prickles.

Although he is standing directly in front of me, it feels as if he is circling me. "Those thick eyebrows," he says, "the flecks in the eyes. An orca on your neck. And she didn't let them bind your head either, did she?" His eyes linger on my throat.

My hand automatically goes to my necklace. Hanging from the leather cord are a tiny wooden owl, a crystal wrapped in blue thread, and a small round ceramic vial with a moon etched into one side and an orca on the other. Things Paya Kuyllay had given to me. The look in his eye is disconcerting. "You knew my grandmother?"

"Who in this region does not?" he says, digging through one of the baskets. "It was my father, Torzhin, who gave her the vial you're wearing."

I do not like the feel of this stranger, the way he acts like he knows me. I want to leave, but my feet refuse to move. *It's the twilight*, I think. *Anything can happen in the twilight, the door between worlds.*

He pulls out a bundle packaged in an elaborately embroidered fabric and unwraps it carefully as he speaks. "My mother left this world as I entered it, but she shows me things from the other side." He thrusts a brightly painted ceramic toward me. "Let's see what Kuyllay's granddaughter can tell us . . ."

I step back, but he puts it into my hands. Chochi flattens himself across the back of my neck as if trying to melt into me and disappear. "Who are you?" I stutter.

The man cocks his head to one side, amused. "I am sure you have heard of me. Pikaq of Acari. An old, very old, friend of your grandmother Kuyllay. From before you were born, child. From before you were born."

His voice is mocking and unpleasant. I can't place where I have heard the name. He doesn't seem like someone she would have called friend. All I want is to leave, but something about the vessel looks familiar. It's shaped like a sea creature arching upward, baring its teeth, with two pouring spouts and a fin on its back.

"Tell me what you see," Pikaq commands. "Feel it. What does this shark tell you?"

I hesitate. The fin is much taller than a shark's. The black lines framing the eyes look just like one of Kuyllay's orca-shaped pots. A column of heads stretches along the sides in ochers and reds. Kuyllay once called them generation lines, each head another step into the past—a string of ancestors belonging to the same *ayllu*, the same community. This pot must have been done by or for someone connected to the Orca clan. My clan. A shiver runs down my spine.

"Ahh . . . you feel the shark's power," he prods.

I avoid his eyes. I do not want to contradict an elder, even one as distasteful as this Pikaq. "I have heard," I say slowly, "that the shark is sacred to tribes in the north." I offer the pot back to him. "What do you see?"

He doesn't take it, but his face is transformed with pride and pleasure. "Ah, so many things!" He passes his hand over the top. "Where it has been. Who has held it. How it has been used. It speaks to me."

Then why, I wonder, *hasn't the pot told him it is not a shark?* He must really want it to be a shark. The speed and strength, the deadly teeth, the tenacious cunning. But every Nasca child knows that the orca is the most powerful creature in the sea. Not only because of their size and strength but also because of how intelligent and social—even playful—they are. I have watched them burst from the water as if in flight, breaching and splashing down, rolling in delight. Unforgettable in their immensity and exuberance. Some say that gods like to take the form of orcas just to enjoy the sea.

Pikaq is obviously thinking about something else. His voice is an ecstatic hiss. "Imagine this ceramic floating with a hundred others, shining on the surface of still waters."

It's suddenly as if I am stepping out of my body into a dream. I see myself place the pot in the reflection pool at the Grand Temple of Cahuachi in the time of the pyramids before they were buried. Specters of ancestors gather around the pool, hovering, strangely alive and present.

Pikaq presses my hands against the pot. My skin recoils at his touch, and the vision dissolves in the reek of his breath. "It called me from the desert," he says, "from beyond the grave."

You mean you stole it from a tomb, I think, trying to pull away from him. He presses my hands even harder. "Feel it," he whispers fiercely, his voice snaking through my head. "Tell me what it says to you!"

A powerful voice startles me. "No! The time has not yet come." As I watch Pikaq's face, I realize that the voice is coming from me.

CALL OF THE OWL WOMAN

He removes his hands so abruptly that I almost drop the pot. I recover my balance and put it on the ground in front of him, then back away. I have a sick feeling, like something has been pulled out of me. Again, my hand goes to the necklace. Kuyllay had said it would protect me one day. Perhaps that day is now.

Pikaq grabs my wrist as if sensing my impulse to run. "That necklace was my mother's. My father had no right to give it away. Take the shark and the medicine it carries. In exchange, give me the necklace."

"I don't want your shark."

"Then take my monkey. Yours needs a good companion."

"I don't want anything of yours."

His face flushes. "You already have something of mine."

His hand is on the vial before I can stop him; in the other is a knife. "I have come a long way to find this," he says. "If you want nothing in return, that is your choice." As he slices the cord, Chochi launches himself at Pikaq's leg and sinks his teeth into the man's calf. Pikaq yelps in pain and slaps at the ball of angry fur as the vial falls to the ground. I scramble to grab it and take off running. Pikaq's screams follow me.

"That belongs to me, witch's child—I will have it back!"

chapter 4
Weq'o's Challenge

I'm not sure when Tachico and Ecco catch up with me, but I do not slow until the village is in sight. Ecco bristles when I tell him about Pikaq trying to take my necklace. He's ready to go back to complain to the caravan leader, but before any fuss I want to tell our parents. "I'm okay," I say, looking back toward the caravan camp. Behind it, the mountain stands solid and reassuring, glowing white against the sky's deepening blue. "Yuraq Orqo," I whisper, "thank you for your protection."

As we approach the plaza at the edge of the dusty farmlands, we can already hear Uncle Weq'o's shrill voice. Clusters of young men surround a group of elders in the middle of an argument.

"I say we wait for Achiq!" Weq'o shouts. He stands taller than most, his dark hair lifted by the wind. His eyes are hidden under heavy brows as he bellows at our father. "Yakuwayri, you may be the Guardian of Waters in this valley, but this mission affects the whole region."

We climb a nearby boulder to get a better view. Yakuwayri's voice booms back, calm and even. "Rest assured," our father says, "all the necessary offerings are being made and we will stop at the temple to make an offering on our return." Many are nodding as the familiar cadence of Yakuwayri's voice rolls through the plaza.

Uncle Weq'o almost never agrees with his older brother about how to manage the valley's dwindling resources. I hate the way he takes pleasure in making people nervous. He delights in feeding people's fears, and he can be so convincing that even I have to remind myself when he's lying.

"If you don't go there *before* the mission," Weq'o insists, "the affront will bring even worse troubles upon us, and you will be to blame!" Murmurs of assent sift through the crowd.

"We have made offerings at Yuraq Orqo," Father replies. "We will be making offerings at Tunga. There will be no disrespect. The temple will receive its due on our return."

"So, you put the tribute to Cahuachi last, then?" Weq'o turns to the crowd as if he has made his point.

Father holds his hand up to the crowd. "Is it an insult to your wife when you embrace your child before her? We honor the sacred at all times, wherever we are, brother. Have you forgotten that the ancient temples of Cahuachi were destroyed because people put the temples themselves above the gods they were built to honor? That is why Takarpu K'iti was built so simply. To remind us."

"And Takarpu K'iti is the temple that now honors the sacred waters. Yet you would go without the priest who serves it?"

I climb a little higher, pulling Tachico up behind me with Ecco's help.

Our father appeals to the crowd. "South of us, only the Acari River has any water. We are going to meet with their water-guardians. For that, we do not need a priest."

"Wrong!" Weq'o yells, trying to rile up the onlookers. "Our priests can tell if the people of Acari have used their magic to take our waters!" The way the crowd buzzes with glee is worrying—a dangerous mixture of anger, fear, and the pleasure of finding someone to blame.

Weq'o's Challenge

"Weq'o, your concerns will be taken up in council," Yaku-wayri replies. "Until then it serves no good to sow suspicion. Go home, friends, and help your families prepare offerings to the Great Mother, that her bounty be restored. Our people have faced worse times, yet we have always found ways to help Pachamama, the Great Mother, our generous Earth, to bring her waters within our reach." He lifts his staff and calls upon the spirits of the sacred mountains, the great Apus from whom the waters flow, our guardians and teachers. He rotates slowly, calling on the sacred directions. Facing north, he honors the wind, Wayra. We join the crowd's response, "We give thanks." To the east we honor Father Sun; to the south, Mother Earth; to the west, the Moon and Sea. I love watching Father. He seems larger, radiant, strong—as if he has stepped into another dimension among invisible allies. He pivots and calls out a final thanks.

We scramble down from our perch as the crowd disperses. Uncle Weq'o is still facing his brother with a look of distaste. "Yakuwayri, I know you are also going to the sacred cove," he says, "to repeat your antiquated rituals with all your amusing sincerity." He makes a derisive sound and seems about to walk away but pauses to add, "Achiq will be here once he finishes his visit to the north. You should wait." He unties a bag from his belt, reaches in, and pulls his hand out with a thick mass of black hair twined around his wrist and an umanqa hanging at the end.

Weq'o holds it up. "You will also need me on your expedition. An umanqa this powerful might even make your little ritual succeed this time." I hate the way he insults our father, but I can't take my eyes off the head. The eyes and mouth are pinned shut with long guarango thorns, but I recognize Tikati, the priest who helped Achiq prepare Kuyllay's umanqa. He had been a friend to our family.

Father's face betrays no emotion. "I had not heard of Tikati's death," he says slowly, "nor of any illness."

CALL OF THE OWL WOMAN

"Tikati had an unfortunate fall. But why not let his *mis*fortune be our good fortune? A sudden death leaves more energy in the skull and makes for a more powerful umanqa. If Tikati had withered into old age, his power could have evaporated with him." Weq'o caresses the head and returns it to the bag. "Some say that the only thing more powerful than a priest's umanqa is that of a child." He shrugs, slings the bag over his shoulder, and strides away, nodding to us as he passes. I don't like the way his glance lingers on Tachico. I think I may hate my uncle almost as much as I hate Achiq.

Tachico's hand suddenly weighs heavy in mine. "Tikati?" he mumbles, his face ashen. He was a skilled bonesetter and a seer, our family's favorite of the temple priests, and the one we most trusted. Tikati also helped Tachico learn how to channel his sense for unseen waters. And now he, too, is gone.

Father places a hand on Tachico's shoulder. "Let's go home." His silence hangs over us as we follow the edge of the riverbed. It isn't until we turn onto the upward path toward home that I start to tell him about Pikaq. Father interrupts as if he does not realize I am talking. "I will need your help preparing for the trip, Patya. I want to be gone before Achiq gets back."

chapter 5
Echoes

I wake up the next morning hungry and stiff, the sun already bright. Through the door I see Mother slicing a length of *wachuma* cactus into round cross sections. She glances up at me.

"Well, she wakes at last!"

"Why did you let me sleep so long?" I grumble. "I was supposed to help Father."

"He'll be back. Tachico went with him to fill the water bags."

"Is there any soup left?"

Keyka nods toward the fire. "Squash."

"Again?" I groan.

"Would you prefer alpaca strips?"

"No."

"There's a little fruit in the basket."

I make my way to the skimpy basket, almost tripping over a dozen squealing quwis as they scurry away from my footsteps. The little rodents have clearly been eating well. And they've been multiplying. Four more little fur balls scurry to follow their mother under the bench. "Will any of these be gracing our bowls soon?" I ask. "Or are they all reserved for your healing work?"

"These are the ones I've been fattening for the wedding celebration."

Disappointing. There are just a few shriveled berries in the basket, and my mouth is so eager for succulent quwi meat that I can almost taste it. I watch Mother slice the cactus. "Another ceremony in the works? Is the wachuma for one of your patients?"

"No. For the Council of Elders tonight," she replies.

I think back to the first time I was introduced to the wachuma cactus brew with Paya Kuyllay's warning. "Wachuma can be a potent ally, Patya, but it is not always a gentle teacher," she said. "Treat it with reverence and respect. Listen. Watch. Let it show you how to work with the energies in plants, people, and with the unseen world." I know that wachuma can be a powerful teacher and guide, but I am definitely not a good student. The brew makes me unbearably nauseous. Let it show the healers what to do—I prefer not to see any more than necessary.

My mother looks up, speaking softly. "A small dose might do you some good. Help you work with those dreams."

I sigh. "What did I say this time?" It is terrible when your mother knows more about your dreams than you do, but that's often how it is with us.

She slides more cactus into the water and begins slicing another length. "You were calling to Kuyllay," she says. "Something about flames."

"Flames," I repeat, closing my eyes. Then I remember dreaming of oil lamps floating in a shallow pool, sparkling among the sea of stars reflected around them. The seven brightest stars of the Harvest Constellation were shining clear and strong, like they used to in years when the rivers ran full. I am back in the dream again. An old shaman hands me a lamp with a seven-pointed flower at the center. When I lean forward to receive it, it begins to spin, turning into a vortex that opens up beneath me. I fall into the center of a flaming whirlwind. Behind the flames, Pikaq

Echoes

is dancing, holding the ceramic orca high over his head. I shudder and jerk myself out of the scene. Mother is watching me. I meet her eyes. "Could Paya Kuyllay see an object's past when she touched it?"

Mother stops cutting and looks down at her hands.

"Could she?" I prod.

"Why do you ask?"

"A man with the caravan says he knew Grandmother. He said his name was Pikaq."

Mother stares off at the hills then murmurs, "Ask her when you dream tonight."

"Just tell me, please?" I plead.

She puts the last of the cactus into the large pot, cleans off her cutting surface, and stirs the soup pot on the smaller fire. Still pensive, she chops some yellow peppers into a bowl, pours some soup into it, and puts it in front of me. "Eat. It will be a long day."

"More squash." I stare into the bowl, but I am thinking about the cactus, how the slices looked just like the flower in my dream—seven points with a circle at the center. What would Kuyllay say about that? Were the dream images a call from the wachuma?

Mother adds more wood to the fire. "Sometimes," she says, "Kuyllay did see things. But not often. It always came unexpectedly." She hesitates. "Have you begun . . ."

"To see things?" I am horrified by the thought of it. "No! But Pikaq seemed to think I could."

"It's a rare person who has that gift," she says. "A dangerous gift. Some things are better left unseen."

"Pikaq reminds me of Uncle Weq'o," I say, recalling the way he held Tikati's umanqa—so smug, arrogant, and challenging. I glance around and lower my voice. "Would someone with the gift be able to see how a person died just by touching them? Could they tell if Tikati's death was really an accident?"

41

Mother shakes her head. "I don't know. But nothing would surprise me," she says. "Tikati was a good man. If he had had his way, your paya Kuyllay's umanqa would still be with us. But Achiq was persuasive, and Tikati had to honor the Council's decision, as we all did. We take comfort in the knowledge that our prayers and offerings will be magnified through her." I swallow the words I would like to say and change the subject.

"Father does not want Achiq to go on the mission. What do you think?"

"That's the reason your father called for a wachuma ceremony with the Council tonight, so we may see the way more clearly." Mother's next words come with hesitation. "Achiq thinks he knows the will of the divine better than anyone. Who knows? Sometimes he is right. Maybe this is one of those times."

"Well, I doubt that. He's up to something. He scares me. So does Uncle Weq'o."

"They worry your father as well. But what is most important now is getting water to the fields, or there will be nothing to harvest when the time comes. The next family to leave could be Faruka's, and Ecco with them."

That is my worst fear. I cannot bear the possibility that both my friend and my brother could leave. "So," I say, "what can I do to help?"

She hands me a large cloth sack. "Let's go get those feathers so you can finish Faruka's wedding cloak."

"But what if we see that horrible merchant?"

"Leave him to me, dear."

The buzz of people and barking dogs fills the air even before the caravan camp comes into view. I press close to my mother as we wind our way through the makeshift marketplace. It is already crowded with people from faraway settlements eager for news

Echoes

and novelties. I pick out some beautiful feathers for Faruka's shawl and for my own costume. Mother uses our alpaca fiber and dried fish to negotiate for the feathers, medicinal plants, and obsidian. We are about to leave when we run into Jorat, who greets me like an old friend. He turns to my mother and says, "You must be Keyka."

"I am. And you must be new to this caravan," she replies.

"I am. My brother did not want to leave his wife, who will soon give birth. So, I am here in his place. I wish we had midwives as experienced as the famed healers of Nasca. Your mother was spoken of in every place I have visited. I was very sorry to hear of her passing."

Mother lowers her head for a moment before she says, "Thank you. We miss her." She looks up again with a wistful smile. "Has your journey been pleasant?"

Jorat hesitates. "Mostly," he says, "but we've had some challenges. Your daughter may have mentioned the boy struck by lightning? His family is less than a day's journey from here. I hope there's someone who can help."

"We'll see what we can do."

They continue talking together, but I am not listening. I keep glancing around, hoping I won't see the strange merchant again. I guess Jorat notices because suddenly he turns to me. "By the way, Pikaq asked me to give you a message. He apologized for being so insistent with you and said he would make you a very good trade for your necklace if you ever change your mind. He is on his way south to Acari now to visit family but will be coming back through Nasca again and—"

I am dumbstruck. "Insistent? He tried to steal it!" Jorat looks shocked. "That man has nothing I would ever want," I add sourly.

"The man always struck me as odd, but I've never heard of him stealing," Jorat says. "This is very disturbing. I will let our leader know not to let him travel with us again." He shakes his head. "The man did a lot of trading. Seems to have an eerie talent for discovering what people most desire. And for getting what he wants. Is there something special about your necklace?"

Mother looks worried. "My mother, Kuyllay, wore it as long as I can remember—until she gave it to Patya."

I suddenly feel drained. "The day before she died," I add. "She told me it was for protection."

Mother puts her arm around me. "This Pikaq has been here before," she says, "and nothing good came of it. Jorat, what do you know about him?"

"Not much. He's a wanderer. Seems to have no loyalties, no responsibilities. He pays well to travel with us but lives like a shadow. Eats alone. Disappears and reappears."

The trumpeting of a conch shell sounds from the fire circle. "Come," Jorat says. "Time to share more pleasant stories."

I am relieved that Pikaq is far away now. We choose a spot on the cool ground, and I let my tension slide into the earth, grateful that Pachamama can digest and transform it like a fallen tree. I relax and listen to the conversations around me as people settle into place. There is talk about crops faring better in Ica than in Nasca. About how much dried fish there is for trade but so little other food and no cotton.

"The only decent harvests have been farther north," Jorat says. "Near the bigger forests where the soil doesn't dry out as quickly." It reminds me of how angry Father got at Uncle Weq'o when he cut down trees to expand his cotton fields. Now those fields are all barren. Father says the roots of guarango trees go deeper than our wells could ever reach. Trees more ancient than our ancestors still tap veins of water deep in the earth, which helps pull moisture to the desert surface, even during drought. Thinking of trees, I fall into a reverie, imagining the world underneath us, following roots through rocks, into underground rivers, to the heart of the earth. Until the sound of another pututu rouses my attention.

Echoes

The leader of the caravan thanks the Nasca people for our hospitality, then shares news from other regions. He answers questions about the predictions from star-readers they met along the way. More weather trouble, more drought. He mentions an increase in Warpa raiders, hunters encroaching into neighboring territories. Caravans taking more dogs for protection. Jungle products being harder to get. Violent clashes between groups. I am shocked to hear of people fighting over food in a place where rivers flow all year round and plants stretch as far as the eye can see. *Let them try living in this desert*, I think.

An old woman asks if it's true that the priests have stored seed and grain near the old temples at Cahuachi. Someone else shouts, "If it is true, it is time that they share their provisions!"

My mother says something so quietly that even I can barely hear it. "If they use the reserves now, there will be nothing left when the crisis gets worse."

A young man stands up. "I have just come from the highlands. They say that Apu Illakata is angry. What have we done to offend the mountain gods?"

I think about the men killed by lightning. The caravan leader says, "It is not for us to interpret the intentions of the gods. That is the work of shamans and spirit-talkers. After the priests and shamans next meet, they will surely advise us."

"Our priests care only about the temples!" another voice shouts. "They are deaf to the voice of the divine that they are supposed to serve. They no longer listen to our shamans!"

"What is happening to us, to our world?" a woman despairs. "How can we right things?"

The caravan leader throws his hands up. "Who am I to answer such questions! I know llamas. I know trade. Give me a problem I can fix, and I will gladly do what I can. But if it cannot be fixed by food, medicine, rest, or negotiation . . . you must ask someone else!"

CALL OF THE OWL WOMAN

The audience laughs.

"But now it is time to hear a story from you—tell us how the Nasca got their name!"

I smile to myself. I have heard so many variations of the legend that I once asked Paya Kuyllay which one was correct. She replied that they all were. "Stories should keep you thinking," she said. "There is never only one way to see something."

"Keyka, you tell it!"

I crane to see who has called on my mother, but a whole chorus is now echoing, "Yes, Keyka, tell it!" "Tell us, Keyka, tell us!"

So she stands up. "Only if you are willing to help," she says. "Drum, hum, or whistle with me. I know you came prepared! Use your rattles and flutes to bring in the thunder, sound the wind, serenade the lovers . . ." She lifts a small ceramic drum and starts a slow rhythm as people pull out their instruments. All I brought was a rattle, but I am ready to follow her cues. The hum of expectation grows with each rhythmic pulse. "You ask about Illakata," she calls out, stopping the beat abruptly, then leans in confidentially. "Some say he has always been angry. Some say his rage began the day his heart was broken—" She holds the drum high, points to our sacred mountain, and takes a long look around the circle. Only the sound of the fire breaks the stillness. "And that Yuraq Orqo was the one who broke it." She resumes a gentle rhythm that builds as she walks around the circle and people pick it up again, weaving their sounds with hers.

"Some say the Apu we call Illakata was once a powerful chief. Some say he was always a god. But all will agree he was master of thunder and lord of lightning and fire. Some say the woman involved was his daughter, others say she was his wife, and some say she was his betrothed. But there's one thing we all agree on—it was Tunga who lured her away. Tunga wooed her with passion and promises, of valleys lush and harvests full, and visions of a

Echoes

magical sea. Young and full of love, they slipped away while the great Illakata was sleeping.

"By the time he awoke to find them both gone, they were close to reaching the shore. With fire and fury, the Thunder Lord followed, storming with terrible rage. He threw bolts of fire to light up the hillsides and sweep the shadows away. The lovers kept running, trying not to be seen, seeking terrain that might hide them. They climbed sharp, rocky hills in search of a cave, dodging his spears of rippling lightning. When a blast made the woman stumble and fall to the ground, her hand lost its grip on her lover. Tunga reached back while she stared, terrified, at the dark cloud closing around them. A quick flash lit up the two desperate arms reaching across the divide. Between them, the granite was shattered and sharp, and stone dust fell in piles around them.

"'Go!' called the maiden through the roar of the wind. 'You must escape while you can!'

"'I won't leave you!' said Tunga. 'He's not seen us yet! We'll hide ourselves here in the rubble!'

"Knowing the reach of the Thunder Lord's rage, she begged, 'Be gone before he arrives!'

"'I won't let him harm you!' Tunga declared, his confidence still strong. 'The King of Thunder and his spears of light have no rights in my domain.'

"Fields spread lush in the valley below, aglow with the colors of maize. Raising his hands, Tunga commanded the winds to carry the grain toward the heavens. Great clouds of corn spiraled and flew as his breath turned into a fine meal. Those clouds hovered and swirled and settled in waves until they covered the ground. When the air finally cleared, a giant dune rose up, hiding the maiden completely. 'I will lead Illakata all the way to the sea, where my mother reigns queen of the waters. They will swallow his fury and drown his rage, and I will come back for you,' Tunga vowed.

CALL OF THE OWL WOMAN

"Her voice rose like a murmur from behind a white veil. 'I will wait for your return.'

"The earth trembled and shook as Tunga raced west, dodging lightning that cracked every stone. The ocean was but a few short leaps away when Tunga called to the sea. 'Mother, open your arms—your son has returned and is eager for your embrace!' Her waves swelled high, but the earth gave a heave and the ground beneath Tunga exploded. A fiery whirlwind of broken blue rock rattled with echoes of thunder.

"'You dared to insult your generous host?' raged the voice of the great Illakata. 'A sniveling coward who sneaks off in the night with a woman more treasured than life?' Rock crashed to the ground, with Tunga beneath, and the great pile of stone covered all. A new mountain of sparkling blue emerged in the new morning's light. A sob rose from the sea, and the breath of her cry caught the last of the lingering dust. It rolled over the plains, still shimmering and soft toward Tunga's buried beloved. The cloud hovered there, on the great hill of maize, and transformed maiden and hill into sand. Yuraq Orqo was born, a new mountain of white, with her face turned toward Tunga forever.

"Illakata returned alone to the snow to bury his rage and his sorrow. His thunder lay silent, the rains ceased to come, and the valleys and rivers went dry. People thirsted and cried and wailed with despair as their lands slowly shriveled and died. They turned to the great hill of sand, the mountain of Tunga's creation. 'Yuraq Orqo, White Mountain,' they pleaded in pain, 'help us, we suffer, Nanasca!' Those ancient words, echoed again and again, 'Nanasca, we suffer, we suffer.'

"The wind carried their cries to the top of the sands and stirred Yuraq Orqo's compassion. She shuddered and trembled, her tears poured in streams, and the rivers filled up once again. The valleys turned green, but those words are still heard in the winds that roll

Echoes

across our plains. The cry of 'Nanasca!' would echo through time, and 'Nasca' would be known as our name."

Mother's drum slows. Her voice softens. "The tears of Yuraq Orqo answered our suffering. We will never forget her kindness. Some say that even now, a magical lake lives at the heart of the mountain and feeds the wells that are not yet dry."

In the hush after Mother takes her seat again, I can't help but wonder if Yuraq Orqo will awaken again with tears to protect us from Illakata's new rage. But even more I wonder why Illakata has a name and Tunga has a name, but the woman they both loved has no name of her own. She became a white mountain, and that is the only way she is known. Just "White Mountain," "Yuraq Orqo." But how was she known before the moment of her transformation?

chapter 6
Wedding Dance

I have been working on Faruka's marriage cloak, fastening each feather with care to withstand even the most vigorous of dances. Tachico is jumping and dancing around the fire, brandishing the spear that Father fashioned for him with the new obsidian point.

"Ready to hunt! Ready to chase!" Tachico chants as he hops from one foot to the other, spinning as he goes. "Ready to bring home some meat!"

"I'm sure you are," I say, trying not to laugh. "Maybe Otocco will take you on his next hunting trip."

Tachico crouches low and rolls his eyes, trancelike, intoning, "Come to me . . ."

"Your prey will fall at your feet, Tachico," I say, trying to sound serious. "You will never need to throw your spear. They will beg you to take them. Who could resist your charm?" I try to catch his spear as he slinks by. Tachico dodges from side to side with exaggerated gestures.

"Tachi," I tease, "why don't you do the wedding dance with us? Faruka and Ecco would be honored." He hops to the side,

Wedding Dance

thrusts the spear high over his head, and turns his back on me. When he shakes his bottom at me, I laugh. "Actually, maybe not. The steps are pretty hard."

Tachico's head jerks around. "I could learn them if I wanted to." He spins again. "But I would never dance with Takiri."

Takiri usually leads most of our ceremonial dances, but he's arrogant and has a terrible temper. He practically grovels around Otocco but picks on Tachico and me for being "roundheads," as if it was our fault that our heads weren't bound when we were babies like our older brothers were. Nasca families prefer the look of elongated skulls because it's supposed to make them more god-like. But on the night before I was born, a woman came to my grandmother in a dream and warned her not to let them bind my head. Something about my destiny. I never really understood why Paya Kuyllay took it so seriously. When Tachico came along, my parents thought it would be easier on me if his head was not bound either. They were probably right.

I had gotten used to people teasing and making fun of me. Questioning my Nasca-ness. I found it easier just to keep to myself or help Paya Kuyllay. When Tachico was born, it was nice having someone get so excited to see me. And it was fun to look after him. Later, when I started delivering medicines for my mother and grandmother, I noticed that people seemed to become kinder. Perhaps they did not think it wise to insult the girl who brought their remedies. Sometimes I think that that might be why Mother insisted on me helping, even though I have no interest in doing what she does. I am just not the healer type.

Tachico was born a fighter. He came out fist-first and scream-ing. They say it was a miracle that both he and my mother survived the birth. But Kuyllay was there, and she has been credited with a lot of miracles. My dad announced that if anyone tried to bind Tachico's head the boy would probably rip off the bindings faster than they could put them back on. We make a good pair, Tachico

CALL OF THE OWL WOMAN

and I. We grew up hovering at the edges, watchful and careful. My father says we are "fiercely self-reliant." Maybe I used to be. I'm not so sure anymore.

I don't enjoy being around people much unless there's music and dance. I'm willing to put up with a lot if it means I can lose myself in the rhythms of movement. I transcend the world around me and venture into other worlds. I can even put up with Takiri. But Tachico is not so amenable. Like now. He stops in front of me, sets his jaw defiantly, and says, "When someone else leads the dance, then maybe I'll join."

We both jump when a voice startles us from the darkness beyond the fire. "Then you'll be happy to know, Tachico, that you won't have to wait." Ecco steps into the firelight with a grin on his face.

"How long have you been there?" I ask, my heart still pounding.

"I just got back from Faruka's," he says. "Her father doesn't want Takiri anywhere near them anymore, so Faruka wants you to lead the dance. That is, if you can talk Farina out of her heartbreak."

"What?"

Faruka's younger sister, Farina, is willful and immature, but she is the best dancer in the valley. And the prettiest.

"You'll have to start tomorrow," Ecco continues, as if I have already agreed.

"I can't."

"People are still talking about the amazing dance you did for Grandmother's funeral."

"I don't even remember what I did there. I did it for Paya Kuyllay. I just let the music carry me."

"So do this for us!"

"But there are twenty dancers for this one!" I argue. "I've only led small groups!" Even as I protest, my mind is already filling with motions and music.

Ecco nudges me, lowering his voice. "The drummer who

Wedding Dance

made that music will also be coming to our wedding, you know. You do remember Faruka's cousin, don't you?"

"I said I can't do it," I insist, but then Ecco's words catch up with me. "Faruka's cousin?"

"You must remember Yantu," he croons. "The drummer who you put into a trance with your singing?"

"That was a song of mourning," I reply as curtly as possible. "And Yantu was kind enough to accompany me only because Otocco asked."

Ecco pats my back. "You'll need to start early. The wedding is only days away!"

"Yantu is only interested in music."

"Of course," he says, nodding.

"We have hardly even spoken. He thinks I'm a child."

"Music is more powerful than words." He pulls me to my feet. "And you enjoy making dances as much as singing. Come on, you'll love doing this."

Farina is younger than me by two years. Everyone knows her for her beauty and her dancing. Her head angles up gracefully in perfect symmetry with her oval face. She carries herself with poise and dances with both lightness and passion. Ecco tells me she was supposedly choreographing with Takiri when her father arrived to discover them in an embarrassing tangle that had nothing to do with the dance. Farina had announced cheerfully, "We can plan my wedding next!" When Takiri merely mumbled excuses and made a quick, awkward exit, she had been surprised and humiliated and hasn't left her bed since.

I find Farina buried under her blankets, whimpering. I sit on the floor next to her and pray silently for the right words. After a while, Farina peeks out from her covers. Her puffy red eyes dare me to speak.

An impulse takes my tongue as I lean close. I whisper, "Takiri is a turd."

Farina blinks at me, wide-eyed. She has never heard me talk that way.

"You just have to step over it," I say. "The sooner we get to work, the sooner he will know that you don't need him."

We meet with the dancers the next morning. We only have six days to prepare for the wedding, but I enjoy the new routine: morning practice in the plaza, afternoons in the shade to sew costumes, and evenings helping Mother prepare medicines. I can feel Paya Kuyllay watching over us and imagine her hovering above us in her white robe and mask as we practice. If we had her umanqa at home, I would have brought it here to be with us. I try not to imagine what Achiq is doing in Palpa now.

I hardly even notice when Takiri loiters in the distance, acting aloof and disinterested but visible. His presence agitates and distracts Farina. I decide to take her with me to make an offering to Yuraq Orqo—some flowers, a small jug of chicha, a charm carved from a sacred *mullu* shell, and a rock with a tree etched into its surface. It's a long walk to the altar, which is at the base of the mountain, so we have some time to talk. Which mostly means Farina. I half listen and make appropriate sounds to let her know I am (sort of) paying attention. We are almost there when Farina sighs dramatically.

"My costume fits well, doesn't it, Patya?"

"Yes. Beautifully."

"You don't think it's childish?"

"Childish?"

"I mean, it doesn't make me look desirable. As a woman."

"In the dance you are a bird, Farina, not a woman."

"I know. I know. I build a nest. I'm supposed to be the spirit of home and happiness."

Wedding Dance

"You also do the courting dance."

"But it's not . . . you know . . . It doesn't show me at my best."

"Your best?"

"I want to be attractive, alluring, not just cute."

"You are the very heart of the dance."

"I know." She sounds disappointed.

"Is this about Takiri?"

She twirls around, then slumps. "He doesn't want me."

I stop to face her. "You are the most beautiful girl in the valley, Farina. You could have anyone you want."

"Except Takiri."

"And why would you want someone who cares more about his own looks than yours?"

"He was fun."

"Such a man will look elsewhere for his fun as soon as you are busy with his babies." I can't believe she still likes Takiri. I pick up the pace or we'll never get there.

Farina trots to keep up with me. "If I were beautiful enough, he would want only me!" I glance at Farina's gracefully sloped forehead and wonder if it is possible that the binding of heads can affect a person's intelligence. "Do you really like Takiri that much?" I ask. "Or just his attentions, his flattery?"

"Ay, Patya! His touch lights fires all over my skin!" She looks about to swoon.

"I bet you toyed with him as much as he did with you. Come on, admit it. Wouldn't you have dropped him happily if someone more interesting came along?"

"Maybe." She thinks for a moment. "Yes. You're right. But I have to get him back first and then find someone more interesting."

I speed up even more. This conversation is making me wince more than the pain from my old injuries.

At the altar on the hill, we sing a prayer to the mountain and place our offerings. I ask Yuraq Orqo to bless Ecco and Faruka, "and

CALL OF THE OWL WOMAN

bless our dance that it may be worthy." I think of how Ecco looks at Faruka with the same puppy-eyed admiration that boys direct toward Farina. Faruka's features are pretty plain, yet it's clear that Ecco adores the way she looks as much as he adores the way she is. It makes me sad to think no one will ever look at me that way.

The final rehearsal is nearly perfect. The newly finished costumes inspire the dancers into even higher leaps and more dramatic spins. Breezes ruffle their feathers, the torchlight sparkles across their masks, and Tawo's drumbeat pulses through the night. When they launch Farina into the air at the end, she floats above the world as if suspended in time, serene and otherworldly, before spiraling lightly back to earth.

I know I need to rest for the big day, but I have trouble sleeping. I go outside to stretch a little, to loosen my hip and shoulder. A knot winds through me, tugging tighter and tighter. I shouldn't be worried. The dance will be great. But Kuyllay will not be there.

I finally get some sleep, but by sunrise the house is a flurry of activity. I'm too nervous to eat, but Mother insists I drink one of her concoctions. "I'm so proud of you," she says. "The dance is beautiful. The elders from the temple may like it so much that they invite you to perform at the next solstice ceremony in Cahuachi." Tachico bumps into me, tripping as he races past. He rolls in the dirt, bounces back up, and keeps running. I am about to follow him when Faruka and Ecco arrive with somber faces.

"Tawo is ill," Faruka says.

"Probably all that chicha beer he drank last night with Takiri," Ecco adds sourly. "He can't sit up, let alone drum."

Tawo sick? If I had eaten anything, I would be vomiting it up right now. We can't perform without our lead drummer. I had imagined a thousand ways we could improvise if a dancer were to be injured, but no one can replace Tawo.

Wedding Dance

I stare past Faruka to the hills beyond, to Yuraq Orqo. Had my offering offended her somehow? Did Takiri have some special favor with the gods that they would allow him to ruin everything? My knees almost buckle under me. I want to curl up and disappear.

Ecco puts his hand on my shoulder. "He'll probably be fine tomorrow. You can present the dance after the ceremony instead."

"No," I say. "We can't let Takiri ruin your wedding celebration." But I can't give up. I have to think of something. "Gather the group in the plaza," I tell them. "I'll be there right away." As they leave, I retreat into the back room, sink onto Grandmother's bed, and hug my knees, trying not to cry.

The dancers and musicians glance at each other nervously. I close my eyes and concentrate on envisioning the dance as we performed it last night. When I open them again, everyone is staring at me, expectant, confused, waiting for me to speak.

"Tawo is too sick to perform with us," I tell them, even though they know already. "But we have practiced hard. His drum has anchored us, given us our heartbeat, but . . ." I try to stand a little taller, pull my shoulders back, hold my chin high, and announce, "We will have to perform without him." Everyone looks worried, but I grow more confident as I speak. "The music has become part of us. Our pulse. If we sing it out as we dance, the audience will also feel that pulse." I tap my foot, letting the melody build inside me until it erupts into a full-voiced chant. There are no words—I just vocalize the cadence. *Ba bum paaah, tat tat, ba bum paaah, tat tat, shoosh shoosh shoosh awah, ba bum paaah . . .*

The others begin to hum along as I walk among them, nodding in time, my hand floating with the melody. By the time we get to the end, everyone is swaying with the rhythm. "All right," I say. "Let's do it again, from start to finish."

"May I?" a deep voice calls from behind the group, and a path parts to let the speaker through. My breath catches in my throat as I recognize the stocky young man approaching me. It's Yantu. He bows timidly. "I saw the rehearsal last night. The music echoed in my dreams all night. I would like to offer my drum in its service. If you would allow me." He kneels with his head bowed and his drum held out before him. I stare at the top of Yantu's head.

There is a hush so still that I can hear his breathing.

Ever since I was small, I would notice Yantu at gatherings. He tended to hover at the edges of things, like me. While others conversed, he would be staring at the ground, tapping out rhythms or whistling tunes to himself. Faruka once compared Yantu to an old guarango trunk: "The kind that spreads across the ground so long it turns to stone. You can lean against the steadiness of his rhythm like a rock, but then he surprises you with a burst of new life, a curled leaf unfolding. He's a strange one." I never thought him strange. I have danced to Yantu's drum. I trust his music. I trust his instincts.

I am jarred out of my thoughts by Tachico tugging at my tunic. "Say yes!"

I take a deep breath and announce loud enough for everyone to hear, "We would be honored."

My mother paints black around my eyes, tapering the line down to my chin. She adds wide stripes of reddish brown and white across my cheeks. I love the feel of paint against my skin. I feel myself transform with every stroke, becoming the small hawk that is my part in the dance. As the stripes dry, my skin tightens, and my face feels increasingly pointed. When she adds the pale-yellow line down the center of my nose, I can feel the hooked beak.

The night I first danced with Yantu, I was also wearing a hawk face. We were in Palpa for a big event. After our group performed,

Wedding Dance

the festivities continued long into the night. Yantu had been whirling across the plaza with his hand drum, and I was pulled into his orbit, drawn ever inward, gliding on the flow of music until I found myself dancing so close, I could have touched him. We circled together like one unit, but we never spoke.

Tonight the hawk feathers at the end of my outstretched arms draw circles through the torchlight as I merge with his rhythms once more. The drumbeat settles in my core and pulses out through my body, through my fingers, through the feathers. When a breeze lifts Yantu's cape, I have to force my eyes to follow the file of dancers, to keep my focus. We are dancing the shape of the tree path. It's the same path that we follow during our ceremonial gatherings on the plains, but it's been recreated here more compactly, filling the plaza for the wedding dance. I have spent so much time on those lines alone after the ceremonial dances, while everyone else ate and drank, that I know some of them by heart, especially the tree. I have explored each curve with the whole of my body, leaning, leaping, gliding, hovering, rolling, sliding, spinning, embracing the space within and without.

The traditional tree dance connects the three worlds—the divine heavens, the elusive but fertile underworld, and the physical world we live in. Tonight's dance weaves those worlds together and centers them in the heart, in the union of two souls, and in the promise of new life. As we dance, we are all transformed and transported until the last beat echoes into the night. The sound of the audience cheering engulfs us as we hold the final tableau, our hands lifted upward, muscles tensed, hearts pounding. We exhale in unison, lower our hands, and step back into the darkness.

After we finish, I am dimly aware of people speaking to me. My mind seems to have traveled far beyond the valley. When I finally come back to myself, I am standing alone in the center of the plaza. Yantu is at the far end, leaning against a tree, staring at the moon. I can hear the party up the hill at Faruka's family

CALL OF THE OWL WOMAN

home, where torchlights burn and music fills the night. When I reach Yantu, I stand beside him and look up at the sky. The moon seems to look back like a bright-eyed jaguar with its eyelid narrowed to study us.

"Thank you for your magic tonight," I say, but my words come out like I'm speaking through a mouthful of cotton.

Yantu leans back against the tree and looks down at me. His lips spread into a shy smile. An amazing smile. "Thank you for *your* magic," he says.

We're so close, we're almost touching. The energy between us seems to pull and push at the same time. I have an urge to lean into him, to rest my head on his shoulder, to merge with him, with the tree, with the night. My breath is suspended in the gap between our bodies. Just as I begin to let myself drift closer, he slings his bag over his shoulder, nods at me, and starts toward the river path. I follow in silence as if he has taken the lead in a private dance. I long to touch the edge of his tunic, just to confirm that he is real, solid, but I restrain myself. I stroll beside him, unable to speak. As we near the path leading up the hill toward the wedding festivities, he veers toward the riverbed where the musicians are camped. I want to stop to ask him why he isn't going to Faruka's, but instead I continue walking at the same pace, taking the fork onto the high trail without a word.

The ground is cool beneath my feet, the air fresh, and the moon a bright-eyed and curious companion. I brace myself for forced conversations at the party, for having to leave this perfect night sky. I wonder what Yantu is thinking. The sound of animated voices and laughter already tires me. Across the narrow valley I can see our house. My feet decide for me. I turn away from the party and let the moon light my way back home. I hope the family will understand.

chapter 7

The Mission

Today is the second day of our traditional three-day wedding festivities, but Father insists on leaving for Acari early tomorrow. Last night I overheard Mother trying to persuade him to wait. "We have no time to indulge the newlyweds or cater to their guests," he told her. "If Ecco wants Faruka's family to stay in the valley, he will have to help manage the water problem."

"Can't you wait until the next full moon to visit Acari, Yaku?" she begged. "I don't have a good feeling about this. I saw shadows in the wachuma. We need you here. Please, just go to the cove now, do the ritual, and come right back. Acari can wait."

But Father was adamant. "We have to know what to prepare for. Achiq is expected to be here in Nasca tomorrow night. I want to get to Acari before he does. I need to assess things before Achiq gets there to stir things up."

"After the last tremor, you said we need to intercede in the unseen realms, that we need our shamans to help us keep earth and heaven aligned and in balance."

"Yes, our shamans can see what the priests do not."

"So take a shaman. Do the ritual. And come back. Quickly."

CALL OF THE OWL WOMAN

"But Keyka, we also need to resupply our stock of fish. If things are stable in Acari, we can be at the cove by the new moon, when the catch is best. Just a few days to salt and dry. We will have barely enough time to collect sea-foam beyond the rocks in accordance with the ritual. Otocco has been prepared and is ready. He will finish the ritual in the highlands while I go to make the necessary offerings at Takarpu K'iti to satisfy the priests. Otocco knows the ritual. He knows the spring. I will send Chanki with him. We will all be home sooner than you think." Mother did not sound convinced, but she stopped arguing.

Ecco isn't happy about having to leave only two days after getting married, but Father is unwavering. Faruka is disappointed, but she also wants Ecco to do everything possible to keep them from having to move away. I hate to think of their family going anywhere else, but Faruka's parents have been considering going north to Palpa or Iphiño. Our aquifers here barely provide enough for drinking water and small household gardens, let alone the farms we used to depend on. Several families from our area have moved to higher lands, closer to the springs fed by mountain ice. The landscape is hard to work, the weather harsh, and there is always the risk of conflict with Warpa settlers, but they say that they have enough to eat.

Those valleys might be better off than we are right now, but as more people relocate, the pressure to share what little they have will only get worse. Father has heard that the Acari River has more water than we do, but they are also having more problems. People divert water before it reaches their neighbor's fields, and they steal food right out of people's homes. Instead of trusting each other and our traditions, *ayni* has turned upside down. Instead of our saying "Today for you, tomorrow for me," people are acting like it's "Today for me, because tomorrow there might be nothing."

They say that bloody fights have been breaking out between ayllus in Acari, and even between clans inside those ayllus. There

The Mission

are rumors about sightings of strange wild beasts that steal live-stock at night. Those wild beasts may very well be human. The calls for ritual sacrifices keep increasing, and now the priests want them to be human. I would not be surprised if the Acari priests have been scheming together with Achiq. Perhaps that is why Father is so adamant to go himself to see what is happening there.

Now Mother is busy organizing supplies and supervising the loading of the llamas so they will be ready to leave before sunrise. I help her pack the offerings, extra water, and ceremonial jugs. I notice that one of the llamas is carrying more spears than usual. "Is Father expecting trouble?" I ask.

She gives me a look that says she wonders the same thing but says, "They hope to see some guanaco on the way back. That could mean a nice feast when they return."

"All the extra clubs, slings, and knives make it look more like he's preparing for battle," I mutter, hoping Tachico doesn't hear.

"They probably want extra protection in case they come across Warpa renegades or raiders," she replies under her breath.

I pray over the divining rods as I pack them. May they help Father find new access to underground waters so that the people of Acari do not come after ours.

Tachico suddenly races past, then ducks behind me. Chochi comes bounding after him.

"You got me, fella!" Tachico laughs and then runs off to pester Mother for some fruit, chattering incessantly. As soon as he runs off, Mother pulls me aside. "Tachico has been underfoot con-stantly. Tomorrow could you please take him somewhere so I can have some peace?"

"We haven't been to the Sumara grove in a while," I suggest. "There might even be some ripe pods, with the seasons acting so strange." Sumara is one of my favorite places—a small, secluded

CALL OF THE OWL WOMAN

grove with an old guarango tree that produces more pods than any other. It's not the season now, but we still might find something, and it will take the whole day to get there and back.

"Perfect." Mother kisses me. "Thank you! Now go have fun at the party."

By the time I freshen up, Tachico is at my side again with Chochi riding in his pouch, ready to walk with me to Faruka's house for the party. "I wish I could go too," he complains as we head down the path. "I want to be a water-guardian just like Father and Otocco and our ancestors."

Our father was named for his grandfather Yakuwayri, one of the greatest of the water-guardians in a long line of great caretakers and protectors. They built the original wells, canals, and irrigation systems that kept our fields fruitful and our thirst quenched through many ancient droughts. That ancestral knowledge and wisdom lives through Father, and his deep sense of fairness has kept our valley peaceful, but it is hard to see him so tired and strained. There has never been a drought as long as this one.

"Father says the earth is still creating itself," Tachico announces.

I smile. "Yep. It's Father's favorite teaching. Volcanoes. Earthquakes. Floods. They can be catastrophic, but like Father says, the earth always balances herself with time. Time that is far beyond our human sense of time."

Tachico points to the dusty hills around us, so brown and lifeless. "These will burst into green overnight as soon as a fog lingers long enough!"

"Right. All they need is a little water."

"Our forefathers harnessed the waters!" he says proudly. "They charted the underground rivers and dug all the way to reach them!"

"That's how we were able to thrive in the desert," I reply, echoing Father's lessons. "But long ago, there was a time when our

The Mission

ancestors lived somewhere very far from here. They had to leave their homelands when their survival was at risk."

"I know," he says, brushing me off. "We still sing songs about them." He begins to recite in a singsong voice, *"No distance was too great, no terrain was too imposing; the ayllu found its way, it always found its way."*

Father's ancestors settled in the Paracas Peninsula but slowly expanded southward. For countless years since, hundreds upon hundreds, even when the rivers changed course, when the winds changed direction, when the earth convulsed and broke open, our people have thrived.

I am proud of my family's heritage. But I worry. Humans are not like spores and seeds that can lie dormant for generations, waiting patiently through season after season when no fog comes to linger. For humans and other animals, it does not take long to die of starvation or thirst. And once they do, no amount of water or magic can revive them. Things of this world are not permanent, Father always tells us—they are just part of a divine dance far greater than we can imagine.

It used to be that when I asked Father about the drought, he reassured me and sent me off believing that things would get better soon. Then better eventually. Lately, he doesn't even answer. He spends more time in prayer, making offerings, and performing rituals for the earth. Now when I ask when things will get better, he seems too distracted to answer. I wonder if, when he prays, my father ever feels like he is speaking to a parent who is too distracted to listen or respond. I think, sometimes, that the earth would not miss us humans any more than a dog would miss its fleas.

While Father has been bending under the burden of his responsibility, I find it odd that somehow his brother Weq'o stands taller. He is always energized, sniffing after opportunity, negotiating favors, and making impossible promises behind my father's back. No wonder Father worries about who to trust, who to watch, and who to fear.

When we arrive for the second night's festivities, Tachico runs off to find Ecco but quickly gets bored when he finds that Faruka's uncles are bombarding Ecco with paternal advice. He tosses a treat for the monkey into the air, aiming it at Ecco's head. It lands in Ecco's hair, and Chochi scrambles after it. In the ensuing commotion, Faruka grabs my arm and steers me off into a quiet corner.

"Tell me what happened after the dance," she begs. "You used to tell me everything. Now that I am your sister as well as your friend, you must tell me even more!"

"I went home," I reply. "I was tired."

"Come on, Patya, don't hide things from me! I wasn't the only one who noticed that you weren't at the party last night." She leans into me, prodding with her shoulder. "Or that Yantu was absent as well. We all saw him waiting for you."

"He wasn't waiting for me."

She shakes her head at me like I don't know what I'm talking about. "Patya, your brothers were waiting there to escort you, but Yantu said they should go. He said he wanted to wait for you."

"But he wasn't even going to the party."

"Neither were you, apparently."

"I was! It's just that when Yantu turned to cross the river . . . I kept going."

"What?

"I went home."

"But Patya! You must have spoken at least?"

"Not really."

"Oh, dear. We need to find you someone who isn't so shy!"

I squirm. "I should have stayed home tonight also."

A group of revelers sweep by, pulling Faruka into their stream. I step back to let them pass, envying their euphoria. Then I notice

The Mission

Takiri break off from a group and come toward me. He smells heavily of fermentation. "Sooo sorry about Tawo," he mumbles, tilting his cup upward to drain it. "The chicha was stronger than we thought." He sways over me.

"But somehow it didn't bother you?"

"No. I'm used to it." He chuckles. I try to step around him, but he grabs my arm tightly. His face turns ugly and serious. "And now they're all talking about Patya and her amazing drummer Yantu. And how you will be invited to dance at the temple for the solstice. When that solstice dance should have been mine!"

I invent an excuse as I try to twist out of his grip. "Don't worry, I have to make a pilgrimage that day." But as soon as I say it, I realize that that is exactly what I need to do. I must make the pilgrimage to Yuraq Orqo that I had planned to do with Kuyllay.

Takiri studies me for a moment as if trying to decide if I am telling the truth. "Good," he says curtly. He releases me with a push and staggers off to find his companions.

I make my way to the far side of the terrace and find a rock to sit on. The valley stretches out under a moon so bright I can see our house on the other side. The expanse of stars is mesmerizing. The sound of someone approaching makes me turn. My heart stops when I see Yantu.

He beckons me. "The view is even better from the knoll," he says, nodding toward the path that leads away from the house. I hesitate. He coaxes, "Let me show you."

I follow him to a gnarled tree jutting out from a bluff. "You have to stand just right," he says, showing me where to position myself. Two branches spiral around each other, creating an eye-shaped opening between them. In the center is the moon. "This is what I wanted to show you last night."

Even the moon seems to pulse in the crisp air. "Why didn't you say something?"

He glances sideways. "You did not know?"

"Know what?"

His cheeks turn the color of sunset. "I thought that you could tell what goes on inside my head. The way you dance . . . You move with my drum as if it were your own heartbeat." He makes an odd sound, part sigh, part nervous chuckle.

Our eyes meet, but only for as long as it takes to look away. In that briefest of moments I feel a connection so strong that when my brother's voice interrupts, it feels like a knife cutting through my flesh.

"Sneaking away again?" Otocco appears with a giggling girl on each arm and two trailing behind. Chanki catches up to him and hands him a gourd. "Thanks, buddy," he says, taking a long gulp while we watch uncomfortably. He offers the gourd to Yantu. "Your friends are looking for you, drummer boy. They are saying that our musicians aren't as good as yours. That Palpans have better rhythm. They need you to help them prove it." My brother looks at me sideways and adds, "But watch out for my sister."

Yantu looks totally confused. "What? Why?"

"Because your musicians will be so overwhelmed by the beauty of her voice that they will be unable to play."

"Otocco," I protest, embarrassed but flattered. I didn't think he ever noticed my singing.

Yantu smiles. "I already know your sister's charms. We will be sure to cover our ears and eyes so we can concentrate."

Otocco nods. "Don't worry about covering their eyes. No danger of distraction there."

He might as well have punched me in the gut. His beautiful companions try not to giggle. I think I hear one of them mutter under her breath, "Poor little roundhead," almost sympathetically. They pivot to leave, and Chanki trails loyally behind him. As Otocco and his troupe disappear up the hill, I remember why I never trusted him.

"You'd better get back to the party, Yantu," I say, trying to manage a smile. "You don't see your cousins often." Yantu leans toward me, but I move away. "I'm really tired. You go." Before he can respond, I am down the path and past the curve. Once I am out of his sight, I start running, heedless of the tears that blur my vision.

The next morning, we set off early for Sumara. I'm glad I have a good excuse to be gone before Faruka comes looking for me. Maybe I overreacted to Otocco's insult, but it was a good reminder not to get my hopes up with Yantu.

I challenge Tachico to a race down the hill, and then we settle into an easy trot. It feels good to run. After all the dance practice, my body feels stronger than it has in a long time, even before the injuries from my fall. We keep a measured pace until we reach the entrance to the small canyon. We have to pick our way along the wall of the gorge for a long stretch, careful of loose rocks and slipping. When it widens, we tunnel through bushes and brambles to reach the grove. Each year, in the season when the pods are ripe, we bring our llamas and alpacas with us and camp out for a respite from the heat. I can't wait to climb the huge guarango at the center of the grove. It is so ancient it was probably here when the first Nasca settled in the valley. Many of its branches are dead or broken, but that has never stopped the old tree from filling up our bags with sweet, chewy bean pods, the sweetest in all of Nasca. My mouth is already watering.

Tachico takes my hand to climb over a fallen tree. "Almost there!" I grin, eager to reach our oasis among the branches, surrounded by a chorus of finches with flickering sunlight seeping through the leaves. We approach the grove with reverence, like a temple. I think of it as one of Pachamama's temples. I can't wait to climb into the gnarled branches of the massive tree, to follow its sprawl across the ground, gaze upon its columns thrusting toward the sky, and marvel at the latticework of limbs and leaves. Even the ones that broke under their own weight still reach upward, buttressed by the lower branches.

"I bet my legs are long enough now to climb to the balcony without your help," Tachico says as we pause to catch our breath before the last thicket we have to cross before the clearing. "The balcony" is his nickname for a set of branches that crisscross just above my head, so thick that they create a kind of floor.

"I'm sure they are," I tell him. I hold up some vines for Tachico to step under. When we finally reach the familiar opening, I boost him up over a fallen log and scramble after him, ready for our usual race across the clearing to the tree. But Tachico stands frozen, staring at a mountain of mangled branches and a charred monolith where the great tree used to be. His voice comes out in a whisper.

"What happened?"

I cannot speak. I was climbing that old guarango before I could walk. Every year we gathered its fruit, its resin, its dried wood. How often had we listened to stories here, watching the fire from high perches, drumming out rhythms in its arms, observing the moon travel through its branches?

Voices come from the edge of the brush, and Uncle Weq'o steps into the clearing with a man I have never seen before. His odd clothes and short-cropped hair mark him as an outsider.

"What have you done?" I demand.

Uncle Weq'o does not seem as surprised to see us as we are to see them. "Making this old tree useful," he quips. "It was half dead, you know."

"Half dead?" I seethe. "It was old before your grandmothers were born. Half dead—it still had more life than you! What is wrong with you? Any fool knows how to thin the forest without destroying the trees!"

"Child," he says, smiling at me condescendingly. "Think of the pots that could be fired with this wood."

The Mission

"Think of the food and shelter it provided! Why didn't you just take the dead branches?"

"But imagine how much more we can grow here without the tree! This is an oasis we can farm. An opportunity we have overlooked." He nods at his companion. "This is Waru, a settler from the mountains. Of the Warpa tribe. I'm helping him start a farm."

"In exchange for what?" I say, knowing that Weq'o only makes deals that are in his favor. I am furious. "This was not yours to give away. We don't have enough for our own people, and you bring settlers to cut down the trees that feed us?"

Weq'o signals for Waru to follow him and then turns back to me. "Don't question your elders, child. You are lucky I tolerate your insolence." He disappears into the bushes, but the stranger hesitates, regarding me with a puzzled expression.

I point at the mutilated remains. "How could you?" I demand.

"Many, many trees," he says with a thick accent, gesturing around him. "I grow food, share with your family." He smiles brightly.

"That was an ancestor tree," I enunciate slowly, hoping he will understand. "Do not cut another."

The stranger stretches his arm forward, opening his hand in what looks like a gesture of peace, then turns to follow our uncle. Two black stripes across a red diamond are tattooed on his forearm. I realize where I have seen such tattoos before. I back away, pulling Tachico with me. I try to calm my breathing as we crawl back through the overgrowth and head for home. I run, glad that Tachico can keep up with me and doesn't ask questions. We only stop long enough to drink water. No waiting in the shade for the sun to soften its burn.

Mother looks puzzled to see us back so early, but I go straight to my bed and leave Tachico to unravel her confusion. I roll toward the wall and pull a blanket over my head, trying to shut out the world. I toss and turn, aching with a terrible longing.

The mutilated tree fills my mind like an ominous shadow. I try to summon good memories—the feel of climbing its branches, lying in its arms, watching the dance of the sun's fractured rays through the leaves, enjoying the company of finches, lizards, foxes, owls. How many nests were crushed when the tree fell? How many animals are scrambling now in search of new homes?

When I go outside, the night is strung with stars and the air is cool. I wrap myself in a thick poncho and curl up in a corner against the terrace wall. One of the dogs opens an eye. I call her in a whisper. "*Ssst*, Wiksa, come keep me warm." Wiksa sidles over and leans her body into mine. The soft rise and fall of her breath lull me finally into a dreamless sleep.

I wake to the sound of voices. Wiksa is gone. The sky is growing light. Llamas are lined up on the path below, and Father is on the far side of the terrace, speaking heatedly to someone I can't see. No one has noticed me in my corner.

"I still say it's better to keep the group small and mobile," Father growls, clearly tired of insisting.

"Fine." Now I recognize the disgruntled voice of Achiq pressing back. "But we must take the boy."

"Tachico does not have the stamina for such a trek."

"He is small enough to rest on a llama when he needs to. Your son shares your gift for finding water. Don't you think it's time to teach him the traditions?"

"There will be time enough when he is older," Father replies. "*You* can worry about what will please the gods, but let *me* worry about getting us there."

"Precisely," Achiq responds, lowering his voice. "If you had waited for me, the gods would not have afflicted Ecco and brought you back."

In the silence that follows, I realize that Father has given in. When they are gone, I find my mother feeding the hearth fire. "What happened?" I whisper.

The Mission

She glances around before speaking, her forehead creased with worry. "Ecco suddenly got so sick he couldn't even walk. They had to carry him back." She hands me a small gourd. "See if you can get him to drink this. I have to get Tachico ready." She also hands me a large empty bowl. "You'll need this."

Ecco's head is heavy in my lap as I coax the medicine down. "Too much fermented cactus?" I try to joke. Ecco just groans, then proceeds to vomit into the bowl until there is nothing left to empty. Pale and shivering, he curls into himself and turns away. I leave him sleeping and empty the foul-smelling bowl outside, far from the house, hoping that whatever caused Ecco's distress has left his body with its contents. I cover it with dirt so the dogs won't get to it. As I refill the water jar, I watch Tachico cross the courtyard, his head high and chin lifted. With great seriousness, he reports to Father, "I'm ready!"

For the first time in days, Father's face relaxes into a smile. "You certainly are."

chapter 8
Kuyllay's Grove

Whatever caused Ecco's misery, by afternoon it seems the worst is over. His face has more color in it, and he is already sitting up, making jokes about the trouble he had to go to just to have time with his wife. But I can tell that it scared him, and the way Faruka fusses over him, you'd think he had almost died. The two of them hardly notice I'm there. I wonder what it would be like to have someone look at me like they look at each other.

I am about to go look for Mother when she suddenly speaks from behind me. "It sure is quiet around here without Tachico underfoot," she says.

"But you're as good at sneaking up on me as he is!" I laugh. He hasn't been gone a whole day yet, but I miss him.

"I want you to go to Kuyllay's healing hut," Mother announces. "We need more fever bark and digestive herbs. And see what else we need to help replenish our supplies."

Mother has been going there regularly to collect medicine plants, but I haven't been back there since Kuyllay died. It's not a

Kuyllay's Grove

long walk, but I just haven't been ready. Kuyllay's hut and garden used to be my second home. Going there will make me miss her even more.

"I haven't had time to attend the garden or look through what's there. It needs your touch." She puts her arm on my shoulder. "Take your time," she adds. "Stay a few nights."

I stiffen. Asking me to stay a few nights is not because there is so much work to be done. She is nudging—no, pushing—me to face the emptiness I have been avoiding.

For as long as I can remember, I have helped tend Paya Kuyllay's garden—bringing water from the well, hanging plants to dry, making simple pots to store them. I also helped with patients who were staying for long treatments or healing ceremonies. Her hut is closer to the river, or what used to be a river, and easier for people to get to than climbing the hill to our home.

I hesitate at the edge of the clearing. A sudden breeze rattles an old set of wooden chimes, a long-ago gift from a grateful family. The tones are as soothing as I remember them. As I step toward the hut, a sudden rustling sound catches my attention. I look around but don't see anything. My skin tingles with the sensation that I am being watched. I wonder if Kuyllay was ever visited by ghosts of patients who were not ready to leave this life behind or if spirits still came to look for her. Perhaps an old soul has come to help me through my own grief. Or a hungry animal is watching from the bushes . . .

I pat the darts under my tunic for reassurance, then wrap my hand around the pouch at my waist, taking comfort from the amulets and stones that carry my spirit medicine. They seem eager to come out. Sunlight filters through the trees, and the air is dusty yet smells fresh with invitation. It's time for a ritual to

CALL OF THE OWL WOMAN

prepare me before I enter the hut. Something to calm me. To help me walk in knowing that Paya Kuyllay will not be there with her soft smile and open arms.

I sit facing the hut and draw a circle in the dirt. After consecrating the ground with a sprinkle of water at the center, I offer a prayer. Blowing across three leaves of the sacred coca plant, I honor the upper realm, the realm of this physical world, and the unseen realm beneath it all. Placing my altar cloth on top of the circle, I arrange my collection of stones, shells, and carvings on it, inviting the spirits of the mountains to guide me. I call on the four directions, and on the earth, the sea, the wind, the sun, and the moon, and send my prayers sailing. After honoring the space, connecting to the landscape, and thanking allies from the unseen world, I begin to feel at home again. I pray that I will be safe here and accomplish what my mother has asked. I pray that I will be worthy of my parents' trust and my grandmother's memory. I hold each object to my chest, thank it, and then tuck it back into my bundle.

As I am about to enter the hut, I pause at the whiff of something familiar and turn to look behind me. A fox darts across the clearing and slips silently into the bushes, the white tip of its tail disappearing with a flick. I sigh. It has been a long time since I heard a fox sing. No good harvests to predict. And not many foxes. Lately I think I've seen more foxtails on Achiq than in the wild. I prefer them in the wild.

Parting the heavy curtain, I step into the half-light of the healing room. Pots of all sizes and shapes line the walls, ones that I painted with images to help me remember what each is for. My first painting ever was a man's belly bursting with worms. Another shows a woman with swollen legs. I can almost hear my paya Kuyllay's voice teasing from the shadows—"two handfuls of this, one of that, a pinch of powder in llama fat."

Taking a large condor feather from the corner urn, I set about

Kuyllay's Grove

clearing the space of any heavy energies that might have settled here in Kuyllay's absence. As the feather passes through the space, tiny dust particles catch the light while following the currents of air. The space seems to glow. I sprinkle some fragrant oils and then turn my attention to building a fire in the pit on the back terrace. Once the tinder is glowing, I build up the fire with small sticks, add some slow-burning guarango from the woodpile, and then poke a long stick of wanqor wood into the flames. It lights quickly, and I hold it up to admire the rich flame for a moment before blowing it out. The dark smoke curls upward from the tip, trailing the heavy sweetness through the hut as I recite blessings for cleansing and protection. Deep orange sparks dance across the charred stub, like dream creatures peering from another world with their glowing eyes, looking both catlike and birdlike at the same time. Kuyllay's voice echoes in my head: *The great transformer who transforms the mundane into the magical.*

Back outside I wedge the still-glowing stick between two stones at the top of Grandmother's *apacheta* and remember back to when we made this special mound of rocks together. "When we make an apacheta, we create our own little mountains connecting earth and heaven," Kuyllay used to say. "It helps us commune with the Great Mother. But we must feed it regularly. Dress it with flowers, with shells. Offer it chicha, give it prayers. Feed it your worries! The earth is eager to digest and dissolve even the heaviest of your worries. And let the apacheta also carry your gratitude to the stars and feed their light."

"I am sorry I have neglected you, my friend," I say, blowing smoke across the stones. I place some small feathers from my pouch around the flat stone on top, then pour an offering of water into the center just as the last spark on the charred wanqor wood flickers and goes out. The fragrance still lingers.

The scent reminds me of Kuyllay's warning that wanqor wood must only be harvested from trees that have died naturally and

CALL OF THE OWL WOMAN

dried on their own. "Some things are worth waiting for," she told me on one of the countless mornings that began with her passing wanqor smoke over my bruised body. It took me months to heal after my fall, and she spent much of that time teaching me about the plants she was using. "The tree condenses itself, distills and refines its essence. The smoke releases and shares that essence. Let it cleanse and comfort you. Let it help you follow your breath to the center of your soul. To the essence that endures. To your reservoirs of healing."

I walk around the apacheta, lost in thought, circling slowly again and again as twilight settles over the grove. Once it grows dark, I lean against the outer wall to watch the stars. Father may be taking his bearings by these same constellations right now. I locate Llama, Hunter, Fox, and the diamond-shaped Portal in the south, a steady beacon for earthly travelers and a gateway for shamans. I wish I could read the sky like the Starwatchers, who had foretold these years of drought. What would they say about what I am seeing now?

The next day, I go through all the pots of herbs, deciding what to take back. Mother won't be using the hut for patients anymore since she is setting up a new one closer to the village, where she is training my cousins to help. She will need as much as I can take back now, and I will bring the llamas to pick up the rest.

None of the ceramics are as nice as what Ecco makes, but they are not nearly as rustic as how I remembered them. It took a lot of pestering to get Ecco to teach me what he had learned from the potters by Cahuachi. At first he would just give me his flawed pots to paint and a bit of paint. I always ran out of reds and yellows, but everything got put to use here. He finally relented and agreed to teach me how to make some simple pots myself. I'm not very good yet at double-spouted jars for liquids but have gotten pretty good at the smaller lidded ones for powders.

In a corner behind a bed I am pleased to find the ceramic

Kuyllay's Grove

drum I had been painting for Ecco's wedding gift. It was almost finished, but I completely forgot it after Paya Kuyllay died. I study the procession of mythic figures that spiral up the sides—a jaguar whose face is ringed with rays like the sun, a sea creature with talons, and a line of umanqas sprouting vines to symbolize abundant harvests for the newlyweds. A fox with wings watches a wide-eyed owl woman balance a crescent moon on her shoulder. It reminds me of the time that I danced the part of Fox in the story about the origin of the first canals, how the pelt against my skin infused me with an odd energy of cunning and quickness. My sense of hearing was heightened. I felt an impulse toward playfulness but also a mother's watchfulness.

When Achiq performs rituals in his fox robes, though, he frightens me. When he wears jaguar or condor masks, he merely looks like a man in costume. But when he dresses as Fox, he becomes almost sinister, a Fox-Become-Man that I would never trust. The version of fox I painted on the drum is a lighter, more magical fox, the way I prefer. I put the drum aside to finish tidying up. I still have time to finish it before I go back home.

By the time night begins to fall I realize that I have barely eaten, but I'm not really hungry. The hut is oddly quiet, and my skin begins to prickle. The moon is low, just above the treetops, and the cooling wind is whistling softly. Somewhere in the distance, an owl calls. I'm not sure why I brought Paya Kuyllay's ceremonial costume with me, but I suddenly feel pulled to look at it again. I unwrap it and stroke the soft, feathered tunic. When I hold up the mask, the hammered silver catches the moonlight, gleaming as if it had been recently polished. Rays circle the face, but only now do I notice that each ray is embossed with a tiny jaguar face. I hold it to my forehead, face-to-face, half expecting it to speak to me. Only the cool of the metal replies, lingering on my skin even after I put it down. My fingers trace the lines, the shape of the cheeks, the lift of the eyes. As the silver catches the firelight, the eyes become deep wells filled with mystery. Mother said the costume was not to be used in public. That it was meant for high ceremony. But she didn't say I couldn't try it on.

I unwind my hair and undress slowly, feeling the night against my nakedness. The fabric drapes loosely over my body, the fine cotton softer than any I have ever felt. I tie the mantle at my neck and let the downy breastplate settle over my chest and shoulders. It feels as if I have worn it a thousand times. After tying my hair back, I swirl the cape through the air in a wide arc so that it floats down onto my shoulders, full yet weightless. As I pull up the feathered hood and lift the mask to my face, the world shrinks. I focus through narrow eye slits, watching the earth unroll at my feet as if it is worlds away. I catch a glimpse of movement in the distance and follow it with my eyes. For a delicious flash, I think I am seeing Paya Kuyllay.

The moon is higher now, peering at me, a great jaguar's eye watching from the darkness. I greet Mama K'illa with upraised arms and feel her light fill me, melt into me, flow into each limb. As my shoulders roll back and my neck stretches and twists, my arms float out, filling with the breeze, rising and falling, spreading through the air as my feet pad softly on the hard-packed ground. I move in a slow circle around the clearing, every muscle alert, every stretch of skin responding to the dance rising in me, flowing through me. My bracelets rattle to the slow, steady rhythm that takes over, that propels me into each quickening step. Soon I am spinning through the clearing, whirling and leaping, the jangle of bracelets peppering the air. The world speeds past in glimpses through the mask. All I can see is the blur of feathers sweeping through the air at the end of my arms, but I am too exhilarated to stop.

From the trees comes a loud, sudden *crack!* that jars me like a slap. I come to a stop at the center of the clearing, breathless, my heart battering my chest as if it wants to fly out and away. The

Kuyllay's Grove

space around me still pulses, and the air is suddenly heavier. An owl calls from the distance and I wonder if I have made a mistake, if I have dishonored Kuyllay by wearing these feathers, this mask. I realize I have not asked permission. I hear Kuyllay in the back of my head: *Ask permission before entering another's space, before entering sacred space. Pause to listen, to feel the shift.*

But it felt so right! I want to say to excuse myself. But I know I did not give that space for choice. I wanted to feel it, experience it. If I had asked and felt answered with a "not yet," would I have resisted such strong temptation?

We must honor the rituals that remove us from the ordinary and take us into the sacred. Kuyllay's words come back to me like a rebuke. I was dancing for me in the ordinary world, not for the sacred, for whatever purpose the costume was meant for. I take the mask off and hold it to my chest. "Forgive me," I whisper to the mask, to the cape, to the whole costume. "But your pull was so strong." *No excuse can erase the action.* Kuyllay's voice reverberates inside me. *Honor our rituals. They are the portals from the ordinary to the extraordinary.*

Something bumps into me and thuds softly to the ground. A halo of moonlight glints off the shell of a large horned beetle that is now wobbling away from me. Tachico would love the little armored warrior as a pet. Of course Father would immediately proceed to explain the beetle's unique job in service to Pachamama. Ecco would study its lines and copy the patterns onto a pot. Mother would ask me to consider how I would respond if it appeared in a dream. Otocco would tease me about looking for meaning in a bug. Or tell me that I am as clumsy as this bug, awkwardly crashing into things.

The beetle doesn't care about its awkward crash, though. It marches across the clearing with confidence, not concerned at all whether I could harm it. I admire its curved horn, thinking how practical it must be to carry your digging tool on your head. And a shield on your back. And wings to carry you where you want to go. I hold it up to the breeze and watch it heft itself back into the night before I turn back to the hut.

Back inside, I take off the costume, fold it with reverence, and place it by the window. "Good night, Mama K'illa. May you bless these robes and let them soak in your wisdom and power." I sink onto my mat and surrender to sleep.

Then my dream world awakens. I am walking with Tachico and Kuyllay, singing as we collect plants. In the dream, I wonder if Tachico is dreaming of me too. "I found an earthmover beetle today," I tell him, "but you'll have to come and catch it yourself." He doesn't answer. No bright eyes or eager smile. Just silence.

The air is unusually still while I work on the drum. Since before the sun was up, heat has been oozing even from the shadows. A drop of my sweat blurs the line I just painted, so I turn it into a circle, which turns into an eye, which stares back at me with curiosity. It was not what I planned, but it does belong there. Now the wing of the wide-eyed owl is looking at me while the owl itself looks skyward. I finish the feathers with brown and orange, enjoying the grittiness of the pigments as they dissolve into each stretch of color across the clay. After I put the finishing touches on the drum, I take it to the firing pit. The walk is not long, but it is far enough that I have to stop twice to adjust my hold. I set it down by the woodpile while I arrange layers of sand and broken ceramic pieces to support the pot in the deep hole. After placing the drum at the center, I fill the space around it and fit in some smaller bowls before covering the whole thing with more sand and building a fire over it. I spend the rest of the day feeding the fire. When the sun starts to set, I even out the coals and leave them for the night. Oddly, the woodpiles seem almost as high as when I started, as if Tachico were here playing one of his tricks on

Kuyllay's Grove

me, stacking more when I'm not looking. They could very well be back from the cove by now, and it would be so like Tachico to come spy on me and play tricks.

As I approach the hut, something scurries through the bushes. I turn so abruptly that my feet catch on some vines and I almost trip. When I kneel to clear the vines from the path, I realize they are covering the old stone-lined *pachamanca* cooking pit. I think of how it used to sizzle and steam with mouthwatering smells as soon as the dirt that covered it was removed. That pile of dirt is still piled beside the pit, unused for such a long time that it seems as hungry as I am for those delicious layers of beans and squash, spicy meats, coal-singed corn, and yucca. Right now, I'd even settle for some bland boiled roots.

I notice a gleam from the window and realize it's a reflection from the owl mask. I can't believe I left it unwrapped and out in plain sight. I hurry, feeling terrible that I have been so careless with Kuyllay's treasure. I wrap it carefully and look around, feeling a sudden urge to hide it somewhere safe. The pachamanca hole, I think, would be perfect, like placing the robes in the earth's womb. What better protection? I find more fabric to wrap around the bundle, line the hole with dry wood, make a bed of unspun cotton, and put the bundle inside. I add more cotton around it, set a wide ceramic plate on top, layer dry reeds across everything until it is almost level with the ground, and then cover it all with a cloth. I heap the mound of dirt back on top and smooth it out. By the time I finish scattering dry leaves and twigs over the dirt, it looks just like the rest of the abandoned garden. Now it will be safe.

The next morning, the wooden chimes wake me early, but the sound has changed. Curious to see why, I discover that dangling at the center is a palm-sized wooden carving. An owl's face peers up at me, with delicate feathers traced along its outstretched wings. On the other side, another face has features

CALL OF THE OWL WOMAN

more like a shaman than a bird—very much like Paya Kuyllay's mask, complete with rayed corona. The soft wanqor wood looks oddly familiar. There are traces of charcoal in the hollows of the eyes. One of her patients must have left it as a gift.

As I scan the trees at the edge of the clearing, flashes of memory play in the shadows, games of hide-and-seek with Tachico. Perhaps the group is indeed back from the mission, and it is one of Tachico's tricks, not from a patient at all. My eyes scour the trees for his favorite perches. "Tachico! You sneak!" No response.

I hurry down the path to his favorite hiding spot, the one Tachico calls his Puma Cave, where thick vines have covered a fallen tree and created a small chamber. I chuckle at the thought of Tachico pretending to be some kind of helping spirit of the hills, stacking wood, carving gifts. I duck under some brambles and squeeze through the overgrowth into the hollow. Light pours through a hole left by a fallen branch, but Tachico is nowhere in sight. I hold still. Slowly, the space around me comes to life. Tiny birds resume their foraging; a speckled lizard scampers up a dry twig. A fox begins to emerge from its burrow but ducks back as soon as it sees me. The whisper of a tremor rolls through the earth and birds scatter. If Mother were here, she'd be trying to pull me out. I crawl back through the brambles carefully. The tremor is over, but if Tachico had been near, he would have come out of hiding to make sure I was okay.

At the opening, my heart races when I see a pair of feet blocking the exit. The frayed sandals and dirty ankles are too big to belong to Tachico. My eyes follow the muscular calves upward. What if it is a demon or a spirit or a half man? Maybe the beasts reported in Acari are real. I hold my breath and pray I have not been noticed.

A hand appears, open in an offering of help. Not beast but human, and not obviously threatening. Reluctantly, I inch forward and accept the hand that pulls me up and out through the

Kuyllay's Grove

scratchy tunnel of brush. As I stand, it takes a moment to absorb what I am seeing, but when the diamond tattoo on his arm comes into focus, I back away without thinking about the thicket of thorns behind me. My body automatically arches away from the pain and lurches forward, right into the Warpa who helped Weq'o destroy the tree in the grove. His hands shoot out to steady me.

"Do not be frightened, Owl Girl," he says in a thick but intelligible accent.

"Owl Girl?" I think of the carving I found in the tree and pull it from my medicine pouch, horrified to realize that he must have left it there. That he must have seen me dance in the owl costume.

He smiles proudly. "You like it?"

My breath locks in my chest and blood drums in my ears. I try not to look at the tattoo, try not to think about how he's been watching me. How he carved the costume that no one was supposed to see. I should be angry and scared, but suddenly, strangely, I am not. I'm not sure what I feel. I rotate the owl figure, watching it change from bird to masked person to bird again. Instead of challenging or questioning him, I just stare at the carving and say, "The costume belonged to my paya Kuyllay. She left it to me when she died."

Something like sadness or sympathy crosses his face. He waits for me to say more.

"Yes," I say reluctantly. "I like it."

I've heard that Warpa settlers have moved into the nearby highlands, and our hunters complain of seeing Warpa hunters in our territory, but the only Warpa I have ever seen, before this one, are the ones who attacked me when I was collecting plants. Yet this one feels very different.

"Why are you here? What about Weq'o and your new farm?" I ask, wondering if he notices the resentment in my voice.

"My new farm, she is there," he says, pointing to the path that leads to a rocky gulch that I often climb with Tachico. He

CALL OF THE OWL WOMAN

gestures for me to follow. I shouldn't trust him, but I do. After a short hike, we reach a sun-filled clearing. The afternoon sun lights up the far side of the gulch that is now leveled into three narrow terraces that look ready for planting. "My work," he says, gesturing proudly. "Waru. Not Weq'o." Somehow, it comforts me that he is trying to distance himself from my uncle. I am impressed that anyone could create even a single-level planting area on such a steep hillside, let alone three.

Sitting in the shade next to Kuyllay's hut, we share strips of dried llama meat and some *pacay* fruit from the Warpa's bag. He has just broken open a large pod and is sucking the cottony sweet fibers off the seeds when a gust of wind rattles the chimes. He tenses and looks around nervously. "Spirits come here?"

"Why do you ask?" I reply. "Is there someone you don't want to see?"

He stares down at his arm. "Many someones."

I follow his gaze to the red diamond tattoo and try not to flinch. After spending the last year trying to bury memories of that same tattoo, seeing it again in Sumara was a painful reawakening. I can manage the ache in my shoulder, the twinges of pain in my hip, but not the vivid memory of what caused them. Again, my skin crawls at the sight, and averting my eyes does not keep my thoughts from going back to that day.

Tachico and I had gone farther east than usual, searching for some of Kuyllay's elusive medicine plants. We stopped in a cave to eat our lunch out of the heat, and he got excited about carving pictures into the soft stone of the walls, so I let him stay awhile while I went farther up the hill to finish filling my plant bag.

I heard the hunters before I saw them—the laughter of people after too much beer. I had climbed some rocks to reach one of the plants and was perched just above the path when four men

86

Kuyllay's Grove

appeared, rowdily joking with each other. Another two, barely more than boys, came staggering behind them. When they saw me, one started calling to me like to a dog, coaxing, "Come, little roundhead," while the others jeered. One grabbed at my foot and managed to pull me off the rock onto the path. Before I realized what was happening, I was engulfed in a blur of groping hands. I almost managed to break away, but one of them caught me and threw me to the ground.

I could not fight them off. By the time they rolled me off the ledge with a final kick, I thought the explosion into darkness would end the agony and bring the death I longed for. But death betrayed me. I woke up in Kuyllay's healing hut with more pain than I could bear.

For the next six moons, Paya Kuyllay tended to my broken body. Mother told everyone that I had fallen while climbing, afraid that if the men of our clan learned the truth, the revenge they would seek would only bring more pain. That could start a war.

Rebuilding the apacheta in Kuyllay's garden was part of my healing. She taught me to offer my pain to the stones and to thank them for sharing my burden. We created a new base with a spiral of stones spinning outward from the center of the old apacheta. We infused each rock with prayers as we built the pile anew. Stone by stone, the ritual helped me find my way back. My body healed surprisingly well, but my soul was broken. And the secret still shames me.

The man across from me seems genuine. His actions are gentle. But even if he is as harmless as he seems, his very presence rips open my scars.

"Your tattoo," I ask, "what does it mean?"

He spits out some pacay seeds and looks at me questioningly.

"The tattoo?" I prompt, pointing to it.

"The mark of our clan," he replies, "the mark we receive when we become men."

CALL OF THE OWL WOMAN

"Become men?" I sputter. I want to scream, to strike something, to strike him. "What kind of men?" I stare at the Warpa. Has some demon sent him here?

He does not look up. "I know what happened to you," he says slowly. "You are the roundhead my cousins thought dead."

A chill washes over me. I pull the blade from my ankle sheath and savor the scrape of obsidian against leather. Time slows as my knife finds its way to his throat. "You knew?" I say, pressing the blade against his neck. "And you dare to come here?" He does not flinch. "Warpa filth! If you came to finish what they started," I hiss, "I am ready this time."

His back rigid, he lifts his chin, letting the blade rest against his skin. His eyes meet mine, and his hands open in a gesture of surrender. "Do as you want. Kill me. I, Waru, promise I am not here to hurt you."

One part of me stands back, hardly recognizing the part of me that holds a blade against this man's throat. "Tell me about the tattoo," I demand. "Tell me what you did to earn it! How does a Warpa boy earn his diamond-striped manhood?"

"Please. Hear me." Waru keeps his hands open in front of him.

I hold the knife against his neck a little longer, then I sit back.

"My brother told me what happened," Waru says. "A good hunt. They celebrate. Too much chicha beer. When they see a Nasca girl alone, they . . ." He hesitates. "My brother, he tried to stop them, but . . ." He falters.

"But he joined them instead?" I hiss. "Did he tell you how they threw that girl back and forth? How they told her she was a bad Nasca because her head was round? How they would do her people a favor by getting rid of their ugly outcast? Did they brag about how much of her blood spilled into the soil? Did that make them feel strong? Did that prove their manhood?"

"My brother," he says softly, "he was—"

Kuyllay's Grove

"A hunter? Ready to skin the girl to take home as a trophy?" I goad. "No, that would have been too kind."

"My brother, he was too late to prevent them. But he ended it. He told me he ended it."

"No one ended it." My face is streaked with tears.

Waru's voice is flat. "Kantu told me to put things right. My brother was an honorable man. He could not stop what happened, but he told me to make it right." Waru stands up. "I brought you something," he says, and disappears before I can respond.

Lingering in his wake is everything I have been trying to forget.

I curl in on myself, crossing my arms over my belly. *One breath at a time*, I tell myself. I feel Kuyllay's hand on my head. Steady. Strong. *One breath at a time.*

The Warpa returns with a large bag made of guanaco hide. He sets it in front of me and steps back, standing erect, formal, his legs slightly apart, as if bracing himself. "For you. From the great hunter Kantu, son of Tika and Noku, pride of his ancestors, beloved of his brothers." His eyes meet mine. "His companions were not so worthy of our clan. They were as cruel as they were careless, and not just in the hunt. They did not honor their sisters or their wives. Kantu joined the hunt to make sure they properly honored the creatures who die to feed our families." A shadow of pain crosses his stony face. "After what they did, the mountains themselves demanded justice. There were accidents. Many accidents. Only Kantu survived the journey home. But he would not speak. He answered no questions. He finished preparing the meat and the hides and then took me to a high ridge overlooking the path they had taken to this valley. Only then did he speak of what happened. 'You must return,' he said. 'Make things right for the girl, for our family's honor.'"

CALL OF THE OWL WOMAN

"Make it right?" I choke on the words. "How can anything make it right? Go tell your brother that your coming here only makes it worse!"

The Warpa's face is unflinching. "My brother chose to step off a cliff. He could not live with the memory."

He stares at the ground, and I try to breathe. "Your brother is a coward. He will never be free. That memory lives in every corner of my being." I am trembling, aching to run, but I cannot move. We both seem to be frozen in place.

He finally breaks the silence. "I do not ask for forgiveness for something so unforgivable. Only that you allow me to give you what he left behind. If you had not survived, I was to give it to your family. I know it will not undo what has been done. But please, know that your attackers will never harm another." He bows toward me, turns, and is gone.

I stare at the bag, but all I can see is that terrible day and the dirt against my face.

chapter 9

Shifting Ground

Whatever he may have said, I do not believe that Warpa. I doubt that Waru is even his real name. It sounds like something that Uncle Weq'o made up. Something easy to remember. A Warpa named Waru. And I doubt that he came for my sake like he says. If Weq'o is working with him, there has to be something else. Nothing Weq'o does is without hidden motives. Even if this Waru does believe he can somehow redeem his family's honor or lessen his brother's guilt, what could he possibly imagine would make any difference to me now?

I stare at the bag. It smells like dried llama meat and bitter spices. The seams are nearly invisible, obviously well crafted. I don't want to go near it, but I can't ignore it. If only the guanaco that once wore this hide had been found by Nasca hunters. Instead it fell to the Warpa who encroach on our territory, steal our game, and take what they want. My fingers reach toward the bag, brush themselves across the hairless hide, and surprise me with how soft it is. Despite myself, I pull the cord at the top of the bag. It loosens easily and the bag opens, spilling tufts of cotton. A length of dark, twisted rope protrudes from the packing.

CALL OF THE OWL WOMAN

My hands don't care that I want to turn away. They give a tentative tug at the rope. Something shifts inside. Another tug. It feels heavy, stuck. With the next pull, an object begins to emerge, with cotton clinging to it. I wrap the rope around my hand for a better grip and tug harder. The packing gives way, and the object slides out so abruptly that I have to catch my balance. It takes a moment for me to realize that what is swinging at the end of the rope in front of me is a man's umanqa. Its eyelids and mouth are pinned closed with thorns. On one cheek is a small red diamond.

My legs refuse to sustain me. I can't think clearly through the repugnance that is rising in me. I push the umanqa away from me, sick and confused. I feel like vomiting. My body heaves, but nothing comes up. Has Waru just offered me his brother's head? What does that even mean for a Warpa?

There is more in the bag, but I do not want to know what. I want him to take it back. I can look for him back at the gorge. But I do empty the rest of the bag. And with each discovery, my insides wither more. One by one, I remove seven heads. Carefully severed, each preserved in the Nasca style. Each with a Warpa tattoo on one cheek.

My first impulse is to leave them here and run to Mother. But she has suffered so much already. How can I bring it up all over again when she's so worried now about Father and everything else? I can't do that to her.

I try to remember all the protection rituals and treatments I have ever seen or heard about. I use all the incantations and prayers. I smudge everything with cleansing herbs, blow protective smoke into each umanqa, and circle them with small piles of wanqor wood set aflame to bathe them in the oily smoke. I summon Paya Kuyllay's spirit to help. I call on the ancestors, on Tuku Warmi, on Mama K'illa and Orca and Jaguar. I ask that they keep me safe from the evil that once animated these heads. I pray for guidance, pray to make choices that will be worthy.

Shifting Ground

Kuyllay's words again come back to me. *Trust the rituals. Begin by giving thanks. There is always something to be grateful for, always something to honor or feed.*

I am grateful that my attackers have lost their power to hurt me or anyone else. I am grateful they became victims themselves. I hope they suffered like I did. I am glad life does not end with the death of the body. I hope that the afterlife will teach them remorse and that their souls will not rest until amends are made. But even as I think these thoughts, I feel a surge of regret. As if one of them is returning from a place of numb detachment, from a drunken foray into a foreign world that seemed like an unreal dreamscape without responsibility—and beginning to reawaken. I wonder if death has released him from his ignorance, awakened him to shame. A strange anguish overcomes me, a confusion of pain, fear, and my own shame. I lean forward and slide to the ground, pointing myself toward Yuraq Orqo, feeling the earth solid against my body. I let it draw my pain down into the soil, deep into the Great Mother.

"Harm done to one is harm done to all," Paya Kuyllay used to say. *Let them feel what I felt,* I think. *Let them understand what they have done. Let them know remorse. Let them learn to protect their sisters and mothers and daughters from men like them.*

It is morning by the time I put the heads back in the bag, all but one. I clear out the firepit. When it is deep enough for the bag, I place it at the bottom and add a layer of branches, crisscrossed, and arrange stones and dirt on top—like a small burial chamber. They will be buried but not forgotten. I will decide what to do with them later. I wonder if Waru thinks that justice has been served. Is it over for him? Has his burden been lifted? Because for me, it feels like it is starting all over again.

Carrying as much as I can, I make my way up homeward,

CALL OF THE OWL WOMAN

planning to come back with a few llamas to load up the rest of the plants and pots. As soon as the house is in sight, the dogs spill down the hill, their tails wagging and tongues lapping. I have to wade through their sticky kisses to reach Faruka, who is busy at the fire. She helps me unload, but when she hugs me, she will not meet my eyes. "What's wrong?" I ask, but Faruka shakes her head without answering. She looks nervously toward the house. "Tell me," I insist. "Has something happened?"

Just then, Mother comes out of the house, deep in conversation with Faruka's father. When she sees me, she barely pauses. "I'm glad you are back," she says somberly. "We are holding council tonight. You can help Faruka finish the preparations."

"Of course," I reply. "Have you had news?"

"Nothing. The omens are bad," she says as she hurries past me.

When they are out of sight, Faruka leans in toward me. "Keyka was bothered by a dream last night," she says. "An undersea lodge where creatures were holding council and human heads hung from the rafters. Since the men were still not back from Acari, and no runners have brought any news, she is sure something is wrong. The elders are convening again, turning to wachuma for guidance."

Faruka and I pray over the brew as it cooks. Its effectiveness depends as much on the spirit in which it is prepared as on the cactus itself. Hours later, we pour it into a jar to cool and I signal for Faruka to follow me until we are out of anyone's hearing. We sit on a wide rock by a wall of tall cacti between the outer terrace and the hill itself. I notice a drooping blossom atop an old cactus.

"Patya?" Faruka ventures. "What's wrong?"

For a moment, all I can do is stare at the wilting flower. I shake my head. "So much energy goes into a flower that blooms and fades in a single night. Doesn't it make you wonder?"

"Wonder what?"

"If it's worth it. How many moons has that bud been growing?

Shifting Ground

That cactus put so much effort into making that flower . . . but in the morning it will be dissolving on the ground." I sigh.

Faruka laughs nervously. "Why so upset over a flower?"

"Not just the flower. Everything. Nothing to harvest because everything dies. We plant again. Another year with no harvest. We plant again. And another. We keep doing the same things. Will it really change if they perform their ritual?"

"What ritual?"

I catch myself, remembering that it is supposed to be secret. "You know," I mumble, "going to the temple, paying respect to the sea . . ." But really I am thinking about my father's mission to collect sea-foam from "the wild waters" beyond the rocks, the ancient tradition that requires that sea-foam be taken to a spring in the high hills where the waters are born. There, the seawater seeps into the soil and the soul of Pachamama, seeding the earth's womb with a new surge of lifeblood. The heavens add their rains so that the waters in the hills can grow and swell until they course through ravines and valleys and give life to the desert valleys along the way. The bond between sea and mountains is sealed by the sacred gift from Mother Ocean to the great Apus.

This year Ecco was given the honor of making the vessel, and I was lucky enough to watch him work. It is stunning. Images of the Great Spirit wearing a feline grin curl around the pot. Heads sprout along its body, their tongues curling into vines bursting with fruits, beans, squash, and towers of sacred corn. Human legs float under the flying body. Beasts of heaven walk among humans, and fins give them freedom to swim through the seas. The vessel is filled with the dance of opposites, ever in pursuit, ever in flight. No one outside the mission will ever see the pot, for it will be shattered during the offering.

I may not understand all the things that keep the balance flowing, but I do know how important it is to attend to the spirits and forces at work in this world, in our Kay Pacha. I honor

CALL OF THE OWL WOMAN

Wayra, the wind, who transcends heavens, mountains, earth, and sea, carrying the rain clouds that sustain our Pachamama and the terrestrial beings of this world-between-worlds. I honor the golden Tayta Inti, his gift of light and warmth. But my heart belongs to the Moon who rules the darkness, who draws paths across the sky each night, growing, shrinking, ever-changing but ever-present. My favorite stories from the Starwatchers are tales of the eternal dance between Sun and Moon. Whenever Mama K'illa rises from behind the hills to greet the setting sun, I imagine the longing between them.

"Faruka," I say, hoping to change the subject. "Did I ever tell you about the time I saw Mama K'illa kiss Tayta Inti?"

She laughs. "No, I don't think so."

"When I was small, Paya Kuyllay took me with her to visit an old Starwatcher. He was standing on a hilltop, watching a black circle creep across the sun. In the village below, dogs were howling, and people made noise with rattles and drums, hammering as if the world would end if they did not. The old man squatted down to speak to me. 'Some think that Jaguar is eating the sun, so they make noise to scare him away. But that's not it, child. It is Mama K'illa coming to stand before her lover. Her shining face is turned toward him, so we can only see her back. But when they kiss, what a spark! In those rare moments when they meet, Tayta Inti looks down with the greatest compassion at us, his children. For when Mama K'illa moves on, he sees us as if for the first time, as if we have just stepped out from behind her skirts. He remembers us. We must salute him, show him we take pride in being children of light and heaven, and show our humble gratitude for the gifts they give us.'

"I looked around, expecting something to fall from the sky. 'Where are the gifts?' I asked him.

"The old man laughed. He took my chin in his hand and blew into my face. I gagged at the strange mixture of smells—coca leaves, bad teeth, and fresh flowers. 'The gift of life, child,' he said,

Shifting Ground

'and all the gifts that follow . . . love and joy, music and dance! But we must care for those gifts, and remember, we must never look directly upon his face.' He held up his hands, weaving his fingers together to create small openings. 'From behind your hands, you can sneak little peeks at what happens when the moon kisses the sun!' He raised his entwined hands to the sky. I copied him and looked through the little windows made by fingers. The whole sun became a black circle outlined against the sky by a thin sliver of light. The noise rising from the valley grew frantic as the world was swallowed in shadow.

"Suddenly, a brilliant flash of light shot out from one side. The old man sighed. 'Ah, they meet! You see? Such a kiss!' The flare rippled for a moment like the sparkle of sun on water, then disappeared again into the darkness. A softer light began to form rays around the dark circle, looking like the pupil of an enormous eye. The Starwatcher stood up and held his arms out in salute. The moon slid slowly past the sun, and the light of Tayta Inti began to grow again, resuming its splendor in her wake."

Faruka shakes her head at me. "I didn't know you were such a romantic," she says.

"Grandmother told me that it is a rare privilege to witness the Eye of Creator." I close my eyes, remembering that great eye that looked back at me then. I am reminded of the huge eye of the orca I saw as a child, how it held my gaze, looking back with something beyond curiosity. But one cannot hold the gaze of Inti without being blinded. "Do you think that Creator ever really looks at us or just looks past us?" I ask Faruka. "Does Creator care at all what happens to our people? Or that there is no water in our rivers?"

To myself I also wonder if Creator even cares about our human lives. About what the Warpa did to me? Or that Kuyllay had died? Or that suddenly I have seven heads I don't know what to do with?

Faruka's voice coaxes me back from my thoughts. " . . . and since Old Man Terzhic is sick again, he sent his son Chanki in his place and told him to agree with anything your uncle Weq'o says." She hesitates then adds, "I know Weq'o is your family, Patya, but I don't trust him."

I dust off the back of my tunic as I stand up. "Neither do I. All he cares about is what he can get for himself," I reply. "I wouldn't be surprised if Weq'o has something to do with the way Terzhic's family always seems to get more water for irrigation than their neighbors. If Weq'o is coming tonight, I'd rather not be here." I pull Faruka to her feet. "I still have a lot to finish at my paya's. Maybe we can go back and work on that together."

As soon as Mother sees us, she pulls me aside. She has something else in mind. "Let Ecco and Faruka take a couple llamas tomorrow to bring the rest for you," she says. She pours some wachuma into a gourd. "It is time you make that pilgrimage you and Kuyllay were planning. Take this with you. Do your own ceremony."

Paya Kuyllay died less than a moon before I was to make my solo pilgrimage to Yuraq Orqo. We made the journey together three times, and this year was to be my initiation. I had imagined myself stepping across a threshold to a new and better self, a place where I did not doubt myself or the world around me. I had just started to feel strong enough for the challenge, buoyed by Kuyllay's confidence in me. But then suddenly Kuyllay was gone, and my whole world changed.

Mother holds me at arm's distance to look into my eyes. "You must go to Yuraq Orqo tonight while we hold ceremony here. Mama K'illa will light your way, and the mountain will show you what we need to know." She nods at the gourd. "The Spirit of Wachuma will guide you."

Behind my mother looms the silhouette of the white hill, shimmering against the deep blue sky. For half a breath, I feel my own self looking back.

Shifting Ground

• ✦ •

Yuraq Orqo is not as high as the great Apus farther inland. The great Coropuna towers above the clouds, visible even from Illakata. The Acari Valley is in Coropuna's realm, a demanding spirit whose icy peaks require many offerings. I am lucky to have been born in the realm of Yuraq Orqo, a far gentler spirit. Even so, I always approach with the same trepidation and respect reserved for the greater Apus.

Since Kuyllay's hut is on the way, I stop to feed the apacheta some flowers and cornmeal and remove a small stone. "I will take this bit of your energy with me," I tell the apacheta, "and will bring you a stone from Yuraq Orqo in exchange." I lay out my altar cloth to prepare my offering for the mountain the way that Kuyllay taught me and set five wooden stakes in the ground. Each has a figure carved at the top. The first is a woman's form, to invoke Earth, Creation, and my family's long lineage of healers. The second has the shape of an owl, for navigating the unseen. The center staff, my walking stick, is the tallest of the group, embedded with shells, stones, and resin from ancient guarango trees. A carved condor perches atop the next staff, ready to invoke the power of its great wings to carry messages to the Creator, and the last holds a crescent moon with a sun carved into the wood below it.

I chant softly, shaking my rattle and summoning my allies. I call on the Apus—Yuraq Orqo, Illakata, Coropuna. I call on the spirits of water, of stars, of wind, of ancient trees, and of jaguar-uturunku, owl-tuku, and hummingbird-q'enti. Placing a bit of llama fat at the center of a square white cloth, I call on the ancestors who have gone before us. On a small cloth, I make a pleasing arrangement of herbs and shells, fresh leaves, and powdered stone of different colors, something to feed the mountain spirits. I fold the cloth into a small bundle, wrap it with string,

CALL OF THE OWL WOMAN

and place it at the center of my altar cloth. As I sing an offering prayer, the sounds of nightfall fill the grove and the moon smiles.

I am tempted to rush through the rituals, but Kuyllay's voice hums in the back of my head: *Prepare yourself. Clear your heart and your mind so you will be open to receive Yuraq Orqo's gifts.* The stone atop my walking stick shimmers in the moonlight, as bright as the night I found it when our family was visiting the highlands. Tachico and I were floating in a rocky pool fed by hot springs, watching the night sky. A ball of light suddenly streaked across the sky, disappearing with its forked tail as quickly as it had appeared. The sight filled me with awe and a strange sense of joy. When we scrambled out of the water to go tell the others, Tachico knocked some rocks loose. I caught one of them, a small green stone. It now gleams from its place on my staff, sparkling like Tachico's eyes. I wonder where he is now.

I pack the offering bundle into my satchel, nestled beside the sack with the umanqa. I am still uncomfortable with Waru's unsettling "gift" of heads. I don't know what to do with them. Maybe I should feel satisfaction that it is me who now has the power to harm them should I so choose. I could sever their ties to the earth, hold their spirits hostage. I could exchange them for favors or talismans. Warriors, priests, and shamans can always make use of umanqas, even cause harm to others if they delve into the dark arts. I could learn how to work them as power objects myself. For now I think it best to use them as offerings to the earth. Which is why I will take one with me.

chapter 10
Pilgrimage

I linger at the edge of the grove, reluctant to leave. I shouldn't be so worried about going alone, but it's easy to get lost on Yuraq Orqo. I've gone to the top with Paya Kuyllay before, but we were supposed to make one more trip together to test my memory of the route. I would lead, but she'd still be there if I made a mistake.

Mother would tell me I'll be fine. Just like Paya Kuyllay, she always tells me I need to trust myself more. "Pay attention," she says. "If you listen to your deepest knowing, you will always find your way." Paya Kuyllay liked to remind me that our ancestors journeyed with no guidance but the inner voice of Spirit. "We would not be here now if they had not trusted that voice." And I always retorted that we only know about their journey, not all the other tribes we've never heard of, because they made wrong turns in the desert and never found their way out. We hear plenty of stories about the Great Crossing but not about why our ancestors made the journey. Were they fleeing something, or were they seeking something? Were they a restless people who finally found a place they liked enough to settle? Or had they left reluctantly by

CALL OF THE OWL WOMAN

force or disaster? Had they known they would never return? I can't help but wonder what it must have felt like to realize you would never see your home again, your favorite tree. But this is different. I'm not crossing the world, just climbing a big hill, barely enough to be called a mountain. I will be back home tomorrow.

A cheerful bark greets me as soon as I reach the riverbed. Wiksa races up to me, nearly knocking me over. "Wiksa! Thank the gods you are okay! And just in time to join me!" I hug the dusty dog close to me, already feeling more confident. Dogs always find their way home. As we cross the trickle of water at the center of the cracked riverbed, I find it hard to believe that people ever approached this river with fear, that flash floods had ever carried away livestock. The wells we pass produce barely anything. The fields along the riverbanks are dry.

It's a short climb over the spine of the hill that divides the Aja from the Uchumarca River. The ridge continues upward until it towers over the rivers on either side. But here below, the two river channels come together on the plains near a spray of rocks we call Serpent's Tongue. As usual, there is no water at all on the Uchumarca side. We cross and veer up into the hills on the far side and find a shady place to rest. By the time we reach the path that leads to the top of Yuraq Orqo it is getting late, and the wind is unusually harsh. I use my shawl to shield my eyes from the sting of blowing sand and concentrate on the ground at my feet. Her head down, Wiksa plows into the wind beside me. As the sun sets, the moon grows brighter, lighting the path toward the summit.

The wind drowns out other sounds as we make our way upward through the cracks in the hillside and boulders along the way. I try to keep an eye out for anything unusual that Mother might consider an omen or a sign, but my thoughts keep circling back to Achiq. I did not like the way he looked at Tachico. I'm sure his crooked smile is hiding something. He has been calling for more and more sacrifices each season, insisting that offering

Pilgrimage

our best livestock will bring the rains. He even wanted to send warriors to raid the settlements in the south to bring back heads for offerings, but Father persuaded the Council to stop him. I do not understand how Achiq can be so certain that he knows the gods' wishes or how so many people can believe that he is the best one to interpret the message from Creator. Achiq experiences the unseen powers as beings that dominate and punish. But how can he be so sure that his perspective is right? I don't think that anyone can really be certain of what the gods want. They are such changeable forces—breathing life into wind and water, heavens and earth. Kuyllay used many different names for the forms they took and the faces they wore. When she sang to them, sometimes she called them Mother, other times Sister. For a good ocean harvest, she called on the Mother of Fish, Grandmother Ocean, Sister Tide, Brother Storm Rider, Uncle Sand Winds, Great Creator. But she did not call them gods.

The folds of rock create a tapestry of uneven shapes and varied textures. In the dusty smell and stark features of the landscape, I wander through the lineages of our ancestors, see them before me, one behind the other, all the way back to the birth of the world. I feel the mountains untangling themselves from the bowels of the earth, wrestling the great waters for their place in the world. I recall how the plains of Nasca came to lie between two ranges of mountains, one that was swallowed by the sea and another whose peaks still thrust skyward through the realms of snow and ice. I feel my heart glide along the narrow valleys cutting through the hills, finding their way to the coastal plains. I follow the waters they carry from the mountains, disappear with them beneath the earth, find my way with them to the sea.

At the last solstice gathering, I asked one of the elders about the wooded oases from the stories they tell about how the earth spread her skirts in luxurious folds where the two-legged humans could find protection and bounty, fertile grounds, and good hunting. According to them the children of the first parents followed the animals to learn from them, to find shelter and water. "If such bountiful places exist, why do our people live in the desert?"

The elder grew very solemn before he replied. "So that we remember, child, always to be grateful for what we have. Those who forget gratitude are quick to destroy what they have."

"Come on, old man," Achiq had interrupted. "Tell her why the waters have left us! Tell everyone why the gods are displeased with their creation. Tell them how the desert will drown us in sand because we have forgotten how to please the gods."

I remember Kuyllay putting her arm around me protectively. She seemed upset but spoke calmly. "Sometimes, Achiq, the gods are not asking for us to pleasure them—merely for us to listen."

They say my family has been in the Aja Valley since before people started counting time. They built their homes among the rocks along the barren hillside overlooking the fertile land along the river, right where the Aja leaves the hills to meet the plains. For most of the year, the local rivers were little more than dry pathways through the hills, but when the rains fell in the highlands, the waters of the two rivers would gather and race each other to the sea. In normal seasons, their merging would swell to overflowing, and the canals filled. Even in times of drought the wells held abundant water. My father is one of the most experienced canal-keepers and the most trusted of the guardians.

When I was small, I used to tag along during the canal cleanings, helping pull out clumps of vegetation and smoothing the rock beds so the waters could flow unobstructed. Once I followed Otocco and his friend Chanki into a tunnel. I did not get very far before I broke into a sweat and had trouble breathing. I was sure that the earth was about to crush me. Otocco had to help me out, and he lost his patience. "Girls don't belong here," he said. "Go home."

Pilgrimage

"Let your brothers do the work below the surface," Mother had told me, drying my tears. "The beast that guards the underworld honors no female but Pachamama. He does not want you there to make her jealous. And you, Patya, are a child of the open sky."

Tachico, on the other hand, had begun helping in the tunnels as soon as he could walk. He quickly learned the location of all the canals and wells and could sense the waters before anyone told him. He would break twigs to use as dowsing rods to track the path of waters as he walked along the surface, and soon he could even tell how deep they flowed and how full they were. Crawling through dark, musty tunnels gives him the most joy, and he does it with the ease of any of Pachamama's underground creatures. He was thrilled to take Ecco's place on the mission to the cove this time, but I can't help but wonder why Achiq was so insistent. Or what suddenly made Ecco so sick. I also worry that Mother is so worried. It is not just that no word has come from Acari or from the cove. It's something she senses, and her senses are always right. I hope they are all okay.

I take note of the position of the moon, pour some water into a bowl for Wiksa, and take a deep drink from my water bag. It is odd not to have Tachico with me, prodding me to go faster or to try a new route. I was surprised by the decision to take Tachico on the mission. He is still too young and fearless for such serious matters. He doesn't realize how dangerous the sea can be. He is undaunted by threats of animals or earthquakes or marauding warriors, as if he assumes that some great magic protects him. Otocco and Father don't keep track of him as well as I do. I am usually there to look after him, check our bearings, make sure we have enough water to drink. I always have a supply of dried llama meat in my pouch for when he gets hungry. Maybe it's no wonder Tachico never fears getting lost, or getting thirsty, or getting hungry. He has me.

CALL OF THE OWL WOMAN

That's exactly why Mother has sent me to the mountain with the wachuma. To check on Tachico. I hope the spirits will show me.

We reach a part of the trail that takes a steep turn and all but disappears where part of the cliffside has broken away. I lift Wiksa across the gap and wait till she gets her footing, then brace my staff against the ground to propel myself upward and forward, grabbing a handhold on the other side. The ground under my back foot gives way and starts a cascade of rocks tumbling downward. I cling to the hillside, my heart pounding as my foot searches for something solid. Wiksa whimpers ahead of me. I slide my foot cautiously forward and test the ground before putting my weight on it. One step at a time. When I reach solid ground again, I pull a hair from my head and press it into a crack. A small offering of gratitude to the earth. "Thank you for holding me," I say, and press my lips against the ground.

Over the next rise the base of the dune comes into view. When I can see the tall pile of rocks that marks the entry into sacred space, I know I am in the right place. I approach the apacheta, say a prayer over the rock I brought from Kuyllay's apacheta, and ask permission to enter. I add my rock to the pile and quiet myself. Night sounds float up from the valley, but the wind has grown still. Nothing stirs. The moon pulses with a strange light behind a thin veil of clouds gathering in a circle around it. "Mama K'illa," I whisper, "you look hungry." I pull a smooth red pebble from my pouch, blow a prayer into it, and place it at the bottom of the apacheta. I lean my forehead into the rocks, feeling the moonlight on my back. A small gust lifts my shawl and sends a gentle shiver across my shoulders. I take it as a sign to proceed.

At the top of the fourth rise, I stop at another small apacheta and add a rough black stone that I had picked up at the edge of the riverbed. The rugged edges of the mountain give way to the tapestry of sand unfolding before me. I start the last push. The

Pilgrimage

dune that covers the mountain glows silvery white where the fine sand catches the moonlight. The going is slow. At first touch, the crust is thick and solid, but it crumbles under the weight of each step. I pause halfway up the first ridge of sand, watching tiny avalanches of sand skid down the surface, lifting bits of bark and insect shells to float across the top like waves rolling onto the shore. Remnants of fabric from old offerings have found their way to the top of the hill, some riding currents of wind all the way from the valley floor. I plant my staff deep into the sand with each push forward until I finally reach the top.

A field of stars crowns the hills that stretch across the northern horizon. To the west Tunga's silhouette stands out in the line of hills rolling southward toward the sea. To the east rolls another set of hills, continuing into the distance, each one higher than the last, like stepping stones to the higher mountains. I fling my arms upward and spin around, welcoming the vastness of the sky, the expanse of the world before me, the marvel of this place.

I sing out happily, "Thank you, Mother Moon!" I sift through the sand and hold up a handful of leaves and feather tufts, letting a brisk gust spiral them away, a gift to the Lord of Winds. As they swirl eastward, I suddenly feel the pressure of time, the imminence of the sun's return. I find a shallow dip on the lee side of the dune with some shelter from the wind. Rising through the sand is a patch of harder ground, perfect to set up my altar. I plant my staff into the earth and consecrate the space with an offering of coca leaves before spreading my cloth on the ground to arrange the ritual objects for my altar. I place a mullu at the center, a thorny oyster shell with purple hues. Then a small chunk of turquoise in the shape of a llama and a dark Pachamama stone for the earth, a twisted seashell for the ancestors, a feather for the wind and mountain spirits, and a bright crystal to honor Father Sun. On top of the centerpiece, I place my wrapped offering. Wiksa settles down next to me, curls up, and falls asleep.

After I pour a few drops of the wachuma brew onto the ground, I salute the four directions, then call on the sacred hills and my spirit allies. I shake my rattle over each object, awakening and engaging their energies. "Let me see beyond the reach of my eyes," I chant. "Let me hear more than my ears. Let me taste the truth of the world and feel what I must do." Tilting the gourd toward the heavens, I drink, trying not to gag at the slimy bitterness of wachuma. Then I sit back and allow the quiet to fill me.

My thumb absently strokes a smooth black stone that I found at the sacred cove a few years ago. A gift from the sea, it fit so comfortably in my palm that it felt as if it had been created for me. The depressions on its surface are almost skull-like, like the hill with three caves that overlook the cove. Whenever I hold it, I feel connected to that place, tied somehow to its energy. Right now, that energy is starting to spin. An impulse lifts me to my feet and I begin to circle my altar cloth, spiraling slowly outward until my feet stop at a rock jutting out of the sand. The heart-shaped stone is the size of a small head but reminds me of a condor's eye. A good place, I think, to bury my offering. I trace the head of a condor in the hard sand around it, as if the rock were its eye, then dig until I have a hole large enough to bury my offering bundle. I hope the arrangement of shells and leaves and colorful powders will please the mountain. "To feed the heart of Yuraq Orqo and invoke Kuntur's great vision," I intone, using the ancient name for Condor, "I give this offering and ask your blessing." I cover everything, smoothing the sand over it as if nothing had been disturbed.

Sitting again at my altar cloth, I imagine Kuyllay drumming for me. Pulsating stars gather into familiar shapes. Everything begins to whirl. As if from the center of a whirlwind, I manage to take my staff and walk to the top of the dune. I plunge it into the sand, anchoring myself in the vortex. The ground opens up below. I grip my staff, trying to center myself in the chaos. "Please, show me what I must do."

Pilgrimage

My staff begins to pulse. I see myself in the Sumara grove next to the ancient tree. Its serpentine body weaves along the ground to the edge of the brambles. A tiny owl ducks into its burrow, and my spirit follows. The dry sand gives way to a path through a moist tangle of roots. A ribbon of water leads me downward into a narrow tunnel. Walls of rock glow with iridescent lichen. The tunnel begins to widen and the path tilts upward. The water continues downward, disappearing below. I walk toward light from an opening ahead. When I step out, I have to cover my eyes. The sea gleams, stretching before me, infinite. Below me is the sacred cove. I am standing at the entrance to one of the three caves. The second cave is visible to my left. The third is just below. I have the sensation of watching a memory of something that hasn't yet happened.

A wave of dizziness makes me tighten my hold on my staff. Suddenly I am on the shore, watching a small stone roll across my feet in the shallow water, the same stone I am holding. The wave retreats and the stone begins to roll back with it. I catch it, just as I did when I first found it. It is smooth and pleasing to the touch. My thumb eddies in its dents and dips. I hold the rock to my chest and look out to sea, beyond the rocky outcrops that frame the cove. A sleek black giant bursts from the water, rolls, and falls with a thunderous splash.

I look down again at the stone. This time I see an orca's face, not the playful giant I met as a child but a fierce orca on the hunt. "Go," it seems to say. "Now."

"But I just got here!" I don't know if I said or merely thought it. I am suddenly at the cave's edge again, looking down. On the beach, my father is bent over Tachico. A stream of blood seeps into the ocean with each retreating wave.

"Go," the voice repeats, low and commanding. Achiq stands at the entrance to the other cave, a strange smile on his face. I slip back inside, hoping he has not seen me, and retrace my steps back through the tunnel, back to the stream, and back to the Sumara grove. Without warning, I am fully present again on Yuraq Orqo. The sky is growing light. I stare at the stone in my hand. It stares back. "Now."

The ritual is over.

I quickly repack my things, the vision still burning. Was this what Mother had seen?

"Wiksa!" I call, but the dog is nowhere in sight. I cross over the next rise. "Wiksa!" A glorious dawn is emerging from behind the mountains. I bring the pututu to my lips, thinking my sunrise salute might bring Wiksa back. I sound it three times to the east, hoping the wind will carry it to my mother to let her know I made it. I send two undulating blasts to the south, imagining that Tachico might hear it and recognize our special greeting.

I pull my shawl tight against the damp morning air and set off in the direction of Wiksa's footprints—a path of small breaks in the crusty surface. They lead me to a leafless tree alone in the fold of a dune. Next to it, a small pile of excrement adorns a low rock. A fox marking its territory. Wiksa is probably in eager pursuit. At the top of the next ridge, I scan the landscape. Sand spreads in every direction, sculpted into waves by the sea-born winds with no sign of Wiksa's prints. I close my eyes, trying to will my intuition to nudge me in the right direction. Nothing tugs. *Have faith*, I tell myself, breathing deeply. I have to place my trust in the mountain.

chapter 11
What Is Found

A damp chill embraces me from behind, pushing me forward. "Thank you, Yuraq Orqo!" I blurt out, opening my eyes. I expect to see some sign of Wiksa, but instead I see only thick, unnerving fog. As I turn to look behind me, the sand gives way. I hold tight to my things as I tumble and slide down the steep slope. When I finally come to a stop, I am choking and spitting sand in the middle of a veil of fog. I have no idea how far I have fallen or which side I am on.

Tales of sudden fogs on Yuraq Orqo have always filled me with dread—stories of people staggering out days later, of people who were never seen again. *I must not panic*, I tell myself. *Be sensible.* A fog can burn off as quickly as it appears. I want to kick myself for not going straight back down the mountain instead of trying to find Wiksa. With her nose, she'll be fine on her own—she's probably already on her way home by now. I, however, have no choice but to wait.

The sand accommodates me like an embrace as I nestle in and try to think. I have been up all night and have a long trek home. A little forced rest might not be bad.

I do not realize I have fallen asleep until I am jolted awake by a dream, screaming, "Now!" I am suddenly upright, remembering the orca from my vision, but I am disoriented. The ache of unfinished sleep grates at my nerves. For a moment, I cannot remember where I am. A thin mist surrounds me, but it is beginning to dissipate. A small clearing opens in front of me. From somewhere just above and behind me comes a strange and lilting song: "*Oh, rain will come, rain will come, but not where it is needed.*"

I strain to see through the lifting fog, but I see no one. The voice gets closer. "*It will tease the seeds, call them out, and let them burn unheeded.*" Could it be that Yuraq Orqo is speaking to me?

A movement catches my eye, and I follow the shifting play of light across the emerging landscape. A woman begins to come into focus, her speckled robe the color of sand and her face tattooed with spots. The song stops. "Are you afraid of death?" she asks. The deep brown of her eyes shimmer like the surface of a well in moonlight. "Are you afraid of death?" she repeats gently, growing more solid as she approaches.

I do not know if I am hearing a vision, a spirit, or a human. What was it that Paya Kuyllay said? *Be open to receive Yuraq Orqo's gifts.* Open. To whatever might come.

"No," I reply, more curious than afraid. "In fact, there was a time when I *wanted* to die." But then the thought of Tachico bleeding on the beach makes me add, "But I do fear death for my family."

The woman takes my hands between her own. She leans down to rest her forehead on our joined hands and suddenly straightens. "You come here wanting to know the future. But it hides behind you, revealing itself only as you step through it." Her words roll through me like a dream. My head fills with images. High mountain peaks. Vast horizons of layered clouds. My home. Kuyllay's grave. The sacred cove. An orca bursting from the water.

What Is Found

"Your brother will need your help to return from the darkness, but what you seek is beyond that," she says. It's like the wachuma has reawakened within me, breathing shapes and colors into the words I am hearing. "Darkness flows through your valleys, plagues attack your trees, the earth is in convulsion, and your people are in the way." The woman places her hands on each side of my head, holding it lightly. She then steps back with an odd twirl. "They think it is a punishment," she says dreamily. "But if you roll over in your sleep and crush an ant, are you punishing it?" She smiles sadly. "Can you be aware of every being and its place in your path? When a creature chooses to live in your folds, it must anticipate your moves if it is to survive. Do you think that making offerings can change that?"

"Our offerings to Pachamama remind her we are here," I reply.

"More important," the woman responds, "they remind *you*. Remind you to think of her. To honor her." She turns away from me and raises her arms. The spotted cloak floats as light as gauze behind her. The mist lifts higher, suddenly revealing the canyon below and the rocky ridge across from us. The way home.

"The tremblings of the earth come from deep within, far from where we feel them," the woman says, turning back to me. "We must listen to her, feel when her energies are with us, and know when to get out of her path." Her words wander and leap, mixing in other languages and senseless sounds. I don't understand what she is saying and cannot make sense of the images that flood my mind. A forest ravaged by blight, branches all but bared of leaves, pitted and diseased fruit pods, men beside animals foraging for food, fighting over bones, competing for puddles of water. White-topped Apus are suddenly bare, islands empty of birds. Trees are being cut down faster than new ones can grow, seeds hide themselves in dead ravines, and rotting fish wash ashore. Each breath I take feels endless. Storms rage, deserts overtake forests, people wail that the gods have abandoned them. Overwhelmed by the

CALL OF THE OWL WOMAN

visions, I curl into myself, trying to stop the flood, to find refuge in oblivion.

I wake up to the burn of sunshine against my cheek. Except for a few trailing wisps, the fog is gone. My body is covered by a spotted cloak. I try to remember where I have seen it, but my memory is hazier than the mists that swirl past. I stand up and scan the landscape. The valley below seems impossibly far away. The sun is not much higher than it was before the fog appeared, but it feels like I have been here forever. There is no trace of anyone. No Wiksa. I marvel at the curious cloak, its softness against my skin. It floats on my shoulders as if I have always worn it. I begin to remember the strange woman. The flood of images. If it were not for the cloak, I would have thought it all a dream. My water bag is full again, and on top of it is an odd pendant, rather like a misshapen jaguar. I slip it into my bag and begin to work my way down the dune, still in a daze.

The sand is heating up, but my progress is slow. With each step, my foot slides downward, causing small rivulets of sand to flow alongside each footprint. I set a steady rhythm, singing one of Tachico's walking songs. To block out the image of him on the beach, I picture us singing together the way we do when out gathering seeds and roots or sitting across from each other in a small ravine, rolling our voices along the valley walls, harmonizing with our own echoes. I remember how, when the wind was just right, the voices of flutes and singers from up the valley would join us in concert.

I finally reach the northern edge of the dune. Sharp, craggy rocks border the narrow gorge. It is so deep that it makes me wonder if the mountain itself broke apart in a long-ago earthquake. On the other side stretches a ridge as jagged as the dune is smooth. There appears to be a path along the edge that leads to the valley floor. A natural stone bridge still connects the two sides, a remnant of a time when the mountain was whole. The rocks at

What Is Found

the bottom look as if they were ripped from the high mountains and deposited by one of the great huaicos that crashed through these hills. I pray I never encounter such a huaico. The stories are terrifying.

The path on the other side looks easier to navigate than the usual route via the sea of sand stretching below me. I have never descended the dune this late in the day, and each step burns more than the one before. The archway of rock looks too precarious. I pause, gazing longingly across the gap before I turn away from the ravine. I am about to tear cloth from my shawl to wrap my feet when a large shadow darkens the ground before me. A huge condor hovers above me. The shadow cast by its wings spans the entire bridge—eerily connecting the two sides. I stare up at the condor and then back to the bridge. Could this be a sign that I am meant to cross it? Or is the condor waiting for me to fall so it can feast on my remains below?

The great bird circles around and lands on the ridge across from me. It turns its head in my direction. *Follow the signs*, my mother always says. But what if I am reading them wrong? How am I to know?

My side of the ravine is sparkling, blistering. On the other side is a firm path to walk on. *Are you going to let your fear get in the way?* I hear Paya Kuyllay coaxing me. How often had she said those words to me?

I approach the edge and place a tentative foot on the bridge. Nothing budges, but I still don't trust it. Sand might burn, but it wouldn't drop me to a sure death in a rocky ravine if I slip. The condor adjusts itself, stretching its massive wings before settling them against its back. The two of us stare at each other for a moment, then the wrinkled head turns to scan the ravine's path into the valley.

"Fine," I announce. I tie my walking stick to the bag on my back, say a quick prayer for courage, and take a tentative step

CALL OF THE OWL WOMAN

onto the span of stone. I try not to look down, forcing myself to focus on my next footstep. I am careful not to look beyond the rock in front of me. As I inch my foot forward, a chunk of rock slides off the bridge and clatters noisily when it hits the bottom.

"Steady," I tell myself, lowering to my knees. I find handholds before sliding myself forward. I make my way slowly, carefully. I am almost across when the condor rises abruptly. A rush of small birds swells up from nowhere. The earth itself seems to groan. Things begin to sway, and a slow, undulating roll issues from within the mountain in a nauseating wave. I drop to my stomach and hold on. My heart empties into the void below.

"Lord of Thunder, have mercy!" I cry, clinging to the shuddering rock as I brace for the jolt to come. A huge rock breaks away from the hill facing me. Time thickens. The rock plummets toward my precarious bridge, yet it seems to move slowly through the gelatinous moment. Slow enough for a thousand thoughts to roll through my head as I watch its advance. Is this my day to die? Was that what the woman meant? Do I have to take spirit form to help my brother? I try to calm myself, to tell myself that if it is meant to be, I will embrace it. I will become one with the great source of all being, my soul free of physical limitations.

I imagine myself on the condor's back, the wind in my face, my spirit greeting the snow-topped Apus. I ready my soul to let go of this world and stare into the face of the coming rock, my head thrown back in a triumphant "Yes!" But the sting of sand in my eyes and the rock scraping against my skin call me back. I tighten my grip. Tachico needs me.

The rock picks up speed as it nears the edge of the cliff and the end of my bridge. It hits another rock and angles slightly, veering just enough to miss the bridge and plunge into the ravine. I concentrate on the solid ground almost within reach. Rocks bounce and crash below. My heart pounds in my ears as I work my way across the last bit of bridge and pull myself onto the

What Is Found

path. I crawl away from the edge and lean into the rocky wall, grateful for something solid against my back. Dirt and debris fill the air. Right before Yuraq Orqo disappears behind a thick cloud of dust, the stone bridge shudders and collapses. Only a gaping hole remains.

At first I cannot breathe or move. My heart is pulsing in my throat. I pull the hood down over my eyes and more scarf up over my nose until the rolling subsides enough to move again. I have to get to Tachico. I have to get home. The ground heaves again and I stumble. Gravel pelts me like hailstones. I regain my footing and scan the terrain. If I could just find an outcropping, a place to shelter. I edge my way forward until I feel a hollow in the wall, then wedge myself backward into the nook. The hill feels solid behind me, and the narrow ledge above me deflects the falling rocks.

I think of my father and the way he likes to drill the family for unexpected crises. "Stay calm," he always says. "Fear wakes you up. Use it, don't indulge it. The ability *to think* is most important. The ability *to do* follows." I repeat it now. *Use it, don't indulge it.* A loud crash shakes the overhang. A chunk breaks off, tumbling down the ravine with all the rest. As I try to scoot farther back into the recess, a cool rush of air comes from behind me. I twist around and discover a gap behind what seems to be solid rock. Afraid of what will happen if the rest of the overhang gives way, I flatten myself against the rock and slide sideways through the opening.

Once my eyes adjust to the dark, I discover that I can stand. The opening goes deep. A thin ray of light threads through a hole in the roof and rolls down a large stone. I move toward it slowly, wary of bats. My lungs hurt and my throat is sore, but the air in here is breathable. Near the stone, I can make out scraps of textile, animal droppings, broken ceramics, and flat stones that look like seats. Several wooden poles stand among the rocks. They could

CALL OF THE OWL WOMAN

be walking sticks left behind or ceremonial staves left as offerings. It is comforting to know that other pilgrims have been here. I know that even mountains can be brought down by earthquakes, but at least these walls feel solid. For the moment, this cave seems safer than being outside.

The thought of home triggers such longing that it hurts. Mother must be so worried. For all of us. It's hard not to imagine the worst. I envision her looking to Yuraq Orqo, calling to me, so I call back, "I am on my way!" The cave shakes. It feels like the hill is falling outside. *I will be on my way*, I correct, *as soon as the mountain is quiet.* I worry for Mother, for everyone back home. For Father and the rest of the team who went south. "Please let them be safe," I pray.

My thoughts travel to places I'd rather they wouldn't, but they have their own volition. I start wondering if it's the ones who are killed quickly who are actually the lucky ones when disaster strikes. A fatal blow to the head would be better than being stuck somewhere, too hurt to move, doomed to die slowly while vultures circle. I start to think about what would happen if I were to get badly hurt here on the mountain with no one nearby. These are not thoughts that will help at all.

I go back to the opening to peek outside, but now there is a wall of rocks blocking the way. A bit of light enters through a small gap at the top. I climb the pile and push away what I can, but there is not enough room to squeeze through. I put all my strength and weight into pushing one of the larger rocks. The rock groans. I take another deep breath and push again. The rock shifts slightly to one side with a loud grinding and then stops, refusing to budge any further. *Think*, I tell myself. I study the way it has lodged among the other rocks. I have helped my brothers move plenty of large stones out of fields with logs and sticks. I jam a pointed rock into a gap between the stones and pound it with another stone until it wedges a little deeper. The rock above

What Is Found

gives just a little more. Again, I lean my whole body into it. Some smaller stones roll to my feet, but the big rock remains unmoved. I drop back to the ground, exhausted.

My staff is too brittle a wood to use as a lever, but one of the sticks in the cave may work. I find two poles of guarango, the strongest wood I know, and take a moment to ask them, respectfully, if they would be willing to help. I do not want to offend anyone by borrowing a pole that might have once served as a sacred ceremonial staff, but these seem content to be of service, however that may be, so I take them to the opening. One is encircled by twine from which hangs a small charm. In the shadows, I can't make out the design embossed on the thin metal, but I unwind the twine and slip the charm onto one of my necklaces. I wedge the pole in between the two stones that look most likely to give way, wiggle it to gain a little space, and then slide the other pole in beside it. I wrap the two ends together with the twine and then bear down with all my weight. The wood creaks and groans and the rock gives way slightly. I pound at the ends to push the poles in a little farther and then lean into it again. This time nothing budges. Again and again, I try, with no effect. I finally fall back in tears. "Grandmother," I plead, "what now?" The earth shudders again, throwing me hard against a sharp rock.

Maybe I am meant to be here as a sacrifice, I think. *Maybe Achiq is right that the Apus are angry and thirsty for blood.* The spotted woman might not think that divine beings need sacrifices, but most of my neighbors believe they do. They believe what the priests tell them. Achiq insists that the earth demands blood and that the best sacrifice involves a child. I may not be a child any longer, but if my blood really could help, really could end the drought, then yes, it would be worth it.

But taking human life does not make sense to me. Making gifts and offerings, yes. That is ayni. Sacred reciprocity. We need to give and share, to honor what we receive, and to show our

CALL OF THE OWL WOMAN

gratitude. We receive, we give. We give, we receive. We keep a balance, aspire to harmony. We receive our harvests and give some back to the earth. Our livestock thrives and we give the best back to the earth. The llama's blood nourishes the soil. Blood is life. And I do not deny that giving one's own life to save another may be the ultimate gift, but offering someone else's life, not by their choice—how can that count as a gift? If Achiq really believes that a human life is what will end the drought and the suffering of our people, why does he not offer his own?

What I sensed on Yuraq Orqo was not a thirst for sacrifice or desire for blood but a sadness for our brokenness. If anything, I think the earth herself leans toward balance, even longs for it. I am comforted that our sacred mountain has the spirit of a woman, a compassionate spirit. One that manifested itself to me, showed me things, and gifted me. The spotted cloak and jaguar charm were given for a reason. I trust that they have a purpose, perhaps to be revealed on my return home. But if I am destined to die on Yuraq Orqo, then so be it. May it serve a greater purpose.

Wait.

Maybe I am not on Yuraq Orqo. I crossed the ravine, which puts me on the neighboring hill, the one my uncles whisper about in late-night fire circles. The one they tunnel into for minerals to make the red and yellow paints, for the shiny metals that are pounded into the finest ornaments and masks. The mines are on the other side of the hill, opposite to where I am now trapped, but I have often heard about their rituals to keep peace with the mountain. No one ever enters a mine without requesting permission first, nor ever leaves without having made the appropriate gifts to its resident spirits. They place skulls deep in the passages and feed them with food and drink and shells from the sea. Women are not allowed in the mines. I remember one who used to bring her husband lunch every day. She usually left it at the base of the hill, but one afternoon she was so eager to see her

What Is Found

beloved that she took it all the way to the entrance. They say that the moment he took the bag from her, a great wind burst from the depths of the mountain. It took the form of a huge dark hand and pulled the woman into the tunnel, never to be seen again.

If this cave is connected to those mines, my presence here might not be well received. What if the spirits of this place are blocking my way out? What if . . .

But I can't think that way.

I call on every ancestor, every ally, and every Apu I can think of. I lean into the stone again. And again. Until I have no energy left. Exhausted, I lean back against the wall. My tunic is torn and sweat stings my skin.

I think of my family, of everything I have not done and still want to do, of my lost chance with Yantu, of all the times I did not cry when I wanted to. I begin to weep. I weep for Tachico and wonder if we will soon meet in the world beyond. I think of the crazy Warpa trying to cleanse his brother's honor, remembering the sadness in his face.

Suddenly, the chatter in my mind stops. My tears stop. Kuyllay's words come to me again. *When in doubt, give gratitude. Make an offering.*

Of course! How had I forgotten? I untie my bundle and place the umanqa bag before me. I had planned to use it as an offering for Yuraq Orqo. But if I am honest with myself, it would not have been in the right spirit of giving. It was more like trying to get rid of the umanqa to erase the reminder. I open the bag and place the umanqa in front of me. "I felt something from you," I tell the desiccated head. "Was it regret? A wish to undo what cannot be undone? Perhaps this is a chance for you to begin."

Thick dark hair frames the leathery face and barely covers the hole at the top for the carrying rope. The tattoos on his cheeks are easily distinguishable—two lightning bolts inside a diamond, like the ones on Waru's arms. I do not remember this face or any

CALL OF THE OWL WOMAN

of the others. Only their markings, the emptiness in their eyes. I take a deep breath. *I survived*, I remind myself. This man is paying for his offense, not only with this life but also with whatever comes next. "You can't hurt me," I tell him, "or anyone else." *Not anymore.*

I hold the head up toward the unseen sky, out to the sides, to the floor. "Let this umanqa be a gift to the earth. Let his spirit protect wayward pilgrims and his vigilance serve as an offering to atone for any harm done in his life," I say. *Not only the damage done to me*, I think, *but any and all harm caused during his life.* "I leave him here, that his remorse may be transformed, that his soul may find peace, and that I may be released." Carrying the umanqa to the center altar stone, I hear something rattle inside the head as it sways on the braided rope. A small rock drops out of the back of the umanqa when I set it on the altar, and I pick up the rock and turn it in my hands. Two rings of white circle it at different angles, forming an *X* where they cross. I place it next to the umanqa and coil the rope beside it. I am about to put the stone back inside the umanqa when something makes me hesitate. On impulse, I hold the stone against the umanqa's forehead. It seems to be what the stone was waiting for. The mountain is quiet. The umanqa feels settled somehow. Like the stone in my hand feels settled. I close my fist over the rock, hold it to my own forehead, and back away from the altar. "So be it," I say, slipping the stone into my waist pouch. I bow to the space around me, the cave, the earth, the umanqa.

My legs tremble, suddenly weak. In a wash of confusion, I hear myself saying, "Stranger, your wrongs are etched in my body and my soul. If there is such a thing as redemption, may you seek and find it."

When I go back to the corridor, I place my hands against the rock blocking my exit. I imagine myself within the rock. I imagine the journey it took to reach this place and the possible paths

What Is Found

in its future. The countless what-ifs following each possible twist. A tapestry unrolls before me, much like the cottony networks in many a soil, the fabric of the earth. "Please," I pray to the core of all being, "open my vision, open my heart, open my path, show me the way." The next aftershock could compact the rubble even more, but if I am lucky, it will dislodge something instead. With my help, it might even open a hole. I position myself at the pole, ready to push when the earth moves again.

While I wait, I imagine a ballad for Yuraq Orqo, a ballad for pilgrims of the future. "*Llaqta Llaqta Piriy, purikoq, Sonqosapa,*" I sing. "Journey, pilgrim, to the great good heart, the heart of Yuraq Orqo." I'm working out a new verse about the journey home, *puriripuy*, when the earth lurches again. I roar, throwing all my weight onto the pole. The rock groans and tilts slightly. I keep pushing against the pole, trying to drive it deeper to keep the rock from falling back into place. But it will not budge any further. I dig my feet into the ground and shout, "Yuraq Orqo, help me!" I push until every muscle trembles. The ground stops moving. The rock rotates slightly and settles at a tilt. A sudden stream of light animates the dust. Only then do I look up.

The opening is above my head. I climb the pile of stones and almost scream with relief. It is just wide enough to squeeze through. I squirm out, pulling my things behind me. I have to close my eyes against the light, but when I feel the open ground, I can't tell if I am laughing or crying.

I crawl over the rubble to what is left of the path. Below, jagged piles of rocks poke through clouds of settling dust. Voices in my head leap out of the silence around me as I maneuver through the rubble, climbing over obstacles and kicking smaller rocks aside. Paya Kuyllay coaxes me forward with a song, Mother's pointing out dangerous spots, telling me to stay as alert as an owl, and Father says to move like a llama, steady, balanced, and ready to shift in any direction.

CALL OF THE OWL WOMAN

With so many scrapes from climbing over sharp rocks, I am covered in a paste of blood and dust. I keep thinking how Tachico would be scampering over each obstacle easily, making it a game. He would not be scraped and bruised like me. Not that I even care about the scrapes. I just want to get home. I can't stop worrying about people getting hurt. Caught in a landslide. Buried by a house. I don't want to give any attention to those worries, so I try to hold other images in my mind—of Father, Otocco, and Tachico moving safely toward home, of family and friends unharmed. I pray as I go, wordless rhythms of hope, gratitude, and trust. I trust Pachamama to get me home. I thank her for sparing me, so far, in the shudderings of her moods. I ask to get out of the gorge without being crushed. But also, should it be my fate that a boulder catches me in its path, I ask that it finish me quickly and not leave me to a slow death, broken and bleeding.

The sun is low on the horizon when I get to easier ground. I sit on a large rock and scan the horizon as I catch my breath. The journey down the mountain has taken most of the day. My legs are scratched and sore, my feet blistered. The ground ahead is layered with splintered rock. I wrap my feet and get up. Before I continue, I run my finger across a fresh gash on my thigh and draw a circle on the rock with the blood. Inside the circle, I draw one line crossing another. *Strength at intersections*, I think, *Pachamama's embrace.*

High on one slope, I notice a familiar cluster of stones. I nod respectfully, remembering that Paya Kuyllay's great uncle was once saved from a huaico by scrambling up that hillside. His two favorite llamas were caught in the roaring mud and rock. As they were swept away, he called from his perch, "I commend them to you, Great Mother! Please receive them as a gift!" Kuyllay always ended the story with, "Pachamama heard his words. She accepted the llamas and spared the valley. And he built the apacheta there to thank her."

What Is Found

I pull the last piece of *charqui*, dried llama meat, from my bag and chew it slowly while I look for the twisted tree that marks the shortcut to the river. I am grateful to be done with the sharp edges of this terrain. My feet are eager for softer ground and the river rocks' more forgiving curves.

chapter 12
Aftermath

At the edge of the riverbed the familiar stones mark the old crossing, leaning against each other like old friends. "It is a privilege to see you again," I tell them with somber joy, patting one as I pass. I have just stepped across the thin bit of water when I hear a familiar yipping. I turn around and Wiksa bounds into my arms. I rub her head and hug her close, holding her longer than she wants me to, but it makes me unbearably happy to see her. "Let's go home!" I say, pointing toward the familiar ridge in the distance. Wiksa bounces at my side. All I want now is to collapse into my mother's arms, to let her put salve on my wounds, to be home.

Before long, the bright yellow of Faruka's house comes into view. It stands out in the haze. So does the red flag that signals the need for a healer. As my eyes adjust to the glare, more red flags come into focus along the valley. The closest is hanging next to what is left of my cousin Uchu's home. I have not seen him much since he moved his family closer to their fields. A group huddles in front of a makeshift tent near the collapsed house. Uchu hurries to greet me. His face is dark with grime, his eyes bright and

Aftermath

nervous. "We heard you were on the mountain. It's a miracle you have come to us now!" He pulls me toward the tent. "It's our boy, Aru. He's not waking up."

"My mother hasn't been here yet?" I ask, wondering how many injuries she is attending to now. Uchu chews on his lip without answering. I press him. "Uchu, what happened?"

"Your mother was hurt," he says, adding quickly, "but someone is attending to her. Please, don't go yet," he implores. "Look at Aru first. Please." He must see the alarm on my face. He stares at the ground. "We heard her leg might be broken. I'm sorry."

I glance toward our home on the still-distant hillside.

"She is not there," he says. "She was with Faruka's family when the earthquake started. Please, look at Aru before you go to her?"

"Uchu, I'm just her helper. I'm not a healer."

"Please, Patya," he insists. "He won't wake up."

They are clearly scared. I try to put on Mother's practiced expression of calm. "I will look at Aru now, but then I must go ask my mother what to do."

Uchu kisses my hands. "Thank you. Thank you." He tells me how their house survived the main quake and first aftershock, but the roof beam fell during the last aftershock. "We didn't realize Aru had gone back in to find something." Uchu's chin juts upward to hold back tears. "You have to help my son."

The group parts for me to enter the tent. Aru is unnervingly still and so pale. "A blanket," I say softly. "Bring a blanket." I place my hand on the child's face—cold as the night air. I pull up his eyelids, listen to his breathing. I wish I had paid better attention while Mother treated her patients. Instead, I usually looked at their ceramics and weavings to get ideas for designs. There is always something much more interesting than Mother's medicine.

However, I do know enough to ask for water boiled with sauco berries to clean the wound and for a particular gelatinous

Call of the Owl Woman

leaf whose name I cannot remember. Thankfully, when I describe it, they know what I mean. While everyone scurries to fill my requests, I unwrap the cloth covering the wound. It is still bleeding where the frayed skin has been torn from the skull. I slice the thick leaf and squeeze its gooey substance onto the skin. I will need to put some on my own feet later.

After bundling blankets around the boy, I promise to return as soon as I consult with my mother. They nod respectfully but clearly hope for more instruction. So I tell the grandmother, "Puma flowers," one of Mother's most common treatments. "Make a strong infusion and give him a few drops at a time. Keep him warm and prop up his legs. Like a mountain, they will give his heart strength." I get them to sing one of the healing songs and can hear them still chanting long after I have slipped away. When I start up the hill, I turn back and notice that they have lowered the red flag.

I worry the rest of the way—hoping that Mother's injury is not too serious, that she will be able to help Aru, and that Tachico is safe with my brother and father on their way home. When I reach the plaza, I freeze, shocked at what I see. The only thing left of the bright yellow house is the wall I had seen from afar. A body lies on the ground, covered with a cloth for the dead.

I sense someone behind me, feel their hot breath on my neck. Weq'o's familiar voice drips with feigned sympathy. "Sorry to hear about your mother."

I have heard him disparage my mother too often to possibly believe he cares. He had opposed his brother's marriage and liked to remind people that Keyka's father was an outsider. Weq'o's voice insinuates itself into my ear. "But you can be proud."

I turn to face him. "What do you mean?"

"A hero," he says dryly, nodding at the body by the house. "Keyka went back in for the mother and baby, but when the wall began to collapse . . ." He shakes his head. "At least she managed

Aftermath

to keep the baby safe. Oh, yes, she was quite the hero. But death did not spare her."

I stare at the body next to the rubble. Mother? Is he saying that Mother died rescuing the baby? Is that why Uchu couldn't look me in the eye? My legs go weak, but I am unable to move. A hero? A wail catches in my throat. My uncle's words blur as he drones on about heroes. I try to focus on what he is saying. "So then Faruka's father went back in and got them out before the rest caved in. But something hit him on his way out. He collapsed. The poor man is still lying there. I'm not sure where they took your mother, but she's already giving orders . . ."

I snap to attention. "Giving orders? She's alive then?"

He acts surprised, as if he hadn't pointed to the covered body when he said her name. "I never said otherwise," he replies. "The bonesetter took care of her first. The hero, after all. And everyone scurries around her now as if she were a chief."

Then Mother is alive! I am giddy with relief. But my relief is quickly replaced with anger that Weq'o purposely misled me. Then the rest of it hits me. Faruka's father is dead.

One of the elders from the Council pushes past Weq'o toward me. "Thank the heavens you are here!" He places his hand on my shoulder solemnly. "We were afraid you would be among the lost."

"I have been lucky, Unay," I reply.

The old man embraces me, then turns back to Weq'o. "The sun will set soon. Casualties need to be taken down the hill. We will meet later in the plaza."

I'm afraid to ask who else has perished. Weq'o draws himself up with an air of importance and waves to a group of men to join him, then goes to collect the body of Faruka's father. My stomach is knotted with sorrow and worry. I whisper a prayer for him, then set off to find my mother.

On the far side of the plaza, women are cooking over open fires. When they see me approaching, they all start talking at once. "Your mother was taken to Pillku's house!" "His daughters splinted her leg. She'll be okay." "The girls are helping Keyka treat the other wounded."

They tell me which houses have fallen and which are still intact. One woman nods to the old woman huddled near the fire. "They found Toti near the river, curled up next to a tree, whimpering about the broken water jars around her. She can't stop trembling. Her sons asked us to keep an eye on her so that they could work on their house."

I take my shawl off and go to comfort her. "*Toti Luya*," I sing softly, wrapping her in my shawl. "Dear Toti . . ."

Toti does not look up but pulls the shawl around her. "*Patya Patya-cha*," she sings back, "little Patya." A deep shiver runs through her. "Did you see how the earth opened? She is hungry, Pachamama. You must feed her. The Great Mother is hungry. You must feed her, Patya, you must feed her." Her eyes stare blankly into some unknown world, clouded like a blind woman's. She hugs her belly. "My baby," she says, though her womb has long been empty and her three sons long grown. She moans, "Don't let them take my little girl." Toti rocks herself back and forth. "She was dancing before my boys could walk. Like a bird, my little one. I saw her in the corner of my eye today, Patya." She turns her face to me. "Do you think she was real?" I remember hearing that she lost her little girl in the same huaico that nearly carried away my great uncle.

"Ah, dear Toti," I say. "Are you not the one who told me that the things we see from the corners of our eyes are more real than the things we see in front of us?"

Toti chuckles. "You must come have chicha with me. And we must make a special pot for her. Will you paint it for me?"

"We will make a pot just the way you want it."

"Ay, Patya," Toti croons, "we will paint it just right, just right . . ." I squeeze her hand. "I will come see you," I tell her, "but I

Aftermath

must go to my mother now." Aru's spirit might also be carried away if I do not get him to my mother soon.

I am scanning the plaza for signs of Faruka's family when I see Faruka herself. We both break into a run and almost knock each other over when we meet. "You're alive!" Faruka says, embracing me. "Your mother will be so relieved."

"And my brothers?" I say, bracing myself for more bad news. Faruka hesitates. "Ecco is fine. Just a bit bruised from helping people who got trapped." She takes my hand in hers. "But there is still no word from your father. The earthquake could have caught them anywhere." She suddenly bursts into tears. "I can't bear to lose anyone else."

It pains me to see her so sad. I hold her close and let her cry. "I am so very sorry about your father," I whisper. "He was a good man."

I think of the way he embraced Ecco into their family. The joy on his face when he placed Faruka's hand in Ecco's and put his own over both in blessing. His deep, resonant voice declaring, "May your lives together be as happy as mine."

I take Faruka's hands in my own. "The men are on their way back to us now. I don't know how I know, but I know." I choose not to mention yet that I also know, deep in that mysterious place of knowing, that Tachico is badly hurt. She doesn't need to know that yet.

She wipes her face. "Anyway, we can't think about that now. Come. The injured are being taken to my uncle Pillku's house. Your mother needs our help." Faruka leads me through piles of rubble to the path.

Torchlight illuminates the large room we step into. People are coming and going, sharing news with muffled voices as they sort medicinal supplies. My mother is propped up on cushions against a wall, bent over a task with one of Pillku's daughters. A few people, caked with dust and blood, wait in the corner for attention. I see Mother glance up as Faruka enters. She holds out a bag without pausing for greetings. "These are ready to take to my cousin Hukato," she says. "He will get them to the families near the river path." She stops and looks back up again. "Patya?" She lurches forward but immediately falls back, clutching her bandaged leg. Before she can say anything else, I am on the floor next to her, wrapping my arms around her, both of us shaking with tears.

I stand in the doorway, my face lifted toward the moon, arms at my side, taking a moment to calm myself. As soon as she heard my description of what had happened to Aru, Mother sent for him and his family. She told me which herbs to boil and which needles to thread, so everything was ready when they arrived. The family stayed outside to pray while we took Aru inside. He's been washed and prepared but is still unconscious on a table surrounded by torches. Everything is ready except me.

I never dreamed my mother would ask me to do this.

When she explained how to clean the wound, how to remove the debris, down to the exposed bone, my stomach wrenched. I cringed at the thought of knife scraping against bone, Aru's bone. "I can't do it," I told her.

"You can." Mother handed me the knife, its dark obsidian sparkling in the torchlight.

I shook my head. "Sewing a tunic is one thing, but this . . ."

"I will guide you," she insisted. "You'll be fine. You've seen blood before. Be thankful the blow wasn't worse, or you'd be cutting through bone as well." She held up her trepanning tools and tweezers for removing skull fragments. "The knife is sharp. Your work will be easy. Trim the ragged pieces, pull the edges together, and stitch the way I showed you. Relax, let the ancestors guide your hands. Let Spirit work through you. If you close the wound well and treat it right, it won't fester. Aru will heal faster than you think."

Aftermath

I do not understand how my mother can stand being the one people come to for everything. It's not just the major injuries and emergencies either. Most of what she does is messy, repetitive work. Sores and ailments, sicknesses and scratches. She spends as much time comforting patients as she does preparing the herbs that speed their recovery. The same plant medicines might help one with inflammation, help another with anxiety. Treat lethargy in one, fungus in another. Not only does my mother seem to know exactly what people need for body and for spirit, but she also has infinite patience and a gift for finding the problems behind the problems. Like the women who come looking for cures to the burning that happens when they pass water but are soon sobbing about how their men have hit them. I know that it is not only drunk Warpa hunters who hurt women.

I admit that I like knowing how fractures and illnesses can be fixed, but I have no desire to be the one trying to fix them. And even more, I most definitely do not want to be known as the one who tries to, but *cannot*, fix something. The one who fails to say the right thing. Who ruins someone's hope. Someone who could not stop the inevitable.

Pillku's daughters, Quri and Nikta, have been assisting Mother for years. They are skilled at caring for cuts and bruises, headaches and heartaches, common ailments—but nothing prepared them for so many injuries all at once. They are exhausted. They've been attending to people all day, and more are waiting for bandaging. Some are afraid to leave after they've been treated. Homes that withstood the first shock started to crack later and may not survive another tremor. Everywhere we look, we see hills threatening with boulders that could break away in a moment and crash through our walls. The slightest trembling of the ground causes panic.

I can almost understand why so many people mutter about the world coming to an end. I overhear some whispering that

CALL OF THE OWL WOMAN

the time of the great prophecy is at hand, the Great Change that Achiq warns of, full of plagues and destruction, the opening of a portal to another world. But Ceetu, the shaman in Palpa and one of Paya Kuyllay's oldest friends, holds a different vision. He says there will be a day when humankind suffers no want, enters no conflict, and lives in harmony with our Great Mother, beloved children of Pachamama. He says a great crisis will offer a gateway to a new world, to more abundance than we can imagine, but that the world must lie fallow for a time like a field and will come back stronger. After a good rest, we will flourish again. I am not sure if that means we will journey to another region during that time—or if there is a veil between worlds we will have to cross. Either way, I prefer Ceetu's vision to Achiq's.

I do not believe that Pachamama is acting against us. The woman on Yuraq Orqo makes sense, like things my mother and grandmother say. The earth has her own rhythms. We humans are not unlike ants in the folds of her skirts. Her attention cannot be everywhere in every detail. Paya Kuyllay used to say, "The shifts that are coming are already felt." She would tell me that, like a child sleeping next to his mother can sense her begin to roll, shamans feel the earth's cycles and hear the plants and animals. Even so, I have learned that even shamans who are good observers are not always good predictors, and people can be very unforgiving. Many a shaman has been stoned for failing to warn people before a disaster. Even now, I hear talk of finding out who is to blame. I have no patience for that. What matters now is tending to the injured, finding the missing, and fixing homes.

And Aru is waiting.

The moon has traveled a good distance by the time we finish, and I step back outside for air. Through the door, the moon's light pours across Aru's face. I thank Mama K'illa, Pachamama, and

Aftermath

Creator that Aru is still breathing. I watch him for a moment, his face calm, lost in the rhythms of sleep. I pour a little water into a shallow basin to clean the blood from my hands and leave some rags to soak. I will finish washing them tomorrow. Aru's family is asleep on the terrace, huddled together under a single blanket. I find another to cover them before going back inside.

Mother smiles up at me wearily. "Come," she says, patting the cushion next to her. I curl into her embrace. I have so much to tell her, but I am overcome by sleep before I can open my mouth.

I wake to the muffled sound of Mother trying to give instructions quietly. The light from the door is painfully bright, and a fresh gust of air sails across the room to greet me. The room is full of bundled deliveries that Quri and Nikta are discussing. Outside someone is asking for help with a nursing baby unable to hold food down. Keyka gives directions for special brews, one for the baby and another for the mother to help her recover from the fright. It is important not to pass the fear into her milk.

As I pull myself to sitting, the ache in my shoulders and feet returns. I try to speak, but Mother shushes me, strokes my forehead, and holds a cup to my lips. I sip slowly, letting the minty sweetness soothe my throat. Mother strokes my arm gently, her eyes glistening.

When I reach the plaza, it is close to sunset. Mother's cousin Hukato is speaking to a group gathered around the firepit. The wood is arranged and ready for lighting. A coal pot waits, ready at the edge. Dusk is upon us. Some women sit nursing babies, some spin thread, and others speak among themselves as they knit. I make my way to where the men have gathered around Hukato, whose animated gesticulations have some nodding, others looking doubtful. "Our main well has collapsed," Hukato says. "Our homes are in rubble. We should take what we can and move upriver. Leave here and start again." I am here to speak for my family, but I feel so small among these men.

Hukato draws a likeness of the river's path in the dirt before him. "Around the bend above Two-Stones is a wide stretch where the Shappa clan used to live. It's far enough above the river to be safe when it rises—may that happen soon—and the low hills give it some protection from rockslides." He looks around, making eye contact with each of his neighbors. "The homes they left behind need some repair, new roofs, and a little clearing, but it would be easier than rebuilding here. We can bring water from the spring." He carves the air with his hands. "Why waste time clearing through this debris when we could be preparing the fields? Fixing the canals? The little water we have is draining away through new cracks every day."

Unay speaks firmly. "My grandfather built the house we live in. The base is solid. I can clear the rubble in a few days. With help, I can get beams up for the roof. We can finish the walls later. I don't want to leave the land that my family has worked for generations. Our sweat is mixed with the soil. We will carry water from wherever we can."

Unay's sister nods, pausing in her spinning to stand up. "We have seen worse," she says.

"But not in times like these," argues a woman with a baby at her breast. "I think Hukato's right. The damage is worse here."

A young man says, "I thought you always said that theirs was the worst spot on the river for farming. Isn't that why the Shappas left?"

Hukato waves his hand in dismissal. "They went to Palpa because three of their daughters married into families with better farmland. We don't want to move to the Palpa Valley."

"Why not? I haven't had a good crop since my oldest was born," says another. "If we decide to move, we might as well go where we'll have a better chance."

Aftermath

"Things are not that much better in Palpa now," Hukato replies. "The river is low. Some of their own people have gone farther inland, up into the clouds. If you're ready to pack up what's left of your home and go to the mountains, that is your choice," he says. "But I'm talking to anyone here who is ready to decide now. It is less than a day's walk upriver, beside the Aja we know."

"If it's so good," asks a voice from the back, "won't others want it?"

"That's why I sent my cousin ahead. We were there just a few days ago, already thinking about it. I'm here to see who else wants to join us. There are six houses in good shape there. If someone else decides before you, you'll lose this chance. Join us. We can start the preparations tomorrow."

I finally get the courage to step forward. "My mother asked me to speak on her behalf," I begin.

"A girl who can't even speak loud enough to be heard?" Hukato scoffs. "Who will join us?" he asks again.

Unay holds up his hand for quiet. "Let the girl speak."

I raise my voice. "My mother asked me to bring her message."

"Speak up, child!" Uncle Weq'o cajoles from the back. I should have known he'd be here with Hukato.

I feel my feet on the ground, imagine myself anchored there like a tree, pulling strength from the earth, pulling it into my voice. "My mother Keyka asks that we take time, now, in this meeting, to remember gratitude and ceremony. Our water-guardians are away on a mission with a temple priest on our behalf. She asks that we act as they would, calling on the spirits of our hills and summoning our ancestors to guide us through the coming days."

People watch Hukato as if expecting him to interrupt. I speak more rapidly. "She asks that we hold ceremony to restore our balance as we make our plans to recover together. She says to tell you that we are shaken but not broken. We will fix what we can, level what we must, and rebuild. We must thank Pachamama for showing us where we are vulnerable and for helping us to grow stronger." I address the women in the back. "We know Pachamama suffers with us, just as any mother suffers when her children suffer."

The group seems to grow quieter as I continue, "Balance is a precious, precarious thing. As the world shifts itself into place again, so too will we find our place again." I see a few heads nod. "As for relocating, our family home also suffered some damage, but we will stay. Faruka's family will stay with us while they rebuild. We have already begun. When my father returns with the group that went to Acari, the work will move even faster."

"And if they don't return?" Weq'o asks, as if the possibility somehow pleases him.

"Then it will fall to us to do what my father would have done," I reply, holding my uncle's gaze. I cannot shake the feeling that Weq'o will somehow find a way to benefit from all this and that, if he chose to, he could undo in a moment what has taken generations to build. His eyes look through me, inscrutable, perhaps slightly gleeful. I hope I am wrong about him.

"Perhaps we're at the world's end," Weq'o says. "Perhaps we are all about to perish. Perhaps the gods have tired of toying with us. I do not put my faith in Yakuwayri or his trust in the ancestors' ways. I do not trust Achiq's rituals to appease greedy gods. I trust what I can see now, what we can do for ourselves. What we have before us. Food to eat. Water to drink. Shelter over our heads. Things that others will want to take from us. I think we will be safer upriver."

"Or perhaps," I reply with all the force I can muster, "this is a challenge for our people. If these are times of Pachakuti, of the great upheaval, won't we be stronger together? Didn't those families leave because they were too far from help when things got bad?"

My uncle just laughs and turns his most charming smile toward the others. "The child has been listening to too many stories. The

Aftermath

Great Pachakuti? Tales her grandmother brought back from her travels have confused her with myths and prophecies that we don't need here." He turns back to me, his face hard. "Before your grandmother came back to Nasca, the earth was calm, the waters were plentiful, and our harvests were good." He addresses the crowd again. "The women of that family are full of tricks and illusions. Just watch! Next, she will probably tell you she had visions on the mountain." He leans toward me, mocking. "Did you see any silver owls?"

I hold his eyes, but it makes me feel queasy. I am aware of the crowd waiting, but all I can see is the same smug look on Weq'o's face that I saw after he cut down the old guarango. I look away. A voice in my head says, *Maybe Pachamama would be happier without humans after all.* I shake it off. I focus again on the earth at my feet, on Pachamama, the great transformer, and then lift my head to face Weq'o. "Everyone here knows that if it were not for those women who you hate so much, your wife would not have survived the birth of your son. And how many others would not be here today if it had not been for my grandmother's medicine? Yes, it is true that before my father changed the water routes, your family had more water, more than most families. You and your friends had the biggest harvests. Enough to trade for the best finery, while others struggled. If my paya Kuyllay helped my father find a way to share the waters more fairly, that is reason for me to be proud!" I turn to the others. "My family is staying here. There is much work to be done. Wherever you choose to live, we need to begin. And a good way to begin is to give thanks for what we have."

"The girl is right," Unay says. "Hukato, do not forget that those who choose to go with you are placing their trust in you. Lead them well. Now, we all need to focus on the work ahead." He holds his hands skyward. "Let the heavens guide us. Let the earth receive our gratitude and give us strength! Let the wind speed our work. May we prosper again."

CALL OF THE OWL WOMAN

As Unay lights the fire, a chorus of voices calls out, "Let it be so." Unay says a prayer for the dead and for the injured and then calls on the spirits of the hills to help us all. "We must each do what we can," he says, then begins to organize work teams to cook communal meals, arrange repairs, care for the injured, search for those still missing, and check with neighboring communities. Hukato and two other families leave with Weq'o to make their own arrangements. I excuse myself and return to Mother.

Mother is propped up with cushions, leaning over a grinding stone. She continues reducing a pile of seed to powder as she greets me, then adds, "Did I tell you that I dreamed of your father last night?" She collects the powder into a small ceramic jar and smiles up at me. "It won't be long now."

I squat next to her. "I should go to meet them," I tell her. "Father may need help."

"You saw it too, didn't you?" she replies without pause. "Tachico is hurt."

I take a long breath, but she holds up her hand. "Don't tell me what you saw. Our visions are filtered through our own fears. We must not feed them but pass through them. Go. Perhaps you can stop the worst from happening." I am surprised by how calm she is. She is always careful and composed with her patients, but I'm her daughter. I know she is worried. I wish she would be open with me, share her own fears. But maybe she's afraid I won't be strong enough if I start carrying her fears along with my own.

Mother pats the bundle next to her. "I have already prepared a bag. Food. Water. Chicha. Healing herbs. And quwis."

I have eaten plenty of quwis, but I don't like preparing them. They are too cute. When their little beady eyes look out of their sweet furry faces, how can I take a knife to them? I admit that once they are cooked, I just see meat. And I love the taste. But it's hard when I think of the quwis used in healing. When they are passed over the bodies of the sick, they help take away the

140

Aftermath

illness, but they are skinned and cut open for study afterward. Their insides mirror what the patient suffers, and that helps the healer know how to treat the ailments, but I'll never get used to it. It is worse than gutting ducks and stripping their feathers. Worse than skinning a deer carcass.

chapter 13

Cahuachi

I do not wait for morning but set out immediately for the temple grounds near the old ruins at Cahuachi. If they haven't reached Cahuachi yet, I will continue south until I find them. I make a short detour to Kuyllay's Grove to pick up more salve for the blisters on my feet. I pack some pouches of our strongest herbs for pain. I take one of the umanqas from Waru's bag, then hide it again. As I make my way along the edge of the Aja riverbed, I pass the juncture where it merges with the Uchumarca River, the beginning of what we call the Nasca River. Following it will take me across the southern edge of the plains, all the way to Cahuachi. After that it will curve northward to merge with the Great River where the foothills end. The path takes a slight downward slant toward the ocean, all the way to the temple. It is good to be walking in the cool of the night, and I am grateful to the moon for her light.

The river used to shrink in the dry season and grow wide again after the rains in the mountains, but there has been no widening for so long it feels like a story from another time. The thin trickle I follow could barely be called a stream. I continue along

Cahuachi

a narrow path of hardened sediment where the long-ago eddies left a smooth trail between the rocks. Occasionally I come to narrow, jagged cracks where the ground broke during the earthquake. How many times has the river's path changed because of the earth's upheavals? Perhaps there was a time when the river did not disappear underground at all. The fact that it does now, however, makes the approach to the oasis all the more dramatic. Every time I make this journey, I feel that sense of trepidation as soon as I pass the last sign of water. Once it's behind me and out of view, there is only the barren landscape stretching ahead as far as the eye can see. Not even a bit of scrub brush. No solitary guarango on the horizon clinging to life through a lucky long-reaching root. To continue walking straight on into the desert feels like an act of faith. A faith I need now.

This time it is not the fear of finding no water. It is the fear that Tachico might be . . . *No.* I don't want to give the dread a name. I don't want to feed my fears by letting images form. Mother's words come back to me. *Through them, I have to pass through them. I will pass through my fears and not let them cling to me.* Instead, I think of how good the air feels on my skin. It feels even better when I speed up my walk. I fill my lungs with the taste of the coming dawn and break into a run.

The path inclines upward, but I keep a steady pace. The old ache that tugs at my hip does not slow my advance, and my breath is steady. When I reach the crest, I stop to take in the view. The path slopes downward again, leveling off as it disappears into a wooded oasis below. The sight takes my breath away with the same delight as always. Behind the distant stand of trees, more hills roll toward the south. To the north, the landscape spreads out into wide, flat plains, about even with the top of the Cahuachi hills to the south. The stars are beginning to fade as the sky tinges with blue. As I stand there, my shoulders begin to tingle with sudden warmth. Light sneaks across the ground in front of me, casting my shadow on the ground ahead. The sun is rising. Today I will reach Tachico. I take out my pututu and trumpet along with the sunrise.

The outlines of fallen temples seem to glow from beneath the sand. It is easy to picture a time when they towered high, when the plazas had been filled with people, and music could be heard in faraway mountains. From the top of the pyramids, people would have watched others arriving from the north, winding their way down the bluffs along the river across from the temple. At night the view of the plains would have been amazing—torches dancing along the paths, lamp-lit ceremonies, the gatherings of clans. The landscape is such a marvelous gift from Pachamama, a perfect canvas, an invitation to create art. Each generation creates their own homage to the earth, to the stars, to the life-giving waters. We build altars or trace out shapes and pathways in places we feel connected to, sometimes near those made by others, sometimes making new ones over old lines that are no longer used. The desert plains are a living palimpsest, with layers over layers, blurring the present with half-erased designs from other eras.

My favorite time to visit Cahuachi is during the summer solstice. Not only are the rock-strewn plains filled with dancers, but I can watch Tayta Inti rise over Yuraq Orqo, watch the mountain wake from the shadows beneath Inti's shower of gold. I have heard many stories about how the pyramids came to be destroyed. None of them mention Tunga, yet I have to wonder if there might have been some jealousy involved. After all, Tayta Inti lingers over Tunga's lover each morning for the three days of solstice, only reluctantly returning to his journey to inch a little farther north with each sunrise. Had he been chased away only to return again to the same spot? I'll have to ask Mother about that.

Father always insists that his own version was the truest, passed down from his grandfather's grandfather. He says there

Cahuachi

was a time when the temples had grown so magnificent that the people started complimenting and paying tribute to the temple itself instead of the water and earth it had been built to honor. The Apus grew jealous of the man-made mountains and sent the largest huaico the world had ever seen. A great surge from the highest lakes overflowed into raging rivers that gathered force to race through the valleys, washing over the foothills on their way to Cahuachi. Angry seas retreated from the shore to gather themselves into a great wall that sucked in all the waters of the world to return in one great wave that rushed so far inland that rivers flowed backward and spit ocean salt from mountain springs. Pachamama heaved. Torches fell. Tapestries caught fire. The wooden beams served as fuel for a blaze that could be seen for days from far away.

Sad, scared, and chastened, people came from every corner of the region to beg forgiveness at the charred ruins. They filled the burnt-out rooms with offerings and then sealed it all with deep layers of sand. Now, when people come to Cahuachi, they come to honor the waters and to honor life. The buried pyramids remind us that no matter how grand the things we humans create, all can be destroyed in a flash.

Kuyllay's version of the story, however, was far more colorful. She spun tales filled with cat-serpents, flying whales, shape-shifters, and talking foxes. She told of prophecies and cataclysms, destruction, and rebirth. But even my paya's story ended the same—with mountains of sand where the pyramids once stood.

Even now, with the rivers nearly dry everywhere else, the sacred waters have remained faithfully present at Cahuachi. People bring offerings from the farthest reaches to honor this sacred place. They consult the priests and healers who live in the shadow of the buried temples, or come here to bury their dead. I have heard that many have stayed.

At the top of the first hill, colorful flags dance with the

CALL OF THE OWL WOMAN

morning breeze, each representing a different family. I spot our family emblem, the sand-colored puma-snake with outstretched arms flying across a deep red background. One hand carries a fruited staff; the other carries an umanqa.

I pass several campsites in the shadow of the trees near the water's edge. People are beginning to stir, but I hurry toward the healer's lodge. Amaruyu is the eldest of the temple-guardians. He is famous for his ability to converse with the great serpent Amaru, who embodies the inner world and knowledge and is deeply connected to the waters within the earth. The old shaman used to be the one who always accompanied Father for the rituals with the sea, but he has become too feeble to make such journeys now. Father trusts him more than anyone, and Amaruyu's skill as a healer is legendary. The thing that worries me is that it is two days' walk to get here from the sacred cove. Tachico might not survive that long if he has lost too much blood.

chapter 14

Amaruyu

A fox skin hangs from one side of the lintel over the doorway to the healer's lodge. Its head and paws dangle as if about to leap onto anyone who enters. On the other side are the head and wings of a large gray owl with amber stones for eyes. In between, a jumble of jawbones, beads, and shark teeth are strung across the opening. At the center hang two umanqas. The legendary shaman Para Waqaychaq, a rain-guardian when the temple was destroyed, was said to be able to command weather and sea. The shaman Yuyaq Cocha was the Keeper of Memory who died in the disaster. According to Kuyllay, Para Waqaychaq's excessive pride was partly responsible for the tragedy. "One must never seek to control, only to influence," she would tell me as we strung twine along the walls to guide the vines in her garden. "Force alone may make temporary solutions, but ultimately it swings back against you." A humbled Para Waqaychaq oversaw the burial of the temple.

I study the rain-guardian's head. Long strands of black hair wrap around and knot at the front like a horn protruding from his forehead. A braided rope exits a hole in the skull, just above

CALL OF THE OWL WOMAN

the knot. He has a tattoo of interlocking diamonds on one cheek, on the other a small starburst pattern that starts at his chin. Thin zigzags overlap above his eyebrows, with a circle of rays at the center, like on pottery—the path of the thunder god's spear. They are all too similar to the tattooed arms of the Warpa hunters I want to forget.

I try not to think about Waru's bag of umanqas, but they weigh on my spirit. The shadows that haunted my nightmares now come in full daylight. And no, it does not help to know that each has already met his death. That bizarre act of vengeance is something I still can't comprehend.

But what happened on Yuraq Orqo left me feeling that something is shifting. When I decided to take an umanqa with me to the mountain, it was as much to get rid of it as to bring an offering. Even though the umanqa is now in a cave far away, I feel strangely connected to it through the stone in my pouch, the one that I found inside the skull. And I am connected to the mountain through them both. I don't know what that means, but it feels important. The way it felt important to bring an umanqa to Cahuachi. Like it can serve a purpose. I just don't know what.

Para Waqaychaq and those before him survived times as hard as these. The effort that it would have taken to bury the old temple is incomprehensible. And before that, how much time, effort, and vision had it taken to build the first underground canals? "How did you do it?" I ask the stony face as if it would answer. What I really want to ask is if he had ever felt betrayed by the gods, but a shudder suddenly rattles my shoulders like a dog shaking off water.

"Enter!" says a voice from the other side of the opening.

I step through into a short passageway that opens into a high-ceilinged antechamber heavy with the fragrance of burning copal. Flames dance in small bowls around the room, which is empty except for a large basket at the far end and a round stone

Amaruyu

pit glowing with red embers. A small woman stands over the pit, sprinkling small bits of copal resin over the coals. Her leathery face is covered with painted lines that disappear into deep wrinkles and resurface on the other sides like lines across the plains. The copal sparks and wisps of smoke carry the heady sweetness across the room. "I am Waqar," she says. "Is Amaruyu expecting you?"

"No. But I think my father might be here."

"Your father?"

"Yakuwayri, of Two Rivers."

Waqar approaches me, her elongated forehead framed by a wide headband with a winged feline creature at the center. A huge tongue protrudes from between its two fangs. The tongue forks to either side, one side sprouting into a pepper plant and the other into a stalk of maize. She strokes her long braid thoughtfully. "We expected Yakuwayri and his group several days ago. Since they left for Acari the moon has passed through darkness and grown full again. I hope they won't be much longer. They promised a good supply of fish." Waqar studies me, her eyes intense and piercing. "And why have you come?"

"I think my little brother is hurt." My cracking voice betrays my worry. I had been feeling so strong, so able to manage things. I take a deep breath and put my bag on the ground. It convulses as the quwis squeal and try to get out. I ignore them. "My mother and I both had visions of Tachico. Bleeding. A lot. I came to find them. To help."

Waqar stares at the bag, avoiding my eyes. "Amaruyu has hardly slept since the earthquake, busy caring for the wounded. But he will want to see you." She gestures for me to sit by the basket. Oddly, it is full of rocks. She follows my eyes. "Before you go in, you must calm yourself. Align with the energies. Only an open vessel can be a clear channel."

She sets a large, flat rock on the ground in front of me and

149

CALL OF THE OWL WOMAN

another in front of herself. Then she selects a palm-sized rock and turns it in her hands, feeling its weight at different angles. It is narrow at one end, like a pointed egg. She holds it over the flat rock, pointing downward, hovering a bit before setting it gently on the uneven surface. She plays with the balance for a few seconds and then lets go. Its tilt looks completely impossible, but it remains there, standing on its own, balanced on that narrow point.

"Now you."

I take a rock from the basket and turn it in my hands, trying to notice where it is heaviest, where it seems to want to lean. I place the narrower end on the base rock and try to balance it like Waqar, but it tips to one side. No matter how I adjust the tilt, it tips over the moment I let go. I keep trying. Then I notice a faint dip in the stone base. It might offer support. I cup the stone as it wobbles and nudge it ever so slightly back and forth until it seems to settle into the dip. Something slips into place as if an invisible column within the rock has suddenly lined up. It stops wobbling. I slowly take my hands away, and it stays upright. I almost clap for joy.

Waqar nods for me to take another stone. When the second rock is standing, I look up with pride. It immediately falls, knocking over my first rock as well. Waqar gestures for me to do it again. It takes time, but it seems like they both stood more easily, as if they remembered their positions. My third rock stands quickly, as if it had merely needed me to nudge it into position. Seeing the three stones standing before me in such an unlikely equilibrium gives me deep satisfaction. I begin to reach for another stone, but Waqar gets up and signals for me to follow.

We enter the inner sanctum.

Tall guarango poles rise toward a ceiling lost in shadow. We pass a table the height of my waist. At the end of the room is a figure seated on the ground with a single flame burning before

Amaruyu

him. My eyes slowly adjust to the faint light as Amaruyu comes into focus. I watch him place a purple mullu shell at the center of the altar cloth before he turns to regard me. When I reach him, he stands, places his hands on my shoulders, and looks into my face, level with his. "Patya, you look more like your father every time I see you. So tall. And so serious."

No one ever tells me I look like my father. I don't know how to respond, so I go straight into the reason I'm here. My words tumble out, hurried and confused. I tell him about my vision on Yuraq Orqo, of Tachico bleeding, of Achiq next to him doing nothing, of my mother's worries. I have to stop to catch my breath, then ask the real question: "Would Achiq really hurt my brother?"

The old healer holds up his hand to quiet me. "They will be here soon." He fills his mouth with fragrant waters and blows a fine mist over me and over his mesa. I relax into the familiar cleansing ritual, grateful. He passes a condor feather over my body in a methodical rhythm, sending currents of air over my back, my arms, my legs. As the feather rises and circles my head, I feel a weight lift from my neck and shoulders. I breathe into the release, let my head drop, and realize how deeply tired I am.

Amaruyu has me sit next to him and begins a low, rhythmic chant. His large hand drum fills the room with a steady heartbeat while he invokes the Apus and local spirits. "Come, Yuraq Orqo, bless this woman-child, our Patya of Two Rivers, bless the ancestors who travel with her." He calls on distant Apu Coropuna, on Amaru of the Deep, Kuntur of the Heavens, and on his Ally Spirit. "Jaguar of the Night, honor me with your guidance, your ease and strength, your vision." With each summoning, my body is washed with new energy. I feel the wind rolling down the hills, the serpent winding its power through my core, the wide stretch of wings riding currents from the heavens, seeing all. I feel the gaze of the jaguar and am ready to follow her lead.

151

He holds the drum close to his ear, hunching over to listen, humming along with closed eyes. Then he stops. Amaruyu's body seems curved around his drum. He looks up at me, but his loose eyelids almost obscure his dark eyes. The extra folds of skin around his neck remind me of an old turtle just barely poking his head out—or an ancient, mythic beast called out of sleep. A sharpness lies behind the softness, hinting of danger if fully roused. I know I can trust him. He straightens his back and faces me. "We have much work to do."

Waqar is approaching us with a bowl when the sound of a pututu in the distance makes us all turn to listen. She waits until the fourth blast wavers into silence before she sets the bowl of wachuma beside Amaruyu. He nods, and she retreats. She lights the torches at each corner of the table, then slips out the door.

Amaruyu prays over the wachuma, pours some into a wooden cup, and drinks deeply. He refills the cup and passes it to me. "Let the spirit medicine work in you. Let it show you what is needed." I tilt the cup back, trying not to gag. I have to force myself to swallow small gulps. Once. Twice. I watch Amaruyu circle the table with a bowl of smoldering herbs. Several jugs are set at either end of the table, along with bowls of ointments and powders. Only at that moment do I realize that Amaruyu had been preparing for Tachico even before I arrived. I take a third gulp.

I try to keep my eyes open, but my eyelids are becoming too heavy to hold. I try to concentrate, to hold a vision of Tachico strong and healthy, but every little noise distracts me. Footsteps. The hiss of a torch. A dog's bark. Images in my mind shatter, dissolve, or morph into glittering lights. Whenever I succeed in coaxing my lids open, Amaruyu appears to be at the end of a long tunnel. Each time I open my eyes, a new lamp has been lit. I slide close to a wall so it can support me and close my eyes against the brightness. In the cool darkness, I think I hear a fox cry.

I awake to the sound of a familiar voice outside. Waqar is

Amaruyu

holding the curtain aside for someone I barely recognize as my father. He is covered in dirt and carrying a pole on his shoulder. He makes his way into the room, slowly, his head bowed. His whole being slouches forward as if the burden he carries weighs on his heart as much as his shoulder. At the other end of the pole is Chanki. Hanging from the pole is a sling of fabric. The inert figure inside its folds is Tachico. Otocco follows behind them, supporting, almost carrying, a young man I have never seen before.

The bundle is lowered onto the table. Father removes the pole and spreads open the cloth. I jump up to go to them but am stopped by the look on Father's face and by the dizziness in my head. I steady myself while they arrange the limp form on the table but keep looking for any signs of movement from Tachico. I can't even tell if he is breathing. They begin removing the fabric he has been wrapped in. Amaruyu leaves some of the bulky bandages around Tachico's shoulders and torso while he inspects the rest of Tachico's body. Waqar blows cleansing smoke over the table, and I wait for my cue. Finally, Amaruyu gestures for me to join him. He moistens the blood-soaked bandages and begins removing them slowly. I follow his lead, sponging the special waters over Tachico's skin, washing away the dust, the sand, the crusted blood. Deep gashes run the length of his leg, dragging purple valleys through skin tinged with the yellows and greens of days-old bruises.

Amaruyu leans into me, speaking into my ear. "Trust the wachuma," he says softly. "Let it guide your attention. Help Tachico find a place to anchor here, in this world. Or we will lose him." I take Tachico's hand in mine, but as soon as our skin touches, I have to let go. It hurts to touch him, and a horrible, suffocating force pulls me downward. I grab the table to catch my balance, to keep from falling, but I am overwhelmed. I was not prepared for this. I am not strong enough. I sink to the floor,

CALL OF THE OWL WOMAN

overcome by shame. How could I have possibly thought I could be of any help?

My heart is racing. My head is spinning. I can't breathe. But beneath my knees, I feel the cool earth offer comfort. Reassurance. "I am here, daughter," it seems to whisper. "Let me share your burden. Pass it on. My depths can hold anything." But I am crumpled on the ground, useless. Still, the earth coaxes. "Even when it feels impossible, you can stand."

I can stand, I think. *Like a stone when it finds its balance.* I remember the stones I balanced earlier, how impossible it had seemed that they could stand like they did. The thought steadies me, brings me back to my breath. Slowly, I pull myself up, mindful of the earth beneath me, imagining her holding me. I stand, looking down at Tachico's small, round face, pale as a fading moon.

"Mama K'illa, protect his wandering spirit," I whisper. "Pachamama, help me bear his pain." I place my forehead against his fevered little hand and feel the vortex pull at me again. My body remains still, rooted where I stand, but I fall from my physical self into a strange and crowded dreamscape. I am searching for something recognizable when a horrible pain jolts through my shoulder. My arm seems to stretch through the sting of salt, the chill of the ocean, the glare of a setting sun. I struggle for air, for ground, for something to touch, but I sink into a fog of nothingness. I let go into the deep silence until I am yanked abruptly back into the center of the pain. I watch my arm, Tachico's arm, the arm I am not holding, disappear into a forest of teeth, shark teeth.

It is a miracle that he is alive.

When my awareness comes back into my body, I am grateful again for the feel of solid ground beneath my feet. Tachico's right hand still lies limp and hot in mine. The sweat on his skin glistens in the torchlight. I begin sponging cool water over his arm,

Amaruyu

neck, and forehead. As I work, I hold images of the people waiting for Tachico at home, Mother, Ecco, Faruka, family, neighbors, friends. I picture Chochi and Wiksa bounding toward him, eager to play. I focus on the things Tachico loved most, his collections of shells, his new spear, his musical instruments. I keep thinking of all the things worth coming back to, hoping he can feel them, dream them, remember them through me.

Amaruyu gently removes the bandages from the other side. His blade peels and cuts them away to reveal the arm bulging blue above the rags tied around the stump of his arm. As I watch the tangle of bandages fall away, a sick hollowness rolls through me. Under the dried blood, herbs, and sand that cling to the dressings, there is nothing below the elbow but splintered bone.

The rest of the night, I feel like I am watching myself from a distance. I am able to watch without retching, to follow orders without hesitation. I witness the sawing of bones and the cutting of withered flesh as if it were a trimming of broken tree branches. I move without thinking through the rest of the day and into the evening until a heavy hand tugs at my shoulder. Waqar is speaking, but I have trouble registering the words.

"There is nothing more we can do now," Waqar repeats gently. I stare at the floor, determined to stay with Tachico until he wakes, but Waqar insists. "Otocco went to check on the llamas but will be back soon. I left you all some bedding. You must try to sleep—you will need your strength for the coming days. I am going to help Amaruyu attend to the stranger now. Go rest." Before she turns to go, Waqar leans in to add, "Come see me in the morning. Look for my flag. The one with the owl."

Father is just outside, sitting on a bench, his head in his hands. He looks as if he has fallen asleep sitting up. I hesitate, not wanting to bother him, but he stirs and reaches toward me. I move an

CALL OF THE OWL WOMAN

uneaten bowl of food and sit down next to him. He is trembling. His frame convulses. I close my eyes and let him weep for both of us. When he wipes his eyes, the dirt smears across his cheeks. His mournful look scares me, and he grips me with a desperation I have never seen. "Patya, help bring him back to us."

I want to cry at how powerless I feel, but I put my hand on his cheek and tell him that I know Tachico will come back to us. He places his hand on my shoulder, unable to speak, holds me tight for a moment, then we go find our sleeping mats. He is asleep before I can wish him good rest.

I look for Otocco and find him sitting at the edge of the hill, looking out over the valley. We watch the vast spread of stars and listen to the muffled sounds of people below, the slow drumbeat throbbing from somewhere upriver. I wait for Otocco to say something, but he doesn't. I don't know where to start, but I need to say something. I want to know what happened. What he saw. What he is thinking. All I can stammer out is, "How can everything continue as if nothing has happened?" He doesn't even look at me. He presses his fingers into his forehead. He is locked inside, somewhere he doesn't want me to see. I move to sit behind him, where I can rub his head and shoulders the way our mother often does. "Let me," I offer. He grunts, but his muscles slowly unknot beneath my fingers. His breathing slows. Soon, he is asleep. I nudge him awake enough to get him to his sleeping mat and then stretch out on my own.

I lie awake, thoughts and feelings twisting through me. I envy Faruka. She has always had sisters and now has a husband to comfort her as well. I wish I had someone to envelop me, to help me cry and rage, someone to help me sink into the oblivion of sleep. But when sleep finally comes, it brings no oblivion. The darkness fills with distorted, watery visions of mangled flesh. Waqar appears wearing the face of an owl and the body of a seal, sunning herself until an orca slides onto the beach and devours her. It rolls

Amaruyu

into the next wave and looks back with a grin before diving into deep waters. Moments later, the orca resurfaces with a great leap. An owl bursts out of the orca's blowhole and flies north along the coast. I follow from the air, riding on a condor's back. When I wake, it is still dark.

I light an oil lamp from the embers and go check on Tachico. I am not the only one who has been restless in the night—I find Otocco asleep on the floor beside him. Tachico's face is so pale, so expressionless it scares me, but his skin is not quite as hot to the touch. I dip a sponge into the floral waters again, thanking the herbs for doing their work, and pass it across Tachico's forehead and neck.

When I step outside, the sky is just beginning to lighten behind the eastern hills. At the top of the hill beside the healing lodge, an orange flag flutters from a small hut. A brisk wind stretches it out so straight that the owl decorating it seems to launch into flight, its wings outstretched against a full moon. Waqar's flag. I hope she is awake.

chapter 15
Waqar

I wind my way upward, past a scattering of small adobe houses and structures made of woven cane, simple rooms added haphazardly over the years—temporary walls that have forgotten they were temporary. Many are anchored at the corners by heavy guarango poles that remind me of tree guardians. Their solid energy emanates patience, perseverance, and self-sufficiency, an ever-present reminder that we humans are short-lived in the great cycles of the earth, a small part of something so much bigger than our own lifetimes. I turn back to look out over the landscape below. The healing lodge is hard to see in the midst of the mini-forest of tall poles that surround and tower over it to support the viewing platform that overlooks the river and the desert plains on the other side. The platform is popular for ceremonial gatherings, a place with a fitting nickname, Takarpu K'iti, place of stakes.

Slightly downriver and still in the shadow of the old Cahuachi, Takarpu K'iti draws pilgrims from the same far regions as Cahuachi used to. Amaruyu lives in a small room that faces the courtyard of a simple complex near the larger ceremonial space.

Waqar

Achiq lives in the same complex on the side closer to Cahuachi, closer to the memory of its grandeur. I have not yet seen Achiq anywhere. I wonder if he came back with the group, wonder what his role is in all of this. I worry about how Tachico will react when he wakes up and finds himself here. What will he remember? What will he be able to tell us? Does he know about his arm?

I linger, appreciating the view. Even though the temples of old are buried now, the landscape is impressive. The outlines of what was once a huge complex still rise behind the belt of green along the river. If it is still so imposing under all this sand, I can understand how people would revere the beauty of those human constructions when they were flourishing. I am glad that people now know better than to let that reverence outshine our gratitude to Pachamama and the Creator God Wiracocha. We still need places to gather, places to honor the waters and converse with the gods who give us hope. Or if not hope, I think, at least an understanding of where we stand in this world. Being in good stead with the earth and her cycles means health and survival. It means celebrating whatever there is to celebrate. It occurs to me that celebration is an important thread in the experience of belonging. I can't remember who used to repeat so much, "If we share joy together, we can weather pain together." Mother? Paya Kuyllay? Or was it Faruka? A woman's voice, though. Definitely a woman's voice. Yes. It comes to me now. Faruka told Ecco at their wedding, "We share so much joy together, we can weather pain together when we must."

Uncle Weq'o's voice slithers into my thoughts in his chiding, disdainful tone. "So simple?" he interrupts. "You think it is all so simple?"

"No." I defy the voice in my head. "I don't think anything is simple."

While I hesitate in front of Waqar's quarters, I study her flag. Large owls must be common where she comes from. From

Call of the Owl Woman

Waqar's way of speaking, I assume she is from the highlands south of the Acari Valley. I'm surprised I have never seen her before, but most visits here have been for large gatherings. Dancing usually takes all my attention. My father is the one who comes here often. Amaruyu is like a favorite uncle to him. Maybe I will find an auntie here for myself. I knock on the door softly.

"You are up before the birds!" Waqar remarks, waving me inside and nearly pushing me onto a pile of cushions. I make myself comfortable while Waqar fusses over something in another corner. She comes back with something to drink and a plate of cold fish. "Just back from the sea, salted and sunned and soaked anew," she says. "You must eat."

I sip slowly at the smooth beverage. "Thank you. This is wonderful."

Waqar sits next to me, watching as I nibble at the fish. "Did your grandmother give you that pendant?"

"Paya Kuyllay?" My fingers automatically go to the carved vial with the orcas, the one Pikaq tried to take. "Yes. She used to wear it all the time," I reply. "The day before she died, she told me I should have it. Like she knew." I shudder. "But she acted so normal. Said she wanted me to have its protection."

Waqar puts her hand on my leg. "I am sorry she is gone."

I sigh. "Me too."

"I do remember her wearing that pendant. She would run her fingers over the orcas on the vial the way you are. That's probably why they are so polished." Waqar hesitates. "But I was wondering about the silver one."

"Silver?" I look through my strings of amulets. "You mean this one?" I rub at it with the edge of my tunic, trying to make out the design through the tarnish. "I found it on a staff in a cave on Yuraq Orqo. I took refuge inside to avoid the falling rocks during the earthquake, but then I got trapped inside. When I saw the ornament, I don't know why it reminded me of Paya Kuyllay,

Waqar

but I suddenly felt her, like she was watching over me. I remember wondering if she could have been the one who left it there. Maybe that's why I took it with me . . ."

Waqar studies me intensely. "That is very possible." She opens a small ceramic box and pulls out a shiny silver charm about the same size. "I met your paya Kuyllay before your mother was born. She was here with Amaruyu and the other healers, tending to the injured after a terrible earthquake, much, much worse than this one. It happened in the middle of a solstice gathering. Kuyllay stayed with us until there were no more wounded to care for. I worked at her side. Many died, but most returned to their homes before the third moon. Only then did she go back to her own home. By then we had become good friends. When she left, she gave me this pendant." Waqar hands it to me.

I lift the cord of my necklace over my head and hold the charm next to Waqar's. It is definitely the same shape.

"May I?" Waqar asks, reaching her hand out for my charm. I watch her rub a white powder over the surface until it begins to gleam. "Cleans well, doesn't it? One of the caravans brought this from a mine in the north. It works like magic." She holds it up. "If you look at it upright, the embossing looks like an owl, a little *tuku*, but lengthwise it looks like a jaguar . . ."

I am awed by the transformation. She hands me the pendant. "Tuku Uturunku," I say, almost in a whisper, as I rotate it in my hand, tilting it to catch the light. I realize I am grinning. "I hadn't seen either one!" Waqar places hers next to mine. Same size, same lines. I stare at them, side by side, and remember the jaguar woman on Yuraq Orqo. While I dig through my waist pouch excitedly, I try to describe how I got lost in the fog on Yuraq Orqo, and how the strange woman had appeared as if taking shape out of the sand, and how she was wearing a spotted robe like a leopard's and kept speaking of strange things until she disappeared. "But she left behind her cloak, and this," I tell

CALL OF THE OWL WOMAN

Waqar, holding the ornament out for her inspection. As she lines it up next to the others, a chill ripples down both our spines. The patterns are the same. Tuku Uturunku.

"Grandmother has been with me, hasn't she?"

"Not just Kuyllay," Waqar says softly, reverently. "These pieces once belonged to Kuyllay's mentor, a great shaman. Tuku Tukuq, they called her. The shape-shifting Silver Owl Woman. Tuku Tukuq lived on the highest mountains in my own part of the world. They were part of her ceremonial attire, metal pieces that overlapped like feathers on her breastplate. The night she died, she gave Kuyllay her robes and mask but told her to take apart the breastplate and give away the pieces. 'You will travel far and wide,' Tuku Tukuq told her, 'and when you meet girls and women of good heart and strong spirit, give them one of these silver pieces, that they might hear the call of the Owl Woman when the time comes.'" Waqar pauses, then adds, "'One day, in a far distant future,' Tuku Tukuq said, 'the scattered pieces will come together again, to rekindle the sisterhood of the Silver Owl.'"

Waqar looks up from the silver charms. "My pendant must go with you, Patya. You are like a little burrowing owl, with the jaguar's shadow poised ready in your depths and Mama K'illa's light shining through you. Tuku Uturunku. You may disappear into the landscape or watch the world from the safety of your burrow, little Tuku, but when danger comes close, you have no fear. You will do what is needed, and you will do what is right. Jaguar, Uturunku, will give you power." Waqar's face glows. She tips her head back as if listening to something in the distance, closes her eyes, and sighs.

"Tuku Uturunku. It has a nice sound, doesn't it? Tuku Uturunku. I can feel you, child, living long enough to see the lineage of the Silver Owl rise again in new form, grounded by Jaguar's strength. While I . . ." Her voice trails off as she reaches for a carved stone on her altar. "I am much more like this old sea

Waqar

lion—every day a little thicker around the waist, a little slower, a little closer to the earth. I am slowing down, readying myself for the time when I shall return to Pachamama. And maybe be reborn."

I stare at the sleek seal carved of stone, tempted to tell Waqar about my dream of the owl flying out of the orca that ate a seal. Instead, I just echo, "Reborn?"

"Such a wonderful thing to imagine!" Waqar says cheerily. "I don't want to wait around in a tomb. I want to sail with my soul wherever it wants to go, to explore this world all over again. I don't care if I am a rock. I want to feel the sun and the moon and hear the water flow and the birds sing." She smiles at me, radiant for a moment, and then grows serious.

"Your brother has a difficult journey ahead. You will have to help him, but the way will not always be clear, and these times will not make it easy. I have seen many pilgrims pass through here. Each brings their own array of fears, secrets, desires, pains, joys. Some come for healing, some to celebrate together, some to seek greater power for themselves so they can have more power over others. I have seen parents tear food from the mouths of their own children." Waqar offers me a bowl of peanuts cooked in their shell, but I cannot eat. She continues, "Our visitors have been generous. Here, we have enough to eat. For now. But we cannot see the future. It's too bad I did not think of this when we had times of plenty, but some of us elders should have fattened ourselves up then. So we could offer ourselves to feed the rest when food becomes scarce. Remember the old story of the whale who threw herself onto the shore when people were starving? She fed the whole village for months! I would have volunteered happily—to eat to my heart's content until crisis calls for sacrifice! What an honor to have my old and tired and fattened self one day become a feast for my friends!" She laughs at the horror on my face. "Come on, don't be so alarmed. There are tribes in the jungle who eat their enemies to absorb their strength. Others who eat their friends to honor them in death and absorb their wisdom." She wags her finger at me. "I would not want you to starve, should things come to that."

"It will never come to that!" I protest, appalled.

"Let us hope not! But just in case . . ." She winks.

"I couldn't!"

"If you were hungry enough, you could."

"There are ways to make our food last . . ."

"But for how long? We may very well have taken all we can from the land here. Our grandfathers' grandfathers coaxed the waters from beneath the earth. Your father and his father expanded the underground reservoirs to feed the canals. But the waters that come to fill them are less and less each year."

"There are more rivers hidden under the desert," I say, trying to sound hopeful.

"Yes. And ever farther from our reach. We must be prepared for change, Patya. But we will not despair."

Waqar holds up her left hand and faces it toward me. With a sharp thorn she scratches an *X* across the center of her palm and then takes my hand to do the same to mine so quickly that I am too stunned to protest. "Be still," she says gently, as she presses her hand to mine. "This is not just about your brother; it is about the danger we all face. Healing Tachico's body will be the easy part. Becoming part of the sisterhood will be a life's journey." She rotates her hand, smearing the blood into a circle, and then releases my wrist. "Tachico will learn to make do with one hand, but only if he can let the other one go. To help him do that, you must retrieve it from the belly of the beast that took it."

"That's impossible!" I object.

"We have allies in both worlds, seen and unseen. You must call on them."

The blood on my palm stiffens into a string of small red dots crossing the circle of red. "I am not like you," I groan.

Waqar

"Wherever you go, you are not alone. Remember that. Kuyllay is not the only one who will help you."

I stare at her hand, recalling the circle I made on the rock the day of the earthquake. What had prompted me to make that mark? To put the crossed lines inside it? Where have I seen that symbol before?

"Waqar," I ask, "what called you to serve the temple?"

"Called me?" She grunts. "I wasn't called. I was left. I had not borne my husband a child after a year, so he brought me here. I did not know that he was taking me as part of his offering when I came with him to the solstice gathering. I had not wanted to leave my village even for a few days, let alone a lifetime. He told the priests that I would serve the needs of the temple better than I served his. He went back with a new wife."

"How awful! You are better off without a man like that!"

"True enough. But it took me a long time to realize that, Patya. Kuyllay helped."

I study Waqar before speaking again. "If I ask you something, will you keep it a secret?"

She smiles, intrigued. "Of course."

"Do you know where my grandmother's umanqa is kept?"

Waqar gives me a long, considering look. Then she takes my hand and dabs some salve onto the scratches before she replies. "No, I don't. Achiq has been keeping it close. He has been trying to summon her power. He had a special ceremony before he went to meet your father for the trip to Acari. I heard him bragging to some of the younger priests that he would bring the waters back by making an offering to the sea more powerful than ever before. A *yanantin*, a dual energy offering, with Tikati's umanqa and Kuyllay's. He planned to take them with him to the south. But after the ceremony, he was very agitated that Kuyllay's umanqa had not responded. The ceremony was dull, tepid. I heard murmurs that perhaps it will not fall to him but to someone else to tap the power of her lineage." The expression on her face is hard to read.

"Where is Achiq now?"

Her face darkens. "No one knows for certain. Your father thinks he went back to Acari after the earthquake."

"But why?"

Waqar goes to the door. "That is not our concern. Right now, we must attend to Tachico." She hustles me out and back down the hill.

I brace myself before entering the healing room. Otocco is gone, and Chanki sits to one side, quietly chanting a prayer I do not recognize. I feel Tachico's wrist, relieved to note that it is not as hot and that the pulse is strong.

"Your brother slept calmly," Chanki volunteers. "Amaruyu is with the sailor now. He said to send you in when you got back." He offers me a bowl of scented water and nods to another door.

I cup my hands in the water to perform the ritual cleansing, ignoring the sting in my palm. I had forgotten about the mystery patient. "Did Amaruyu say anything about Tachico's quwi reading?"

"The first one died before he could skin it properly," Chanki replies, adding quickly, "but he was encouraged by the second. The first absorbed too much pain. But Amaruyu says that Tachico has much strength left, and his insides were not harmed."

Even though I am familiar with quwi readings, they still make me uneasy. I can't stop myself from imagining what it would be like to absorb another's pain and then have one's skin peeled off. How could such a thing please the gods? I had heard that priestesses in the northern Moche territories are sometimes skinned alive—and then buried with great honor in elaborate tombs. Did the women offer themselves, or were they forced? Was it a last resort after quwi ceremonies and sacrifices were not enough? Or did those women believe the ritual could save a loved one, someone whose life was worth more to them than their own? What if such a sacrifice would save Tachico? Could I do it if I thought it was the only way to save him? Would it be easier to do it if there were a medicine that could keep me from feeling the pain?

Tachico's complete stillness scares me. It is as if his body has no spirit to animate it. "We must draw his soul back," Waqar tells me again, "and hope he is not too far away to hear us."

I stroke Tachico's cheek gently and whisper in his ear, "We'll have a concert, the two of us, when you are better. All our favorite songs and a few new inventions. And Otocco will take you hunting, so you'd better come back soon before all the guanaco are gone!"

In the other room, Amaruyu has finished cleaning the stranger's wounds. The deep cut across his scalp is swollen and red, but Amaruyu has given him something to sleep deeply. The patient does not stir. He has me hold the skin closed while he sews the gaping wound together, then applies the poultice. He shows me how to prepare a new one to apply at sundown. When he leaves, he asks me to help Waqar bring more blankets.

I wrap a cloth around the stranger's head to hold the poultice in place, relieved that he is sleeping so soundly. I take my time, fascinated by the shape of his head, the slope of his brow, the full lips. He is slightly darker than my people, his skin remarkably smooth and taut across his cheekbones, as if stretched to fit a drum. When I dab a bit of cream onto his broken lips, they curl back reflexively, revealing large teeth that are unusually white. I'd like to find out what he chews to keep them so bright. I wonder what he looks like when he smiles. I study his face, trying to guess whether his eyes would be soft and dreamy or glinting and sharp.

CALL OF THE OWL WOMAN

Waqar pauses next to me. "He's a pretty one, don't you think?"

"I hadn't noticed."

Waqar chuckles. "Well, do you think you can stop looking at him long enough to help me bring those blankets?"

We wind through a confusing maze of corridors until Waqar finally stops at the entrance to a storeroom. She piles my arms with blankets until I can barely see over the top. On the way back I follow close behind her. After a couple turns Waqar stops so suddenly that I run into her, spilling my stack of blankets onto the ground. As I kneel to refold them, a slightly nauseating but vaguely familiar cacophony of smells escapes from a curtained room beside me.

"What's in there?" I ask. I don't wait for her answer. Leaving the blankets on the floor, I step through. A narrow opening at the top of the back wall lets in just enough light to silhouette some hanging herbs, enough to help me navigate the large room. This is more than just a repository of herbs. The walls are lined with shelves—one full of dried medicinal plants, another covered with carved stones, another with shells and other ceremonial objects. In the corner are musical instruments—ceramic *antaras* and trumpets, flutes of bone and cane, and drums of all sizes. But the smell that had caught my attention came from what was hanging from the beams at the center. My eyes come to rest on the rows of umanqas. The hair on my neck rises and my skin tingles. There are at least fifty, maybe double. Could Kuyllay's be among them? Are they trophies from old battles that will be used in offerings for burials or new buildings or for requests for divine favors? Are they revered ancestors brought here to guide the priests and shamans? Or are they used in ceremonies just for show?

When I was small, I never noticed anyone wearing more than three or four umanqas during ceremonies except occasionally,

Waqar

when very elderly shamans dressed for high ceremony with full costume regalia, adorned with their strings of skull cap necklaces and their belts dangling with umanqas. Lately, however, even at simple gatherings there are priests and leaders who wear them like braggartly boasts. It's not unusual to count eight around one man's waist, ten attached to another's cloak, as if simple possession equaled power.

Waqar makes a small cough from the other side of the curtain. I quickly survey all the rows but do not see Kuyllay. "Paya," I whisper, "are you here?" Waqar clears her throat in warning. Reluctantly, I make my way back toward the corridor, but as I near the exit I notice a large ceramic in the corner, a pot as tall as me. On it hangs an elaborately embroidered tunic, its cloak lined with foxtails and necklaces of bone. It looks like a costume ready and waiting to be worn. Disappearing behind the folds of the cloak is a belt of umanqas. I pull the cloak open. There at the end of the string of umanqas is the face that smiled back at me my whole life. I fall to my knees, placing my forehead against Kuyllay's. A flurry of images flows through me, a river of journeys and adventures, of stories and laughter, comfort, and advice. I want to weep with joy—I have found my paya Kuyllay!

Waqar coughs louder.

I run my fingers over the thick rope of hair. "I'll be back," I promise. Then I slip out the door, the curtain falls into place behind me, and Waqar restacks the blankets in my arms. Her eyes ask if I found anything. I look down, hoping she interprets my downcast eyes as disappointment. I am not ready to tell her. Not until I have a plan.

chapter 16
Mishka

Amaruyu has already sent a runner to Keyka with the news that Father will be home soon. I will stay with Tachico until he is strong enough to make the journey home. The fact that Otocco and Chanki will go to the mountains to finish the ritual is still secret.

"And the sailor?" I ask.

"We'll see," Amaruyu replies. "His injuries were already festering before he reached shore. Head wound, knife cuts, broken ribs. Likely from a fight. We do not know what happened before he reached the cove. Since he doesn't speak our language, it may be a while before we find out what brought him here. Boats from the north are seldom seen this far south, and those always have several sailors. Odd that this one was alone. Keep an eye on him. Give him more of the sleep medicine if he wakes. He'll have a better chance if he can rest until the fever is gone and the wounds begin to heal."

When we change Tachico's dressings in the afternoon, Waqar opens the cane shutters to let in the sun. She fans the smoke from

Mishka

a small burner, sending the aromas of wanqor wood and sweet-grass across the room. Tachico's pallor is beginning to lessen, and the new scabs are forming well. I am finishing my ministrations when Otocco stumbles in, smelling strongly of fermented chicha. He leans against the wall and slides to the floor.

"Gimme something," he mumbles, "to stop the dreams."

"Patya, take him outside," Waqar orders. "I will prepare something for Otocco to help him sleep tonight, but please get some food into your brother. He will need strength for the trip home."

I pull at Otocco's arm. "Come on."

He mutters something, grabs my leg, and tries to pull himself up, nearly dragging me down to the floor beside him.

"Less go," he slurs.

Once he is up, he leans heavily against me while I guide him out the door. We pass Chanki, who is talking to a man who introduces himself as "Punawa, at your service."

"I need to get Otocco some food," I tell them, as if to explain our slow progress.

"Let me join you," Chanki offers, slipping into place beside Otocco and wrapping my brother's other arm around his shoulders.

"May I suggest a visit to Lady Mishka?" Punawa says. "There is always good food there. I'll show you the way." He takes my place, and the two men stride ahead with my older brother between them.

"Lady who?" Otocco mumbles.

"Mishka, whom the gods have favored," Punawa replies. "The Oracle. Mishka, who serves the great goddess from her nest of abundance." His voice booms like a storyteller launching into a favorite tale.

"This Mishka has enough food to share?" Chanki asks, dubious.

"Food to share and drink to spare! She receives so many gifts and offerings of food that there is never a lack. If Otocco will tell her a story, that will be better than food for Lady Mishka."

171

CALL OF THE OWL WOMAN

"She exchanges food for stories?" I ask.

"She does. She is always eager for tales of travel, adventure, and unusual occurrences."

Mishka's hut is beside the old temple grounds at the edge of the settlement. A young boy greets us at the door and then disappears into the shadowed interior. Punawa tells me, "Don't be surprised by anything."

The woman we meet inside reminds me of the voluptuous ceramic pots that are used for fertility offerings. Her round, smiling face tops an even rounder body, which is seated on a cushioned bench. Tattoos decorate all her visible skin and, I suspect, unseen skin as well. Mishka laughs merrily when Punawa bows with a great flourish. "My hungry boy is back!" She chuckles. "Bring us food!" she instructs, and her attendants reappear with bowls piled high with varicolored beans and a steaming stew. "Such tender alpaca," Mishka sighs. "A young one got caught in a rockslide. Pachamama sent her to us."

I had not realized how hungry I was. "Food first, conversation later," Mishka announces. She turns to me. "You are in a hurry?" I am taking second mouthfuls before swallowing the first ones.

I stop self-consciously. "I just want to get back to my little brother," I say, but her eyes are on Otocco.

"It looks to me like you have another one right here to worry about," Mishka replies. "Come with me when you have had enough to eat."

As soon as I finish my plate and lean back, Mishka nods toward an opening in the back of the room. "Follow me." She rocks back and forth on her seat until she gathers enough momentum to launch forward and upward. She steadies herself with an ornate staff and makes her way slowly toward the partition of woven reeds. The other room backs into the hill. Three of its walls are of adobe, but the back wall is recessed into solid earth, with a seat sculpted into it. It looks as if the woman and the hill behind her

172

Mishka

had been created together, as if Mishka had once been a piece of earth that had simply stepped out of the rock in human form. The earthen wall is covered with markings—the same inked symbols that cover her body.

Mishka looks toward a view that is barely visible in the gap between the wall and the roof. "Yuraq Orqo is stirring," she says. "I feel her. In order to see her well, you have to climb to the top of the hill behind us. But you do not need eyes to feel her. The sands that shift across her body also blow across my own." She closes her eyes. "Your friends come to me for food, but you are here for something else."

I glance around the room, not sure what to say. Fever bark and dried thistles hang in bunches from the ceiling; ceramic jars line the walls. A large jug in the corner is tilted over a smaller bowl, with water still clinging to its lip. "I just came along because . . ." I begin, trying to remember the sequence of events that have brought me here.

"You came because you needed to consult me. Like your father did at the beginning of his journey."

"My father came here before going to the sea?" I shake myself. How stupid of me! Mishka is *the* Oracle, the last of an ancient lineage of women who have served Yuraq Orqo, of women who receive visions from the future. "Yupaychana Mishka, honored one." I bow to her, embarrassed that I had not known who she was. I would not have wasted time eating if I had realized who she was—someone who could tell me what I needed to know. I hope she is not insulted, but I can't wait. "What was revealed to you?"

Mishka adjusts herself on the bench and leans her staff against the wall. Her jowls quiver as she breathes in deeply, closing her eyes. "One cannot argue with what will come," she says slowly, "or see beyond seas filled with thunder and shadows. Fate is the path we follow and destiny is where it leads, but the territory ahead only becomes clear as we enter it." She opens her eyes and takes my hand between hers. She blows over the X that Waqar scraped into my palm and nods to herself. "You have begun an important journey."

Yes, I realize. I have. Going to Kuyllay's Grove when I did set me on a path I never imagined for myself. While Father and his group made the journey to Acari, I have been on my own journey. The trek to Yuraq Orqo, through the fog, through the earthquake, back home, and here, to Cahuachi. But all I want now is for this journey to take me back home as soon as possible. Father's journey is almost over. How could mine be just beginning?

Mishka leans back, swaying slightly and humming to herself. Her voice comes as if from a great distance. "Many people come to see me. Sometimes I see visions that answer their questions; sometimes I do not. Sometimes I see things that they have not asked for and do not want to know. It is not my choice what I see. It comes as it will, when it will. I merely float. I notice every sensation. I listen. I watch. I feel . . ." The movement is small at first, as she rocks forward and back in a steady rhythm. Little by little, the range increases to one side, then the other in a growing arc, forward, back, swaying, hypnotic. She is lost in some inner dance. Her breath exits her lips with a soft whistling sound.

After a while, her voice begins to emerge ever so softly. "Sometimes," she says, "I feel like I am slowly, silently exploding. Bits of me everywhere. I become everything. I am the rolling hills, the folds of rock, deep ravines, hidden springs, spilling water from within. I'm an underground stream on my way to the sea. I am the mountain caressed by the wind, by the lover's kiss that crosses the desert." Her voice becomes a whisper. "Sometimes I am a vessel, disintegrating slowly, slowly, far from breaking but bursting within. Only my will holds the vessel together. Light tunnels through me, shines through each piece I let go of. One day I will let go of everything and become one with the stars, shining from

Mishka

every pore." Her movement slows. She becomes still. Her skin stretches moonlike across her face as she smiles like a sleepy cat. "That is how I want to leave this world, to become a star in the great forever."

I am mesmerized by her face, lulled by her voice.

She opens her eyes. "You came to see me," she says with sudden brusqueness. "What do you want?"

"I hadn't thought. I mean, I didn't know . . ." I sputter, flustered by the abrupt change.

"Nothing is an accident," Mishka says. "A casual meeting, an ugly crime—anything can become significant when you are on a quest. What is your quest?"

"I . . ." I falter. "My little brother, Tachico . . ." I begin nervously. Then I remind myself why I am here. I straighten my spine. I level my gaze and meet Mishka's eyes. "I came to help."

Mishka sits back, nodding. "Yes. I see." She leans forward, sniffing at me and then at the gust of air that enters from the gap in the ceiling. "If I am not mistaken, I think you know your next task?"

I answer without thinking, like my tongue was ready before I was. "Waqar says that I must bring his arm back from the belly of the beast." As I speak, the looming presence before me transforms. The Oracle is no longer Mishka, a woman, but the mountain herself, singing in a chorus of voices—the woman of the spotted cloak, Kuyllay, Waqar, Mishka, the ancestors of long ago.

The mountain-Mishka leans forward onto her staff, and it seems to grow as she grips it. "Gather your allies," she says to me between breaths as she draws herself upward. "You must find them." When she is standing fully upright, she thumps her staff on the ground. She is huge. Solid as a boulder. Centered, tall, imposing. "Find them," she commands. She peers over my head as if into a far, far distance, shudders, and then sits down.

"But for now," Mishka says, "call the others in."

CALL OF THE OWL WOMAN

· ✦ ·

The three men are huddled over a table. Otocco and Punawa are engrossed in watching Chanki carve something onto the face of a flat river stone. "That's a really sharp point on your knife," Otocco says, and Punawa nods. They do not notice me waiting to catch their attention, but I don't mind. I need to catch my breath. I do not know what to make of Mishka. So I also watch Chanki pull the knife across the stone. The design reveals itself in the lighter color beneath the surface. "There's your orca," he says, handing it to Otocco, "scar and all." Otocco stares at the rock, fixated, looking for something in the image.

I clear my throat. "Mishka wants you to tell us what happened."

Punawa raises his eyebrows at me and glances toward the back room. "It looks like it's time to earn our meal." He places his hand on Otocco's back and guides him toward the back room. Chanki lingers at the table, gathering up several small, flat stones. I recognize some of the symbols.

"Divining stones?" I had never imagined Chanki would be interested in such things.

"Some people read leaves. I prefer rocks."

"Northern tradition or southern?" I pause. "Or Brotherhood?"

He looks up at me from under furrowed brows. "You know about the Brotherhood?"

"I've heard stories."

"As have I. Their traditions are too dark for me. I seek understanding, not power." He puts the last of the stones in his pouch while I study him with new interest. I never thought of Chanki as a person with much depth. He always shined in games—strong, not as fast as my brothers, but with much more endurance. He was usually quiet but always quick to answer his father's demands, and Terzhic is a very demanding father, one with a cruel streak.

176

Mishka

Until now, I actually kind of assumed Chanki would follow in his footsteps.

Punawa waves us over. "Mishka is ready," he says. "I will be out here if you need anything."

"Perhaps I should wait out here as well," Chanki says, glancing at the door nervously.

"She doesn't bite," I tell him. "Come on. You were there too. You may have seen things that Otocco could not. Please, I need to hear it all." He rises reluctantly and follows me to the chamber.

The three of us stand in a semicircle while Mishka blows aromatic waters into the air and waves leafy branches through the mist, fanning them as she recites a series of prayers. "Sit," she says to Chanki and me, indicating the cushions on the floor. She gestures for Otocco to approach her. Her voice fills the small room, sonorous and soothing. "Otocco, son of honored water-guardian Yakuwayri and revered healer Keyka, grandson of Kuyllay who guides us from the other side." She fixes her gaze on him. "Brother of Ecco the potter and Patya the seeker and Tachico the wounded. Tell us, now, what happened at the cove."

Otocco glances first at Chanki, then at me. I have never seen him look so uncomfortable. He has none of his usual confidence.

Mishka tells him, "You are in sacred space, free to speak your secrets. What you say here will not be repeated unless it is by you yourself."

"I . . ." Otocco lowers his head. "I failed my brother."

"I did not ask for your opinion," Mishka says, suddenly impatient. "I asked for your story. The moon was waning when your father last came to me. Now it is growing again. Tell us what happened during that time."

chapter 17
Otocco

"The sacred cove," Otocco begins, his eyes meeting Mishka's. "Have you ever been there?"

She regards him with curiosity. "It frightens you."

"Have you been there?"

"In this body? No. But I have seen the caves. The hill with sunken eyes, ever watching; the tongueless whisper of secrets. Yes, I know the cove—and the ghostly face that guards it."

"The great beast," Otocco mutters. "From the moment we arrived, I had a bad feeling. But I went in like I was told. I climbed up to the lowest cave, the mouth. I crawled over the sea of bones to find a place to bury the offering. My father says they were llama bones, but they did not look or feel like llama bones to me. Achiq knows. He says the hill is a sleeping beast, always eager for human meals. I made sure to keep hold of my jaguar amulet the whole time, or I might not have made it out. The enchantment is strong there."

Mishka closes her eyes and leans back. "Tell me your story, Otocco. Paint me your picture."

Otocco starts pacing, his hands pressed against his forehead. I

Otocco

can't tell if he is trying to remember or trying not to. He goes to the wall and stares at the chaos of pictures. Just above his head, a likeness of the sacred cove is sketched in red pigment.

"Yes," Mishka intones, "go back. Take us with you. Tell us as you go. Don't think about it."

Otocco's fingers trace the outline of the hill rising above the beach and the arches rising from the bay. He turns back to Mishka. "We were coming from Acari. Their high priest wanted to present his offering to the sea together with Achiq's. They were trying to outdo each other the whole time. Did you know that they believe we have better irrigation not because of our engineering but because of our priests are more powerful than theirs? They say that a woman bewitched an Acari sorcerer and stole his most sacred stone, and that is what caused the drought. They sent their priest to ask the sea for help getting it back.

"It took us a day's walk to reach the cliffs. The sun was just above the top of the arches when we got to the edge, sending long shadows from the rocks and streams of light through the openings—like beacons straight to the caves. We were just in time. Since I was supposed to bury an offering in the cave, I left the others to take a shorter route."

Otocco hesitates before continuing. "The tide was low when I got back from leaving the offering, but it was still going out. Tachico was helping Chanki with the fire, singing fishing songs. Father was at the water's edge, making his offering for a good catch. I caught up with him at the first arch. It is always like stepping into another world." He sighs.

"Achiq was coming back from the far end, where he had made offerings with the Acari priest. The wind and waters were whipped into an angry mess. Achiq waited at the edge of the surf with me while Father waded in up to his knees and placed the package on the water. The cloth opened as it sank, leaving ashes, grains, and flowers floating on the surface. A wave rolled past and

CALL OF THE OWL WOMAN

carried them back toward us, coming to rest at Achiq's feet. He muttered something like, 'Mama Cocha has rejected your father's gift. It's a good thing she accepted ours.' I told him not to be so hasty in his judgments. Then a big wave rushed in and carried the flowers back out. The sea had tasted the offering and returned for it. Achiq just turned and went back to camp."

Otocco starts pacing again. "The next few days we were busy setting the nets and bringing in the catch, keeping the sealskin floats repaired, drying fish, collecting urchins and clams, and readying ourselves for the most important ritual of all. On the last day, it was my job to collect—" He catches himself. "It was my duty to get what we had come for," he says stiffly.

"Otocco," I coax, "Mishka is the Oracle. There are no secrets from her. Chanki was with you on the same mission. And I know more than you think. Please go on."

My brother takes a deep breath. He looks in my direction but stares right through me to that other place. "The moon had grown. It looked down on us like the eye of a jaguar ready to pounce. Everything was ready. The llamas were packed and waiting. The floats were oiled and inflated. I took one and Achiq took the other. We each had a jar tied to our waists for collecting the sea-foam. I went in on the south side of the arches, and Achiq was going in on the north side. Father held my safety rope and Chanki had Achiq's. I went in first, letting the rope unwind, hoping the currents and rising wind would not make it too hard to get back. I was nervous. I had seen a large shark that morning, and we had to wait until it left the cove before we went back out to gather the last of the nets. The entire day had been strange— sudden fogs, winds rising abruptly and then disappearing. The water was colder than usual when I reached the last of the arches. I looked back to shore but couldn't see over the waves. The waters were churning, and it took all my strength to keep from being pulled toward the rocks, but I got the foam and turned back. By

Otocco

then I was praying with every stroke. I did not want to become another victim of the wild waters. I asked the sea to protect me, to send power to my arms, to get me back safely. I did not know there was another who needed that protection more than me." He holds his head as if it is about to burst, then spins to face Chanki. "Where were you? You were supposed to keep an eye on him!"

Chanki jumps up. "I told you, Otocco. I was with your father, watching out for you! Achiq sent me to help hold the safety rope when you kept disappearing behind the whitecaps. He said he would wait to go out until you were safe—and that the Acari priest would take my place with Achiq's rope. So I went to Yaku-wayri. Tachico was having fun. Achiq was going on and on, telling him how brave you were and how Tachico would one day do the job as well as his big brother. When I walked away, Tachico was singing a fisherman's song. They were having fun."

A shadow crosses Otocco's face. "*Fill my nets and fill them fast and keep the beasts away . . .*" he drones the song.

"Yes," Chanki says, "that's the one. ' . . . *Let us live to feast tonight and fish another day.*'"

"Well, it didn't keep the beasts away, did it?" Otocco snarls.

"But you did live, Otocco. And so did he."

"Did he? Have you had a good look? He may not make it, Chanki. We may lose him."

"Otocco," Mishka croons, "do not lose hope. Tell us what happened. Tell us what you saw."

"What I saw? I saw wild waves and sea-foam. All I could see of the shore were the three fires lighting up the caves on the hill. I saw angry waters stretching to the horizon. Then I saw the other float, passing the arches and moving southward in my direction. But it was not Achiq riding it. It was Tachico, and he wasn't pad-dling. It looked like he was slumped over. I paddled hard in his direction, looking for his safety line to grab a hold of it, but I

CALL OF THE OWL WOMAN

couldn't see any markers, no rope. Because no rope was attached. With the wind's help, I got close enough to see his face. That's when my own rope pulled taut. I could see him, but I could not reach him. His hands barely had hold of the netting. He was unconscious, with a streak of red flowing from his arm. I yelled, I splashed water, but I couldn't wake him. I sawed at my line to cut through it so I could get to him. I knew it might mean getting pulled out to sea with him. It might be impossible to get both floats back to shore, but I had to try.

"I had cut most of the way through the rope when a huge swell lifted me. I had to hold tight to keep the wave from throwing me off the float. I lost sight of Tachico, and when I could see him again a huge fin rose from the water between us. My safety rope was stretched so tight that when the wave lifted me again, the rope snapped. I slid toward Tachico down the slope of the wave. The shark surfaced right next to him and nosed at the float. I begged Mother Sea to protect Tachico and wept with gratitude when the shark turned and started back to the open sea. I paddled toward Tachico with more power than I had ever felt in my life!

"Then the shark turned. It came toward us, picking up speed until it rammed Tachico's float so hard he flew right off. The shark went after him, and when they came up, Tachico was hanging from its mouth."

The room is silent. I stop breathing, imagining the horror. Chanki slumps into himself, looking away from Otocco. He winces when Otocco continues.

"I froze. The shark went back under. I thought everything was over. The shark disappeared again into the water. I just stared at the surface, at the shimmering streaks of gold and pink, the stain of red as the sun finished setting. I had failed. Tachico was gone. I had failed him. I had failed our people. The ritual would not be completed. I would not return. I was numb. I wanted to drown before the shark came back for me.

Otocco

"Another wave came, and again I watched from above as the slope steepened below me. I prayed that the shadow at the bottom was some ghostly being come to take me to the other world. Salt water stung my eyes. It was hard to see, but the shadow that took shape in the twilight was not the shark. It was a boat—like something from an ancient story. The bow looked like a monster's head. A sailor stood at its helm, his hair blowing wild. I thought I saw him lean over the side of the vessel and pull something from the water. Something that was balanced on the head of an orca."

Otocco's voice catches. "I still cannot believe what I saw," he says. "Tachico was alive."

He faces me. "I always thought you liked orcas because of our paya's stories about shape-shifting sea-people. I thought of orcas like sharks—just bigger, deadlier, smarter—but I had never seen one myself. Yet, impossibly, there she was. An orca. A gentle giant. Upright in the water, balancing Tachico on her head. She was holding him up so the sailor could reach him. Have you ever heard of such a thing? Once Tachico was in the boat, the orca turned to me. When I close my eyes at night now, I see her. I see that face, that expression. It's as if there is a person inside, someone like us in a different body. Another soul looking back at me. She was . . . amazing."

"She?" Mishka asks.

"She had a baby nuzzling against her side. Little next to her but twice my size. And it was watching me like a curious child. It swam in my direction, circled behind me, and pushed me to the boat."

Otocco stares at the ground. "I wouldn't be here if the gods had not sent them."

chapter 18
Mochico

I wish Otocco had agreed to stay. If only one more day. I understand why Father has to return home as soon as possible. Our people need him. Mother needs him. But I would feel better if Otocco could have stayed longer. Is it really so urgent that he get the sea-foam to the hills right away, or is it more that he can't bear seeing Tachico like this?

Otocco completely dismissed me and my concerns. "Chanki needs to go home to his father. Terzhic's illness has been worsening," he said. "And I have delayed too long already. The mountains are thirsty for rain. Each day without water takes us closer to . . ."

I interrupted him. Accused him of leaving me with a stranger we know nothing about.

"Patya," he told me, "the sailor is no demon. He is a man who used the last of his strength to pull us from the water and get us to shore. He is in a foreign place with no familiar faces. He has more cause for worry than you, little sister."

I gave up arguing, and now, as I change the stranger's bandages, I linger over his face, so different from ours. His forehead, his nose, his cheeks. A sailor. He looks harmless enough asleep,

Mochico

but I can't help but wonder what he was doing so far south. Why was he alone? How did he get injured? Amaruyu said that the head wounds happened before the encounter at the cove. I bathe the cuts nervously, afraid he might wake, although it does feel different, knowing that he rescued my brothers. From a boat. I've never seen a boat before, let alone a sailor. What Otocco told us is more the stuff of myth and legend. I once saw a remarkable bowl with such a boat painted on its sides. The caravanners who showed us the piece said it came from the northern coast, where the Moche people make ceramics so beautiful that they could rival our own. What I remember most from the caravanners' tales about Moche fishermen and seafarers, though, is that they make boats by weaving reeds into the shape of a crescent moon in honor of Mama K'illa. The boat on the pot was not only curved like the moon, but at each end the reeds were shaped into feline heads with long fangs.

I remember the boat well, but I also remember the other side of the bowl—a procession of roped prisoners walking across a field, their blood dripping into the soil. But what really makes me queasy is that the Moche are the same people rumored to sacrifice their priestesses by skinning them alive.

The sailor tosses with fever all night. He seems to be getting worse. I wipe away the sweat and apply the cooling tinctures while he mumbles in his strange language. By morning, the fever is breaking. Soon, he begins to accept food, though he is not very communicative.

Tachico barely moves. He sleeps. Moans occasionally, especially when I dress his wounds. When I try to feed him, he swallows, but not much. Mostly, he sleeps. I talk to him, sing to him, but his body seems empty, lying here, wasting away. It's like he's not really there.

CALL OF THE OWL WOMAN

I can't believe that the sailor is up and walking, and he's figuring out our language. He points to the water jug, and I say, "Water?" He nods. I pour him some from the jug, and he repeats the word "water." He repeats it! Very well, in fact. Then suddenly, like a huaico, he unleashes a stream of Moche words and points to himself.

"Slowly!" I laugh, holding up my hand to stop the barrage.

Then he points to me and says, "Patya." Points to Waqar and says, "Waqar." He points to himself and says something, expecting me to repeat it, but I cannot make the same sounds.

So I point to him and say, "Mochico. We shall call you Mochico."

"Mochico," he repeats, considering. "Moche. Mochico." Then he smiles, baring a wide set of gleaming teeth. He is radiant, happy with himself. Then he pats his stomach and looks at me expectantly.

"Hungry?" I say, making the motions of eating. "Are you hungry?"

He grins in reply. "Mochico are hungry!"

It is incredible to see him learning so fast. He follows us, watches everything we do, repeats things he hears, tries out words.

His recovery is so different from Tachico's. Waqar helps me coax liquids down Tachico's throat, but he is barely responsive. Amaruyu keeps trying different herbs, but nothing seems to make a difference. I leap to Tachico's side every time he moves, every time he sighs. Each moment I'm convinced that he is on the verge of waking. But he remains deep in his coma.

"We need to get him home," I tell Waqar.

"As soon as we can do it safely," she says.

"And my paya Kuyllay as well," I add.

Waqar narrows her eyes at me and shakes her head. "Kuyllay's umanqa would be missed. Achiq's rage would be felt from here to Palpa."

Mochico

"Not if he doesn't realize she is gone," I reply. "Not if another takes her place." I fetch my traveling bag and pull out the umanqa I brought with me. For the first time, I tell her the story of the Warpa hunters who hurt me and left me for dead, about the one who had tried but failed to stop them and could not live with the injustice and shame so he delivered all of their heads to his brother Waru, charged his brother with the task of making amends, and then stepped off a cliff. I tell her about the seven umanqas Waru delivered, and how I took one to Yuraq Orqo and left it in the cave as an offering and how it helped me escape. "And now this one can help Kuyllay escape from Achiq. Will you help me transform it to look like Kuyllay so we can make an exchange?"

Once Waqar gets past the shock, I know she can't turn down the challenge.

We go back to Waqar's home so she can consult her divining stones. Once everything reassures her that the ruse can work, she agrees. If we can make the switch without anyone knowing, then Kuyllay's umanqa will go home with me.

Waqar finds the right pigments to match Kuyllay's tattoos, cotton for filling out the cheeks and chin, and special oils. We set to work to transform the umanqa. The result bears an uncanny resemblance to Kuyllay—the same size and shape, the same round cheeks, the same markings. We braid more hair into his so that it will spill out with the same effect as Kuyllay's. Now we just need to wait for the right time to make the switch.

Amaruyu agrees that Tachico may have a better chance of recovery at home. All the visible wounds have sealed well. He sends word to my family to send help to take Tachico home, making

CALL OF THE OWL WOMAN

it clear that Tachico has not yet woken but is now stable enough to travel. He wants them to be prepared. Waqar follows Amaruyu's instructions for filling gourds with herbs for poultices and infusions and treatments for bathing the wounds. I scratch pictures into each of the gourds to remind me what each is for and the places near home where each herb grows in case we need to replenish supplies.

When Waqar asks me to accompany her to the storerooms to help her find a particular herb, that is my cue. The Warpa umanqa is hidden in one of my bags. I follow her through the maze of passageways until we reach the right door. Before we enter the room she performs a ritual of protection and asks permission for what we are about to do. We do not enter until she is satisfied that we are welcome.

The air is heavy with the aroma of medicinal plants but also dusty and dry. The huge pot is still dressed in the same ceremonial attire, the cloak folded just as I left it. The light is low, but I could swear there is a glow around Kuyllay's umanqa. The guarango thorns holding her eyelids closed seem to tremble as if she wants to open her eyes. I am so eager to release her from Achiq's belt that I fumble with the knots. I make myself slow down. Once it is free I set the two umanqas next to each other on the ground. It is complicated to switch the turbans and get them exactly right. Changing out the carrying cords takes longer than it should, and the delays are making Waqar nervous. She has been praying silently, but I can tell her prayers are growing more fervent. I gently tuck Kuyllay's umanqa into my bag. I'm in the middle of attaching our modified umanqa to the belt when the sound of nearby voices makes me freeze.

Waqar holds her breath.

We stare at each other. I try not to panic.

I can't tell who the voices belong to—definitely not Amaruyu, but they're vaguely familiar. Perhaps a couple of the temple

Mochico

assistants who have been coming and going all week. Their footsteps pause outside our door. We hear an unfamiliar voice ask, "Are you sure he doesn't need us to bring anything?"

Waqar slips silently into the shadows. I am on my knees beside the costume. I have nowhere to hide. The cloak draped over the costume almost reaches the floor, so I lean into the pot as close as I can and pull the cloak across me. I watch the door. The curtain moves, and a hand pulls it open. All I can see is the back of the man at the door. His companion says, "The only message was to meet him. He'll be back soon for whatever else he needs."

The curtain closes. The footsteps recede.

I let out my breath and hear Waqar let out hers.

I finish the final knot, then adjust the cloak so that it looks the same as it had before, slightly covering the umanqa. Before I turn to leave I notice an odd light stretching from the bag holding Kuyllay's umanqa toward the Warpa's, tucked into the shadowed folds of the cloak.

Waqar sees it too. "It is done," she says.

I feel a sense of rightness, an odd sort of justice. The Warpa hunter who had rallied the others to assault me had been a man who found pleasure in hurting women. That same man, through his umanqa, will spend the rest of time clothed as a woman, addressed as a woman, and called upon for aid in healing others long after Achiq is gone. Perhaps the man will come to learn something in death that he did not learn in life. Perhaps, in the process, he can begin a journey toward redemption.

For me, the most important thing is that my paya is returning to the family that loves her.

I go to see Mishka again before we leave. The Oracle receives me in the back room. I inhale deeply as she fans the wisps of fragrant smoke over me. Mishka speaks slowly between long breaths

Call of the Owl Woman

without looking up, as if in a trance. "It is good you have come, Patya. It is good you will go. You have much to do and much to learn." Her voice lowers a register as she continues. "You must take into yourself that which seeks to harm you. Take into yourself that which almost killed you. Transform these things into something new." She pauses, listening to something that I cannot hear.

"Violence comes from those who fear what they cannot conquer," she intones. "This is not new to you, Patya of the Great Tinkuy. You know what it is to be overcome," she says, "but not conquered." Her voice fades, and she begins to rock back and forth. "Those who attacked you . . . their actions returned to haunt them. The circle turns and justice finds a way. The owl in your pocket remembers what she sees from both sides. Trust the man who carved her."

My skin prickles. I have not told anyone, not even Waqar, about the owl carving Waru gave me. How could Mishka know? I have trouble concentrating on what she's saying.

"What disappears returns," Mishka croons. "We tell stories that bring things back. Know this: There is no evil that will not one day collapse into itself, cleansed by the fire of truth and reborn in the waters of remembrance."

She beckons me to her side. "We don't always come to see those truths in our own lifetimes," she says, placing a hand on my shoulder. "A river of souls flows through and beyond time, through despair and pain. Some get caught in the eddies, trapped in the regions of suffering. When we transcend our own pain, we help free others. Our victories, however small, are victories for them as well. Liberations." Mishka begins to chant in an ancient language, passing her rattle over me in a soothing rhythm. I let the sound wash through me. I feel the pulse of vibration turn into rings of light, overlapping, connecting, encasing me in a translucent shell. A sense of strength fills me. The sound anchors me,

Mochico

connects me to the greater pulse of the earth and the music of the heavens. I am floating yet rooted. Connected to everything.

Then Mishka's voice calls me back.

"You have work to do and damage to undo." The Oracle places her hands over my heart. "When you free your brother, you will free yourself." She places her hands on either side of my head. "When you free yourself, you will free him." She places a hand on each of my shoulders. "The beast will not let go until you dance with your demons. Dance until they know that they cannot hold you. The way out is to dance through the heart of it. Wrap yourself in threads of light. Let the light do its work. Let this cocoon of light prepare you, repair you, nourish you, protect you. It is a sheath to shield you until it is time to emerge. Let it transform you."

I feel, more than see, the Great Mother embrace me, wrapping around me like a soft alpaca fur, filling me with both comfort and melancholy. The ache for home, for the familiar, rests beside a deeper ache, the ache that life itself must feel for the womb of the world that gave it birth. There is a sweetness to the ache, the promise of the nameless joy that comes with every rebirth, every liberation, every freeing of a burdened soul. Everything passes, she seems to say—hunger, abundance, anger, passion, joy, pain. Rivers will swell. Rivers will empty. Tides ebb and flow. Come and go.

A gust of wind sweeps past the altar, spilling one of the jars and sending a stream of pungent liquid toward my feet. Mishka sniffs at the air. "The Sand Winds. They will be strong this season," she says. "But not quite yet. A dangerous fox slinks beneath their cover. Expect the unexpected."

My mind turns the corner into another awareness as I watch the liquid creep through the dirt. A fine cloud of sand settles over the stream like a delicate skin. As it slithers toward me, I feel the shadow of Jaguar on my shoulder and a soft buzz hovering at my ears. Hummingbird whispers, "Reclaim what is yours."

CALL OF THE OWL WOMAN

· ✦ ·

I still feel a little dizzy when I reach Amaruyu's quarters, my senses overwhelmed by Mishka's world. Finding Chanki and my good-natured, big-headed cousin Umasapa waiting for me hits me like a breath of cool air, a brisk clearing of my head for the trip at hand. They have brought two llamas with them for the journey back, and Waqar is already packing the remedies into their saddlebags.

We all retire early to rest so we can depart a few hours before sunlight. Chanki and Umasapa carry Tachico in a fabric sling, the way he had been carried before. The pole between them balances on their shoulders as if it weighs nothing. I match their stride, walking beside Tachico while Mochico, showing remarkable endurance, follows with the llamas. Although the landscape is the same one that I passed through only a week ago, everything looks different—as if I am from somewhere else. I watch Tachico sway as we walk, wanting more than ever to ask Chanki for more details about what happened at the cove, but it takes too much effort to talk. I put one foot in front of the other.

As the outline of Cahuachi recedes into the distance, I think about how long I have been without my mother nearby, without our routines and talks, our sharing of dreams every morning. She must be consumed with worry by now and probably trying not to show it. I do not want to add to her burden by telling her everything that has happened. Waru. The heads. The cave. The woman on Yuraq Orqo. Kuyllay's umanqa. Not now. Not yet. I want my mother to know, to understand, but I must wait for the right moment. When things are calmer. There is no need to worry my mother any more than she already is.

Images hover and roll through my mind like waking dreams while I walk. Women and men from legends, myths, and ancestral tales seem to fill the air around me. When the sky begins

Mochico

to lighten behind Yuraq Orqo and her silhouette sharpens, she seems to grow larger, to come nearer. We stop to wait for the sun's first rays. Chanki and Umasapa rotate slightly to face the sun. The sling continues to sway gently between them. I reach in to hold up Tachico's head and tilt it toward the sun so that he can feel its light on his face. "Tayta Inti smiles on you, Tachico," I whisper. "Good morning, little brother. Time to wake up." A flicker of movement crosses his face, but his eyes do not open. "I'll let you blow my pututu . . ." I coax. His face remains motionless, but I imagine the hint of a smile settling on his lips. I sound my salute to the rising sun, then put the shell away and try to get him to swallow some water. I say nothing for the rest of the journey.

When we reach the tinkuy of the Aja and Uchumarca Rivers, I stop to blow a call to announce our return. By the time we are in sight of Faruka's house, she is already down the hill and racing toward me ahead of the others, her arms outspread. I sink into my friend's arms. Faruka's hug keeps me afloat when my knees go weak at the nearness of home. Ecco joins us halfway up the hill and walks with Mochico, trying to communicate with him while Faruka fusses over me.

The savory smell of stewed quwi reaches me even before I see the house.

chapter 19

Home

M other is standing at the door to her uncle's home, leaning on a crutch. She radiates warmth and welcome as she strains to see us through all the people. Voices are hushed as if in unspoken agreement to not disturb the sleeping boy and the heroic sailor. A crowd gathers around Mochico, full of curiosity but keeping a respectful distance.

Chanki and Umasapa carry Tachico up the hill, past neighbors who line the path. Their pace is steady and quiet. When they reach Mother, they stop. She strokes Tachico's face tenderly, her eyes glistening, repeating his name softly, reverently, as if to welcome a newborn child.

Ecco and Mochico reach Mother right before me, just as Father appears at her side. He greets Mochico gratefully, then puts his arm around me and squeezes. He looks so much better than when I last saw him. He scoops Tachico into his arms and carries him inside. Mother reaches to pull me close, and I melt into her arms. She holds me for a long time. Before she lets go, she brushes the hair from my face, looks into my eyes, and says, "Thank you for bringing him home."

Home

Father places Tachico on the bed, and Mother settles herself at his side. They had prepared Tachico's bed near the door, with a view of the cooking area where he would be close to household activities—hearing, even if not seeing. "Let me sit with him awhile," she tells me. "Go get yourself something to eat with the others. We put your favorite peppers in the stew." She hugs me again. "And make sure the sailor eats well."

As I go to join the others, I glance over my shoulder. Mother is checking every part of Tachico's body. I know the shoulder is still discolored and badly bruised, but she'll be happy with the way the skin is healing. I'm sure she will appreciate how well the broken bones have been set, but I turn to walk more quickly, wanting to be out of sight before she gets to the missing arm.

I find Mochico with Chanki and Umasapa already finishing their third helpings. I fill a bowl, already savoring the aroma of my favorite foods. Umasapa soon leaves, eager to get home. I sit next to Chanki and pull a small leather bag from my pouch. "Perhaps these will fit in your collection?" I offer him two small, flat stones, one etched with a hummingbird, the other, a tree.

He smiles and nods. "Your favorite ritual lines. They have good stories to tell."

"Please, take them," I say. "They are yours. Thank you for your help."

He closes his fist over the stones. "It's just ayni," he says. "I know you would do for me, and I am happy to do for you." He bows awkwardly, adds the stones to his pouch, and turns toward the path home.

I call to him, "Perhaps one day you can carve an orca into a stone for me like the one you gave Otocco?"

He pauses to look back. "Of course."

"Chanki," I add, "when you're ready . . . would you tell me what you saw at the cove?"

He lowers his eyes and mumbles something that sounds like, "Yes, sure."

He is gone before I can thank him.

With my parents and brothers staying in our uncle's home, every corner already has an extra sleeping mat. I show Mochico to his bedding, next to one of my cousins. I try to explain my family to him by drawing pictures on the face of a flat rock, using water and a frayed stick brush. I name each of the stick figures under one roof, representing my family, then figures representing Faruka's family under another. I end by showing Ecco going to Faruka's. Mochico gets it.

He draws a figure for Faruka and one for Ecco, then adds a tiny third figure and circles the three, saying, "Ecco and Faruka. Family." He points down the hill toward the house he had seen them go into.

"Yes." I smile, surprised that he could know when she had just learned of it herself. Faruka's belly has not even started to swell yet.

Later I lie in my bed unable to sleep. I am glad to be home and relieved that Tachico is finally with our mother. She will bring him back, I am sure of it. After all, she and Paya Kuyllay brought me back—even when I did not want to return. After the attack, the pain made me long to be somewhere else. I imagined myself as a star, flowing with other beings of light far and wide across the night. Bodiless. Mindless. Undefined. Unfeeling. But I came back from that unfeeling place. Now I am here. And it is Tachico who is wandering the other realms.

I decide to go outside to watch the sky and find my parents sitting by a small fire. Father glances over his shoulder as if afraid of being overheard. "What's going on?" I ask.

Home

He looks at Mother as though weighing what to tell me. "We're glad you're home."

"And . . . ?"

"Things are complicated."

I shrug. "When are they not?"

Mother's voice is somber. "We've been hearing rumors . . ."

"Achiq?" I ask, assuming that anything worrisome will likely circle back to Achiq.

She sighs. "Your father just met with a messenger. You might as well hear it too. You are no longer a child to be protected but a young woman who needs to know the world she's facing."

Father says, "You know that Otocco was assigned to take the sea-foam to our high hills to complete the ritual. Well, Achiq was supposed to do the same in Acari territory. It was our way of showing mutual support. The other priests liked the plan. But when Achiq went back to Acari he did not continue to the hills with the sea-foam. He rallied the people there and told them a different story, that a demon had come from the north to steal our offering for the sea. He told them that the offering was Tachico. As a water-guardian's son, he was an honored prize, the highest sacrifice. He told them that Orca and Shark were fighting over who would receive the offering for Mother Sea when it was stolen away by the demon. Achiq claims that Orca is angry. Shark got the arm, and now Orca demands the rest. He says all the gods are angry now. That the drought will get far worse unless the boy is returned to the sea and Orca is satisfied. People are afraid."

I am horrified. "The orca wanted to protect Tachico, not eat him! She saved him from the shark. She helped the boat to shore. And why do people keep calling her 'he'?" I exclaim. "If they think the gods are angry, why doesn't it occur to them that the gods might be angry at the shark for taking Tachico's arm? Angry that someone lured Tachico into the water? He would not have been on that float without help. And that help probably came from Achiq!"

CALL OF THE OWL WOMAN

"You're right," Mother says. "It is more likely that Achiq is the one who angered the sea. Mother Moon has been watching over our boy!" Mother speaks of Mama K'illa tenderly, as a member of our family. The sun, Tayta Inti, might rule the day, but Mama K'illa steers the waters of life and love. She is the goddess who guides my mother's world.

"Achiq likes to stir things up," Father continues. "He looks for ways to keep people distracted. To keep them from doubting his ability. He wants them to believe he is the key to balancing the forces of nature. Everyone is happy to have the temple priests read the stars and weather, to announce times to plant and when to clean the canals. After all, they are usually right. They know how to read the signs in normal times. But there are also times of change, shifts in weather. A faraway volcano can block the sun or stop the rains. We can't predict everything. Most people are happy just knowing a little. And most people don't really take Achiq as seriously as he takes himself."

"But what about the ones who do believe him?" I ask.

"There are always a few gullible people, Patya. But most people here think Tachico's survival was a miracle, something the gods granted. Achiq does not like that at all. The gods are supposed to favor him, a priest, not a mere boy. Especially a boy who's the son of someone who dares to challenge him."

"That man is always trying to undermine you," Mother complains. "He sets others against you."

"Because I don't do things his way."

"Which, my dear husband, is a good thing. You are the one who works to keep things fair." Mother takes his hand to go inside. I follow them in. I pray that Achiq never discovers that I switched the umanqas. I don't want to create more trouble for my parents.

I help Mother plaster Tachico's chest with a warm, unpleasant-smelling mud that she says will stimulate his heart and wake

Home

his senses. She smiles when his nose curls away at the odor. "You are strong, my boy. You'll be climbing trees again before the swallows return to the sea," she whispers. When she glances up at me, I smile back wearily, painfully aware that I have more doubts about Tachico's recovery than my mother does.

I try to get some sleep.

Tachico does not wake up the next day as Mother had hoped. Nor does Chanki return to answer my questions. She busies herself with organizing the medicine pots Amaruyu sent. I can't help but wonder how she manages to maintain her veil of calm composure.

I refuse to think about the possibility that Tachico might not recover. I concentrate on feeding him, preparing nectars so sweet that he smiles sleepily and swallows. He seems lost in a land of dreams that hold him just below the surface of waking. Mother watches the moon and prays for guidance. She confides in me that she does not know how long to wait before holding a ceremony to call his soul back, only that he's not ready yet.

While Tachico shrinks a little more each day, Mochico grows stronger. He is an odd mixture of melancholy and enthusiasm. When he is trying to communicate, he is relaxed and animated, but when he thinks no one is watching, he looks pensive and preoccupied. I am still puzzled over what brought him to our shores and what he might have left behind. Had he been embarking on some adventure, or was he escaping a tragedy? Had he set out alone or with comrades who were lost along the way?

I have started learning his language, finally mastering the elusive guttural sounds. I name things. He repeats my words, then tells me how to say them in Moche. Little by little, we have been building a common vocabulary. I try to get him to tell me his story by sketching in the dirt. He outlines a deer on a spit, platters of food on long tables. He points to a figure near the center

CALL OF THE OWL WOMAN

with a triangle tattoo by his ear, then points to himself and the triangle by his own ear. "You!" I chirp. "Mochico!"

In the scene that takes shape in the dirt, Mochico holds a tall spear and stands next to what looks like the leader of the group, seated in the middle with a large headdress and ornamented tunic. He sketches the horizon with the sun over the ocean, then points to our northeast horizon. He mimes sailing and rowing a boat, then draws another picture, this time of the boat on shore and a group of warriors approaching it with clubs. One club lands on Mochico's head. The arm that holds that club has a diamond on it, crossed by two lines.

"Warpa," I say, not hiding my discomfort.

"Warpa kill." He sketches two Moche sailors on the ground with an X over each eye, surrounded by a big pool of blood. "Dead," he says. He draws the Warpa taking the Moche weapons and supplies upriver toward the mountains. Then he draws himself getting up. "Not dead." He draws the boat sailing away. He scrawls a big X over his companion. "Friend. Dead."

"I am sorry," I tell him.

He keeps going. We have to find a new spot for him to draw. Waves. Birds. Sun. Hilly shores. Then he draws an orca and her calf leaping from the water beside his boat. He touches his forehead, touches the figure of the orca, then falls silent for a long time. He motions for me to follow him to the edge of the terrace. He points to Yuraq Orqo and to his head, closing his eyes. "In sleep," he says. "I see orca. I see shark. I see sand mountain."

He pulls me to the firepit and takes out some half-burned sticks, using their tips to draw more detailed pictures on a large rock. He draws the sacred cove with the hill of the three caves. He points at the top two caves that look like eyes and says, "Fire." The fire had drawn him toward the cove. He pulls out more charred sticks and draws the orca with her calf in front of the cove. The shark with Tachico's body hanging from the mouth

Home

by his arm. The mother orca ramming the shark's belly with her head. The shark floating upside down while Tachico sinks. The orca surfacing with Tachico's body draped across her back. The boat with Mochico pulling him up over the side. Otocco on the inflated sealskin at the top of a high wave, then Otocco climbing into the boat.

He points to the picture of the orca ramming the shark. "Shark strong," he says. "Orca more strong."

chapter 20

Revelations

Mochico is eager to help with the work around him. He still gets dizzy when he bends over, so he can't help with the canal work. Instead, he helps string herbs for Mother and paints ceramics with Ecco. His style of drawing reminds me of the Moche pot that the caravanners showed us—simple lines, realistic figures, clear outlines. But Mochico can also imitate Ecco's designs perfectly. Even Ecco is impressed by how quickly Mochico has learned to prepare the pigments for paints and slips. He has already warned me that I will have to find something else for Mochico to do when Ecco starts working on the ceramics for the next solstice festival.

Only the finest vessels are used for the high offerings, and those are chosen in competitions. Usually works by artisans of the old temple lineage are the only ones selected, but one of Ecco's was included last time. He prefers to work alone before competitions. He needs total concentration, beginning each morning in prayer, blessing the clay before shaping it, entering what is almost a trance state. He allows no interruptions while he works. Until that time comes, though, he is happy to have Mochico's help with the everyday ware.

Revelations

Ecco is also learning Mochico's language. We all practice by naming animals, plants, body parts, geographical features, basic actions. We make up songs to remember the words and sing them to Tachico while he sleeps. Maybe when he finally wakes up, he will surprise us by knowing a new language!

Every night, while twilight settles over the valley, I sit with Tachico and tell him about my day. I know that, even unconscious, he would be eager for all the details. Chochi scampers in and out while I tell Tachico about the houses being rebuilt, about how they had finished repairing the cracks in the canals upriver. I joke about how Ecco still complains that my designs on pots are too different, too strange, but that I don't mind. I happen to like that they are a little wild. Unique. I tell him what Faruka is weaving, who Mother has treated, and I ramble on about my dreams. Especially the one about the Sumara grove. "The old tree called us to make something with her broken parts," I tell him. "She told me to bring you back to build forts the way we used to. She said the birds miss us. As soon as you are strong enough, we'll go. You, me, and Mochico." Tonight, when I get to that part, Chochi climbs onto my shoulder and tugs at my hair. "And we'll take Chochi too," I add, "if he will stop pulling my hair."

I worry about Tachico. I worry about my parents having to deal with so many people needing help. I worry that Otocco isn't back from the highlands yet. Mother insists he is fine and that she would know in her heart if he wasn't. And yes, I know that Father wanted Otocco to go farther inland to find out what the Warpa are doing, but still . . . Otocco is alone. "He can take care of himself," Father insists. I am about to say that he could not fight off a whole group, but Father pats me reassuringly and adds, "Patya-cha, most Warpa are peaceful farmers. They are not a threat."

CALL OF THE OWL WOMAN

When I remind him of the raiders that people have been complaining about, he brushes it off. "A few hungry renegades." When I tell him about Mochico's encounter up north, he says, "That's different."

Father does not know about what happened to me. Mother and Paya Kuyllay had feared that if the men of our community knew, they would not have hesitated to seek revenge. Not just on Warpa men, but on their sisters and daughters. So they let everyone believe what Tachico thought when he found me at the bottom of the cliff, that all my injuries came from the fall. Of course no one would ever know why I really fell. They kept the whole thing secret. To protect more innocents from being hurt, they said. To keep one incident from escalating into terrible violence. Something possibly even more terrible than my own.

I do know that not all Warpa are violent, and I do understand that Otocco knows how to be careful. What worries me is that he might not want to be. He might actually want to walk into danger, might actually hope to find violent people. He left Cahuachi in anguish about Tachico. He had faced death alone in an angry sea. He had even hoped for death when he thought the shark had killed Tachico. The Otocco who came back was somber and subdued, different from the Otocco who used to tease me without mercy. I saw how afraid he was that Tachico might still die. If Tachico doesn't make it, I worry that Otocco won't want to keep living. What's worse, I don't think Otocco believes that Tachico will survive.

My relief almost chokes me when Otocco finally returns. Like my heart is too full to fit and rises into my throat. I swallow the sobs that want to come out. He wouldn't like the fuss. He's somber still, but calmer. He reports that the earthquake didn't affect the highlanders as much as us, and he felt no threat from them.

Revelations

Otocco has returned as a softer version of his old self. He sits with the sleeping Tachico, patiently describing his whole journey while leaning back against the rock wall with closed eyes, reliving it all. My muscles strain with him in the jagged climb to the high plateau, cutting through thorns and brush to reach the ledge where the waterfall used to be. When he reaches the part of the ritual where he pours the seawater into the old spring's mouth, there, at the source of the Uchumarca, I feel his enthusiasm. His voice grows stronger. The sense of hope grows with the telling.

"And you would not believe what happened when I threw the pot into the spring! It shattered with such force that some of the pieces ricocheted off the rocks all the way back up to my feet!" He lifts a shard, waving it as he speaks, as if Tachico were watching, spurring him on. "The piece that came back had the eye of the orca, Tachico. It came back because it was meant for you." He places it in our little brother's hand. Tachico's face registers no change, but his hand closes over the fragment. The orca's eye peers out from between his fingers.

Otocco leaves the next day to help repair the canals and homes along the Trancas River. He announces that he will stay there until everything is done. Mother receives the news silently. She wants him to stay closer to home, but even with everyone working long days, it will be months before they can mend all the damage from the earthquake. It's obvious to me, if not to Mother, that Otocco does not want to be here. He cannot bear to see Tachico this way.

With Keyka unable to walk, Quri and Nikta manage most of her tasks. When Old Man Terzhic dies, it seems strange that his widow sends for me, not for my mother's helpers. I beg Mother to send someone else. Anyone else. "Terzhic is a very important man," Mother reminds me sternly. "Chanki himself brought his mother's request that you be the one to help prepare him for burial."

"Why didn't he ask me himself then?" I complain. "He has avoided me since we returned from Cahuachi."

"He was in a hurry. His mother is beside herself. She never believed Terzhic was so close to death. She also sent for Achiq. I have sent word to your father to come quickly with your brothers."

On my way to Terzhic's, I hear rumors that the old man's last breath was used to curse someone. I wouldn't be surprised if it were true. At some point in his life, Terzhic fought with nearly every man in their village. He complained about everything from water allotments and irrigation plans to who was chosen to sponsor local festivals. He was quick to anger when his children were not given positions of honor and bristled if he thought his wife was not deferred to properly. Terzhic cultivated the land that his parents had worked—the section closest to the well where the water was most abundant, at the beginning of a major section of canals. No one lived upstream, so there was no one who could restrict or redirect the flow of water.

Terzhic insisted that his ancestral lineage came from the Creator Wiracocha himself. Even though it was my ancestors who built the wells, the puquios, the canals, he claimed that the waters that fed his fields were sacred gifts and the first offerings to Pachamama. He argued that his having a greater share of water was right and good. Ensuring better crops for him would ensure better crops for everyone. He convinced his neighbors that the Apus would bring fertility to their lands only if Terzhic's own crops flourished. His neighbors helped him cultivate his fields before tending their own.

Terzhic's public offerings were always given with grand display. Yet when it fell to him to host a festival, he would provide only the bare minimum while deriding others who did not contribute generously. His bullying tactics were effective. Everyone

Revelations

contributed double when he hosted, so his festivals were the grandest, and he happily claimed credit.

The rumors that he used sorcerers to harm those who opposed or offended him still make me nervous, but I remind myself that even if Terzhic traveled through life governed by greed and resentment, his death may still offer him a chance to be released from the meanness and cruelty that poisoned his life. Nevertheless, the dead who are displeased when they come back on the fifth day to look for food often stay to haunt those who offended them in life. I do not want to give Terzhic any reason to bother me from beyond the veil, so I must take extra care with the preparations.

I try to focus on something positive about Terzhic so I can concentrate better on the work. *He loved his family*, I tell myself. *He loved his family.*

Terzhic's home is filled with the heavy fragrance of burning copal. Nuqta, his widow, watches sullenly as I unpack my herbs and oils. "Has your brother come out of his sleep yet?" she asks.

"No."

"Then it's true?"

"Is what true?"

"That the sea still holds his spirit hostage?"

I glance up as I arrange my jars. "What do you mean?"

Nuqta busies herself with the burial linens. "This is the finest cloth I've ever woven," she says, smoothing the gauzy fabric. "The gods have always blessed our cotton. My husband knew how to please them."

"Why do you think the sea has my brother's spirit?"

Nuqta holds the fabric over her heart and sighs dramatically. "If your father had been serving the traditions humbly and correctly, he would not have held his son back from the honor offered him, and we might now all have water in our wells." She brushes the hair from her husband's forehead. "My Terzhic knew these things. The gods blessed his cleverness with good harvests, the

CALL OF THE OWL WOMAN

best wool, and many children." She looks at me pointedly. "And gave good husbands for all his daughters. Perhaps if Yakuwayri's mission were more successful, even you would have a husband and my Terzhic would still be alive."

I reply formally, "I don't understand what you refer to, honored aunt. Chanki returned with a good catch, did he not?"

"Don't pretend with me, child. You know the mission I speak of," Nuqta snaps.

"If you are referring to the mission of which we cannot speak, then surely you know that the offering was completed." Even if Nuqta chooses to disregard the tradition of secrecy, I am not comfortable speaking of it openly. But if there was yet another secret objective for the mission, I want to know. I have been suspicious of Achiq's actions and motives, but I always thought of him as an opportunist, not a killer. Yet either he did nothing to prevent Tachico from following his brother into danger, or he deliberately put Tachico in harm's way. I remember after the tunnel collapsed on Tachico how Achiq implied it would have pleased the gods if Tachico had spilled more blood. And his comment about a child's umanqa having the most power was more than unnerving. I think of the morbid pleasure Achiq seemed to take in Tikati's death, but would he actually murder someone? I am angry that he makes Tachico's injury sound like a lost chance to gain favor with the gods, but I have to wonder if he had planned it all along.

If Nuqta believes a human offering is necessary, then others must be thinking the same thing as well. Had Achiq been sowing the idea before they left? Had Chanki played a role? Is that why he avoids my questions?

I try to remember what Chanki told Mishka . . . He had left Tachico with Achiq, at Achiq's request. Left them talking about fishing. Achiq told Father that Tachico was so eager to fish that he ignored all his warnings. But I doubt Tachico would have

208

Revelations

gone out without encouragement. Achiq said he was preparing an offering for the sea when Tachico "snuck out on his own." He suggested that perhaps it was because the sea had called him. To a greater purpose. Why do I always think that when Achiq talks about greater purposes and the gods' will, it has more to do with Achiq's hidden purposes?

I swallow my growing rage and try to pretend I have no idea what Nuqta is talking about. "Your son is a great fisherman," I say. "He brought back a very impressive supply of dried fish. I don't think the sea would have shared such bounty each day if she were unhappy with their visit."

"Chanki's father didn't send him to catch fish. And your father will need much more than sea-foam to get the gods' attention." I am startled by the hatred in the old woman's eyes. "When my great-grandfather headed the Council," she hisses, "he knew how to honor the gods. There was never a lack of water."

I hold my tongue. It is true that Nuqta's great-grandfather led the village council during a time almost as bad as these. But it was our clan who located the underground rivers, my ancestors who guided the canal building, who irrigated the fields. There have always been water-guardians and diviners among my people. Nuqta's great-grandfather took credit for the aquifers, the canals, the sacred wells, for everything. Both Nuqta's and Terzhic's clans are good at claiming credit for other people's work.

"What was Uncle Terzhic hoping for from the mission?" I ask, trying to keep the suspicion out of my voice.

"What every man hopes for. Strength. Health. Another season." Nuqta hands me a vial. "Be sure to add this oil of snake to the ones you use on his skin." She unwraps a golden breastplate and sets it on the side table next to the tunic. "And polish this well. He must look his best."

I recall Terzhic's regalia from the last solstice gathering. How impressive it was when he stood facing the sunrise, resplendent.

CALL OF THE OWL WOMAN

The way the gold reflected the sun's rays made it seem that light exploded from his chest.

With that memory comes another, one from stories of old, about a young girl dressed all in gold on a solstice sunset, standing atop the hills at Cahuachi. About how she was as bright as the sun itself, brilliant with pure splendor, and how she crumpled after as her blood spilled into the goblet that would inaugurate the new canal. That was what Nuqta's great-grandfather had done as leader of the Council the night before inaugurating the new canals. The next day, as water flowed into the fields, the people celebrated his ability to please the gods with the sacrifice, not the engineers who had designed and built the canals.

Nuqta makes a great show of holding the burial mask up for me to appreciate. The sun-face sprouts rays in the shape of snakes, each studded with shining stones and polished shells. "A generous offering to the sea might have given my husband another season. But since it was not to be so, at least he will go to the next life with honor, shining like Father Sun."

I look from the mask to Terzhic's withered face, the sunken cheeks, the circles under the eyes that are being held closed by silver disks. He looks oddly peaceful in death, a body that has surrendered, however reluctantly, to its final rest. Nuqta lowers the mask gently over his face and turns back to me. "Now it falls to me to finish his work." She places a bowl of flowers at his feet and mumbles something unintelligible that could have been either prayers or complaints, then announces, "I will bring my daughters to help. While I am gone, polish that mask until it shines brighter than any you have ever seen."

I stare at the floor. "As you wish, Aunt Nuqta."

Nuqta grunts as she makes her way to the door, then adds, "Your family might want to think twice about keeping that stranger in your home. He will only bring more trouble."

I wait until Nuqta's footsteps are no longer audible before

Revelations

turning to my task. I stare at the body on the mat, so much smaller than he looked in life. The mask is lighter than it looks and seems to leap in the air when I lift it from Terzhic's face. I fumble to keep from dropping it. Not only would Nuqta be furious and accuse me of dishonoring the dead, but what if Terzhic's spirit took offense enough to come after me? I catch my balance, take a deep breath of relief, and tighten my grip on the mask.

Then I look down.

Terzhic's eyes stare back at me. They are wide open, shining out of their dark sockets. A sickly grin spreads across his face.

chapter 21
Monkeys

I try to look away from the dead man's eyes. My heart pulses against my ribs. I want my hands to put the mask back on his face. I beg my legs to take me out of this room, but my feet won't move. My hands won't move. I am frozen, staring into his face while the disks that had covered his eyes thud against the ground.

I tell myself to breathe. Break the spell. Breathe. The incense chokes me. Outlines of the old man's face begin to blur. Voices nudge from the shadows—my mother telling me to see beyond my eyes, Kuyllay whispering about other realms. But I still cannot breathe. The air thickens with an unearthly mist, and my throat tightens against the urge to cry. *Please, let me breathe.* I remember Mother speaking of fogs that linger near the dead, of strange happenings in the times nearest death. Why can't I remember what she said? Why can't I MOVE?

Suddenly, he blinks.

I gasp for air.

He blinks again, like a baby waking from sleep. His leathery wrinkles soften into a swirl of color that floats just above his skin, sparkling like dust in a gentle sunlit breeze. The strange haze

Monkeys

hovers and shifts above the corpse, morphing slowly, forming and unforming itself into different features as if unsure of the shape it wants to take. Then it settles, relaxes, eerily at rest. But the face that looks up from the table is Tachico's. A look of confusion crosses his face. He looks past me, through me. He seems lost. And then he is gone. The face is Terzhic's again. The eyes are closed. Whatever spell was holding me breaks at the sound of commotion at the door. Nuqta is arguing with her daughter. "It has to be tonight. I know your father. He will not wait all five days to return for his meal! We must have food for him here tonight and for the next five nights. We must make sure he is satisfied. I will not have him following me around!"

I lower the mask back onto the yellowed body. His face is as stiff as before Nuqta left. While mother and daughter bicker, I squat to pick up the discs and slide them back into place under the mask.

Nuqta strides over to me, announcing, "I have changed my mind. My daughters and I will attend to my husband. Everything must be perfect." She shoulders past me and reaches for the oils. "Leave these. I will send for you if I need anything else."

I bow my head and slip out of the room, happy to be free of this place.

The walk home is unbearably long. Shadows swell from behind boulders as if reaching for me, only to be sucked back into the darkness just before they touch. I speed up as if that will help. They say the veil between worlds grows thinner near someone who is still crossing, but I never imagined it thin enough for Tachico to peer through from another realm. I have heard of the dead speaking through the living but not of the living speaking through the dead. I have chanted and rattled for Mother when she enters other realms, and I have seen her find pieces of the soul lost during great fright or pain. I have watched her cure children of their scares and help hunters reclaim their courage.

CALL OF THE OWL WOMAN

The time has come to do that for Tachico.

The thought that Nuqta and Terzhic were hoping for Tachico's death shocks me yet doesn't surprise me. It fills me with fury. What dark pact has that family made with Achiq? I break into a run. Mother must bring Tachico home from the beyond before we lose him forever. I feel him drifting away, lost and confused, being swallowed by darkness.

I miss Tachico. I think of how he always got underfoot and annoyed people but made everyone laugh. How he would beg Kuyllay for stories, and how, when she was busy, he would beg me. Especially for stories about monkeys. He never tired of hearing monkey tales, especially the one about the monkeys and the giants. That story hovers at the edge of my thoughts like a song eager to be sung. I let its rhythms drive my feet toward home.

In the ancient age of darkness, giants ate what they could find.
They lived in caves and ate the bats and fed on their own kind.
The monkey clan hid well in trees, but always lived in fear.
One day, they begged Creator, "Please take us far from here!"

Creator's mood was generous; he understood their fright.
He banished all the giants and bathed the lands in light.
He folded all the earth in waves and built the mountains high,
Then exiled all the giants to the dark and frigid side.

Those mountains formed a solid wall that kept the monkeys safe.
Abundance filled the newborn world, a fruited land of grace.
But a wily little monkey grew so bored of light and fun
That he went to ask Creator at the setting of the sun,

"Where do you go when darkness comes? What lives beyond the
peaks?"

Monkeys

The sun replied, "A place, my child, where giants eat the meek."
"Not me!" said Monkey, curious, and set off on his own
To see what really happened in the fearful giant zone.

So, Monkey hid in a chicha jar,
*   where he watched the giants from afar,*
Not knowing of Creator's plans to rid the giants from the land.
The clouds unloaded heavy rains,
*   unleashed a flood from hills to plains.*
Poor Monkey child was swept away
*   and would have died that very day.*

But he grabbed a leaf that floated by
*   to shield his jar from the pelting sky.*
When the waters finally left the land,
*   the jar came to rest on a gentle sand*
Where Yuraq Orqo, hill of white, begged the sun to end the night.
When Monkey's head at last peeked out,
*   Creator called him "brave and stout!"*

"The world," he said, "must start anew
*   with two-legged creatures as clever as you!"*
He formed some new beings with agile hands,
*   able to walk and run and stand,*
Friends for Monkey, with warmth and mirth,
*   who promised Creator to care for the earth.*
Thus came the humans, molded from clay,
*   and gone are the giants of long-ago days.*

Tachico used to recite the story to anyone who would listen. Sometimes that was only Chochi. "It's about your brave ancestors," Tachico would tell him excitedly, "and a little adventurer just like you!" He would describe the giants with gusto and always

CALL OF THE OWL WOMAN

managed to find a clay jar big enough to hide in when he acted out the curious monkey. I wonder if he dreams of it now—of that jar, floating in the darkness, not knowing where it will take him.

When I reach Mother, she is patiently coaxing food down Tachico's throat. I pull her aside to talk. She is not surprised by what I tell her. "Terzhic is passing between worlds," she says, "the veil grows porous around him. And you, Patya, are becoming more sensitive. Enough to see into that beyond. Enough to see that we . . ." She takes a breath. "We are not reaching Tachico." Her voice is steady, but it does not have the confidence I'm used to.

"Your brother is lost, Patya. Untethered and wandering."

Her anguish pains me. With as much conviction as I can muster, I tell her, "Monkey can help him find his way back."

She tilts her head as if listening to something in the distance, then nods slowly. "Of course," she says. "He loves all things monkey. His favorite stories. His favorite pet."

"His favorite ritual walk," I add.

She almost smiles as she talks to herself. "Monkey energy . . . Yes, it might get his attention. Summoning it with ceremony. Amplifying it. Yes, a beacon to help him find his way back."

"We can use the path," I add. "He really, really loves the Monkey Path."

"Yes," she says. "When your father's clan gathers on the plains to walk the Dog Path, Tachico always heads straight to the monkey as soon as we complete the rituals."

"Exactly. While everyone's feasting, he's off spinning down the other path, and I'm always right behind him. I know he'll feel us walk it. It will bring his attention back here, back home."

Mother shakes her head. "Carrying him there would take too long. The thread between his soul and his body is stretched thinner every day. We—"

"We don't need to make the trek to the plains," I interrupt. "We can make a small version of the path right here. Like we

216

Monkeys

did with the Tree Path for Ecco's wedding dance. I've walked the Monkey Path with Tachico so many times I could draw it from memory. The campground area that the caravan used would be perfect."

"Yes!" She looks at me as if suddenly actually seeing me. "Achiq will be using the plaza for Terzhic's rituals." She takes my hand. "We must work quickly. And you, Patya, will be the one traveling beyond the veil. You will be the one to find him."

I stare back, confused.

Me?

Tachico and I have explored a lot together—valleys, hills, plains, caves, ravines. But traveling beyond the veil into unfamiliar worlds, into other realms? That's the territory of spirit-talkers, shamans, priests, healers who know the way back. People with experience. Like Mother.

Not me.

I tell her as much, but she says, "Where do you think you go during your dance-trances? Where do you think your visions and dreams come from? Those realms are not foreign to you."

I can't believe I let her convince me.

We plan it out. Mother will stay beside him, pray over him, anchor him physically. A few dancers will follow me on the path, pounding our rhythms and design into the earth so Pachamama herself will echo it. While my feet connect me to this world, my spirit will fly beyond it. My father and brothers will stand at the corners, keeping the space safe for us.

We go back inside and sit together in silence beside Tachico, sharing the weight of the unknown, the crushing fear of losing him forever.

That's where I am when the dogs start barking and Chochi seems to fly through the door. He buries himself in my lap.

In the opening behind him looms the figure of Achiq.

chapter 22

Achiq

Chochi burrows his head under my arm, trembling. I am on my feet before I have time to think. "What did you do to him?" I glare at Achiq, turning my shoulder to keep Chochi out of his reach. There are only two people Chochi doesn't like—Uncle Weq'o and Achiq—but when Achiq came for Paya Kuyllay's head, Chochi had not been scared of him. He had tried to defend Kuyllay from Achiq's knife. I wonder what Achiq has done to make Chochi so afraid now.

Achiq addresses Mother, lifting his head as if speaking to me is beneath his dignity. His haughty whine grates at me even more than Nuqta's. "Your vicious monkey," he begins, curling his lip around the word "vicious" as if he enjoys the taste. "Your vicious monkey behaves as badly as your daughter, Keyka. You should do something about that before one of them attacks someone less forgiving than myself."

I don't care if he is a high priest. His arrogance makes my blood boil, and I am ready to bite the man myself.

Mother replies with a respectfulness I know is forced. "Revered

Achiq

Achiq, you honor us with your visit. Is there something we can do for you?"

How can she stay so calm? So careful, so smooth. So fake.

"The purpose of my visit is to honor Terzhic," he says, as if correcting Mother. "Terzhic was a valued leader in this community and a generous contributor to the temple. His burial must be given proper importance." I chew on my lips to keep from saying something that will get us all into trouble. Everyone knows that anything Terzhic gave to the temple was done for show. He got far more favors from the priests than he ever gave.

"Rest assured," Mother replies, "we will assist his family in every way we can." She gestures to me to help her stand. "As I trust that you will assist our community in every way you can. The earthquake hit us hard. Yakuwayri and his team have been busy with canal repairs. Homes need rebuilding. I hope you bring support, perhaps some of the food stores from the temple?"

"You are not the only people suffering," he sniffs. "What would be best for all our ayllus is to make right our relationship with the gods. Once they are satisfied, balance will return to our lands. The rains will return to the mountains, the rivers will fill, the guanaco will return. It is your family, in fact, that holds the power to end this suffering."

Mother stands before him, silent. She will not give him the satisfaction of responding or asking how.

Achiq puffs up like an angry rodent. "Your son, Keyka. You say he once offered his blood to Pachamama, yet you defy the gods by keeping his body after they claimed it."

There it is. He has come for Tachico.

Mother leans toward him as if to confide a secret, but her voice is loud enough for his guards outside to hear. "Divine will is difficult to decipher, as you well know, Achiq. Everyone looks to the temple for guidance, but the drought has only worsened.

CALL OF THE OWL WOMAN

Perhaps the gods are testing us, as you like to say so often. Perhaps the gods claim Tachico for a destiny you have not anticipated. Perhaps they are visiting with him now as his body heals. You would not want to disturb their work, would you?" She meets his eyes. "Perhaps they have accepted Terzhic's life as an offering?"

Achiq steps back. "Do not try to talk circles around me, woman. We are at the edge of the solstice. We must complete our offering before our Father Sun, the great lord Tayta Inti, begins the journey back to center. Terzhic's funeral wrapping has been completed. He will be honored here tomorrow and return with us to Cahuachi to be buried and honored in the solstice ceremony. His tomb will be prepared there. As will your son's. If, as you suggest, Tachico is resting with the gods in spirit, he will rest even better when his body is released to them completely. When the sun sets tomorrow, you will begin his funeral preparations. My sacred knife will complete the ritual. Tachico's burial bundle must return with us as well."

His face, cold and hard, turns from my mother to me. "The temple guard will stand watch here to see that you comply. Defy me and you will condemn others to die as well."

Mother's calm unnerves me. She answers coolly while my heart burns in my throat. "We will honor the wishes of the gods, as you have stated. Allow us our own ceremony for Tachico tomorrow. If the gods will him to live among us, they will bring his spirit back to his body before you return. If their desire is that he go with you, so be it."

I am stunned.

Achiq, satisfied, turns and leaves.

His guards remain, standing rigidly along the path below our home.

chapter 23
Ceremony

A gentle morning light bathes the grounds where we gather to create our Monkey Path. At the southern edge I dig a small hole in the shade of the old guarango. The soil is dry and packed but gives way. As soon as it is deep enough, I kneel and press my forehead to the dusty ground. "Bless us with your healing, beloved Pachamama. Please accept this offering in gratitude." I hold my offering up toward the east where the sun is about to rise. "Bless us, Tayta Inti," I pray. "Shine your way into the shadows to light the way back for Tachico." I hold it toward the northern hills. "Creator Wiracocha, send us winds of hope, lend us your strength and wisdom." Finally, I hold it toward the west. "I call on you, Mama Cocha, beloved Mother Sea, to help us return our beloved brother, who has left his soul in your loving hands while his body mends. His blood has mingled with your sacred waters, which makes him your son as well. Great Mama Cocha, his flesh has fed your other children—please accept that as his offering and release his soul from your watery depths. He is but a small thing in your vastness but so huge in our aching hearts. We ask that you help him find his way back to his body, that he may walk among us again."

CALL OF THE OWL WOMAN

I bury the offering with reverence. "Pachamama, through your eternal embrace with your sister Mama Cocha, help it be so." Ecco has made a drawing on a small cloth that we use as a pattern, the way weavers use grids for their designs. Marker stones along the ground guide me as I scrape the design into the dirt with my staff, outlining the path, the map for my journeying. The line starts by creating the tail. I hold a rope attached to a post at the center and create a spiral, gathering the rope slowly as I circle around the post, closer with each round, keeping the path aligned with the marker stones. Four times I pass around the post while I work my way in toward the tip of the tail, then I pass it four times again going out. When the tail is complete, I continue scratching out the long sloping curve of the monkey's back and continue up to shape the head.

After outlining the ears and neck, I drop down to trace the wide embrace of the monkey's arms. I will place Tachico's mat there, in that open area, just above the hands. It will be as if he is being cradled by a giant monkey. Tachico and I used to make up stories to explain why the second hand has only four fingers while the other has five. Maybe it was bitten off by a puma when the wily monkey escaped its grasp, crushed by a rock in a landslide, or chopped off by a sorcerer for a magic stew. I imagine Tachico making up a new story about a monkey who lost a finger while fighting a shark.

I move on to trace the monkey's belly and legs and create the line that exits down and out under the tail, parallel to the line that entered. On the pampas that line continues out of the monkey and zigzags around. The extra line length is good for organizing big groups, but all we need is the body. I step back to look. From the ground I can't see the whole shape clearly, but I feel it. Otocco signals from the hillside that it looks good. Faruka and Ecco follow behind, widening the line for the dancers to see it better. When we finish, we are all caked in a mixture

Ceremony

of dust and sweat. The Monkey Path is ready. Unlit torches stand ready.

We prepare ourselves and return in the late afternoon. Mother and Father bring Tachico on a stretcher and place it inside the circle formed by the monkey's arms. After setting out her bowls of herbs and hot coals, Mother lights some fragrant incense on either side of Tachico. She sets a Pachamama stone by his feet. Carved into the stone is the round earth mother figure with a serpent sliding up over her shoulders and a frog atop her head. Her navel holds a stone of soothing blue. Just above Tachico's head I place my talisman pouch embroidered with spirals and stars.

Mother has painted an image of the Monkey near Tachico's elbow, with the tail above the bend and the rest of the body below it so that Monkey will always be facing him, arms wide open. She unrolls her leather tattoo kit with its needles and powders. During the ceremony, prick by prick, she will add the ink to make the image permanent.

I put my special bag on the ground next to her and lean into her ear to speak. "I have a confession."

I still haven't told Mother anything about how Waqar helped me substitute another umanqa in its place. She doesn't even know about the other umanqas yet. But having Kuyllay's umanqa here is why I am confident that the ritual will work.

Mother rests her hand over mine before I can open the bag and holds up her hand to stop me from speaking. "Whatever you are about to tell me? Don't. I can feel the power of whatever is in that bag, but do not show me. What I have not seen, I cannot answer for. What no one else sees, they cannot report."

Her hands cup my cheeks as she leans her forehead into mine and whispers, "I am sure that whatever you have done, it has your grandmother's blessing."

No one but Waqar knows about sneaking Paya Kuyllay's umanqa out of the temple, but I wonder if Mother's special vision, or

CALL OF THE OWL WOMAN

the wachuma, showed her something. I want to ask her if she knows about the Warpa and the other umanqas, but this is not the time.

When I left Cahuachi with Paya Kuyllay's umanqa in my bag, the feeling of triumph gave me a surge of energy and confidence. The secret buoyed me, like having a hidden weapon. But with Tachico's decline, that confidence began to wane. Nuqta made me see how dangerous Achiq is, even when he is away. All this time he has been stirring up trouble, maneuvering to take Tachico from us again. Now Terzhic's death and Achiq's return make Tachico's recovery even more urgent, but it also feels more possible. Without realizing, Nuqta also helped me realize the need to summon Mother Sea for help.

I trust that Monkey Path will help me reach Tachico. Paya Kuyllay is with me. The energy from her umanqa radiates from the bag. I feel it move into the ground and up through my staff. I twist the point of my staff until it is well anchored in the earth, next to the Pachamama stone by Tachico's feet. I kneel and place the bag against the soles of Tachico's feet, holding my hands over it in prayer. "Paya Kuyllay, thank you for your protection and guidance. Please keep Tachico from harm. Hold the thread between us while I dance between worlds. Help me find what he lost. Beloved Paya, help me bring him home." I look up to Yuraq Orqo and call on her spirit. In her honor I have painted my face and legs with spots. Feathers cloak my arms, and strings of beads swish softly from my neck. I am ready.

I look up as the drums begin. My heart leaps to see Yantu leading them. As if he feels my eyes on him, he looks right at me and smiles his shy smile. The jolt of connection buoys me. I feel at this moment as if anything is possible.

A chorus of antaras, panpipes, and flutes join the drumming, and my feet itch to move. The music pulses and vibrates through the ground and echoes back from the hillsides. It charges me, fills me.

Ceremony

Mother sings the opening prayers as I lift my rattle and melt into the rhythms. She chants her prayers over Tachico and over the gifts brought in offering: fresh flowers and dry seeds folded into a cloth in a pot to be buried, sweets and llama fat, rare and fragrant resins to be burned after dark beside the mountain, a delicate bundle of herbs and colorful ribbons for the waters to carry our prayers to the sea. The offerings will be embraced in the other realms as part of the ritual exchange—taking Tachico's place so that he will be free to leave. Eight people circle Tachico, humming steadily, their hands hovering just above his body.

Mother cues me to rise. I take the cup from her hands, drink the bitter brew, then give it back and open my arms for her blessing. As she circles me with her rattle, I close my eyes. The sound spirals around me. Her voice mixes with the rhythm of the seeds in the gourd and the rustle of dry leaves as they shake. "Let the spirits guide you. Let the wind speak to you. Let the ground carry your feet and the sky carry your heart. May you find what you need, may you serve the greater good, may you return with the answer to our prayers." I begin to vibrate along with them until my feet insist on moving toward the entrance to the path. I circle Tachico with my own rattle, then pass through the opening between the monkey's hands and dance my way in steady steps toward the line that will take me into the monkey's tail.

Dancers stand waiting and ready along the line. One by one, they join the procession behind me, marching, twirling, dancing along the path, singing songs of remembrance. I let myself drift, feeling my body navigate the solid world at my feet while I merge with the mystical world of the soul.

I am lifted by the music, floating high above the path even while my feet follow the pattern in the dirt. I do not need the wachuma for my soul to journey to the top of Yuraq Orqo, though I welcome its company, the glistening taste of light in the landscape, the hum of life in the stones. The pulse of the drums carries

Call of the Owl Woman

me, carries my prayers to Sun and Sky, Wind, and Water. I honor them as I dance and honor the directions each time I face them as the circle turns for each loop of the tail. In the second circle, I meet my allies jaguar-uturunku, owl-tuku, condor-kuntur, and serpent-amaru, and feel their presence beside me and within me.

By the time I am moving along the third ring, I am an empty column that becomes a vessel of sand caving in on itself. Inwardly, I let myself slide downward into a tunnel that begins to form. From the sand emerges Mother Snake, her back rising up to meet me. I hug her close as she slithers through sand that pours into a crevasse. We slide downward, plunging into an underground river that spirals on and on, into the heart of the mountain. Mother Snake grows larger, twisting and shifting until she becomes the curving spine of a winged serpent with talons that scrape along the walls of the tunnel. Wherever she touches, the rocks glisten like living gems, painting the path behind us with light. I hear the rumble of waterfalls just before my stomach lurches with a sudden drop. In the sudden emptiness, our fall is broken by the spread of her wings. She eases us onto a great lake at the heart of the mountain with barely a splash. The water awakens around us in sparkles of greenish light amid the cold stillness of an enormous cavern. She glides in a wide arc then circles inward, leaving a glowing spiral in our wake. There seems to be something floating at the center.

I become aware that in the physical world, my feet have reached the end of the monkey's tail, the center of the spiral in the path, and my body is leaning into the sharp curve that leads the way back out, but my attention is on the world inside Yuraq Orqo. I begin to merge with the winged cat-serpent being, seeing through her eyes, hearing through her ears, knowing through her knowing. My sight, our sight, sharpens. The dark shape at the center comes into focus—a raft made of reeds. Lying on the raft is a body—still, quiet, unmoving. Tachico.

Ceremony

The luminescent spiral around us begins to dissolve into darkness as I, too, dissolve into the magical being, no longer a separate rider, no longer "I" but "we." A sudden current pulls us, and the raft, toward the far side of the cavern, toward the sound of water tumbling over rocks. We reach the raft just in time to curl our wings around it to shelter it from the growing turbulence as the river carries us away. I cannot see Tachico. The water spins us like a bubble of light through the darkness until the mountain seems to open before us. Solid walls disappear as if Pachamama herself is transforming to protect us. Every part of our body is alert.

We plunge again, pulled underwater so far down our lungs ache from the weight of it. We can't breathe in this vast and endless landscape of rock and sand and strange flowing plants. The bottom of the sea. Our wings fold into a tight hug around our body. Our legs pull in. Our claws web and stretch into fins. Our spine arches upward. We change, shift, congeal into a new form. Into Orca. Our lungs are suddenly huge, full of air. We are in the other realm, we remind ourself, a place with different rules. We embrace Tachico with this new self, this "our" self, this otherworldly "we-ness." Tachico, too, begins to change form. We watch him slide downward in a slow spin, the water turbid around him. When it clears, an orca calf appears beside us, drifting in sleep. Tachico the boy has become the young orca ready to be awakened.

On the ground, my feet tread the long stretch across the monkey's back and around its face and ears while Mother's needles mark the path, each prick anchoring Monkey's shape into Tachico's skin. Still, he does not flinch.

Here, in this other world, we nudge the calf gently. We sing the songs Tachico likes to sing but with the calls and whistles of the orca tongue. Slowly, swaying in familiar rhythms, Orca-Tachico begins to stir. Within us something stirs as well. My human feet stomp the earthly ground. The drums feel like echoes of my footsteps, tracing my path and launching me forward. I feel carried by the rhythms, connected to the earth through the beat of Yantu's drum. I am more than me in this underworld, vibrating with the pulse of many beings. Sounds bounce back to us in images and images become sound. We are Orca.

We surface in the sea in view of the three caves of the sacred cove, carved like a face in the hill before us. We flinch when we see the shark, as if we can remember Tachico's pain ourself, feel the ripping flesh cloud the water with streams of red, hear the splintered bone. We watch Tachico's arm pass through the jaws into the shark's throat. We feel, see, hear orca's teeth rip through the beast, sense the ceasing of its heart, watch it sink, watch it bleed, watch other fish feed on the sudden gift from the sea. In the wreckage of its carcass is all that remains of Tachico's arm. I remember Waqar's words, "Tachico will learn to make do with one hand, but only if he can let the other one go. To help him do that, you must retrieve it from the belly of the beast that took it."

I hear again Mishka saying, "You have work to do and damage to undo." I remember her hands over my heart as she told me, "When you free your brother, you will free yourself. When you free yourself, you will free him." What does it mean, to free him? Release him from his coma? His fears? His body, his life?

While my other self physically dances into the monkey's fingers and through the monkey's arms around my sleeping brother, inside my spirit and soul, we are together, we are Orca, we are the sea. We have found Tachico's bones, his flesh-become-food. In this realm we reclaim what was lost, absorb it, transform it back into its state from the Before. The calf awakens and nuzzles into us, Mother Orca, the restorer. We rise together from the water in a glorious leap, fly over the cove, above the caves, high enough to see the thread of river coming from our valley, the ridges that hide other valleys, the peaks beyond them. In the sunlit spray of moisture, Tachico untangles himself from his orca form and

Ceremony

lands his boy self onto this orca's back. He hugs our dorsal fin with both hands and whoops with pleasure.

The air fills with the cry of gulls, the complaints of seals jostling for space on the rocks far below us, the wind singing of mountains and sea. What surrounds us changes us. Feathers and wings replace our orca body. Tachico hugs the rippled flesh of our condor neck as we soar higher, catching the updraft off the sea. We follow the river's narrow ribbon through the desert, inland toward the thickening green that marks Cahuachi. Yuraq Orqo looms beyond. We glide in a slow circle around the mountain of sand. Jaguar woman stands with her hands at her chest in a gesture of prayer. She crosses her arms over her heart and bows in our direction as we approach; she waves us on as we pass. A fox darts down the hill and disappears among the rocks.

Within moments, the rocky plains come into view, with scattered lines and figures ornamenting the surface. We hover over the Condor Path, letting our shadow fill the wings etched across the ground, savoring our connection, then veer toward the Monkey Path. Tachico's excitement is palpable.

On the ground below, a small figure races our shadow toward the monkey, and we recognize Achiq's fox form, even at this distance. He looks up at us expectantly with eyes no mask can hide. We have seen him as Fox before. He studies Tachico with a predator's eyes, intent on catching him, determined to ingratiate himself with his gods by serving up Tachico. He does not recognize me within this Condor form. We circle again, watching the fox watch us.

At the same time, my physical self spies Achiq in his human form, standing beside the strange merchant I encountered with the caravan, Pikaq. They are watching the dancers from the edge of the clearing as I pass through the feet of the monkey on the path. Achiq knows better than to intervene in the middle of a ritual, but I feel his shadow following me. Somehow, Pikaq's shadow is attached to his. Together, they weigh on me, heavy and ominous.

CALL OF THE OWL WOMAN

It feels more urgent than ever that we reach Tachico's sleeping body.

In spirit realm we fold our wings back and dive at the fox, our talons outstretched. Fox hesitates, meeting Condor's eyes as if looking for something he cannot find, then turns and runs. As we near the ground, our form becomes Jaguar, overflowing with Uturunku Spirit. Tachico grips our fur as we land on the sand. I, in a new "we," relish the graceful ease as we glide past Fox. We gather momentum and force, charged by the plains themselves. I am in many places and forms at once, aware of these joined spirits, the energy of the earth, the sky above the hills, the currents of the sea, the body I am physically present in that follows the line where my family is gathered. Father paces a circle around my little brother. My older brothers, Umasapa, and Mochico tend the corners, ready for the dimming light with torches in one hand, rattles steadily pulsing in the other.

Jaguar's power feeds my "I" and my "our," our "we." We pulse with the strength of muscled legs, speeding our mythic selves from the Monkey Path on the plains to our Monkey Path at home. Moisture from our breath beads on our whiskers and dries in the arid wind. We leap in a great final stretch, up and over the monkey's head and into its outstretched hands, just as my physical self arrives at my brother's side. Soul, spirit, and body merge and split and swirl until Tachico's soul body slides down my back and I crouch to let him off. I blow into the heart of his soul, and Tachico dissolves into himself.

Mother blows across Tachico's chest as I kneel beside him, exhilarated and out of breath. "We are back, Tachico," I whisper, blowing against his forehead. Mother's arm rests on my back, helping me anchor again into my own body. As the drumbeat slows, I feel Yantu's gentle support as Tachico's soul weaves itself back together within his body.

Ceremony

I can feel Mother's feelings too. She waits. And watches. And worries.

Then I become aware of something else she is feeling.

As Tachico's soul is being remembered back into his body, so is his memory. And along with it, the physical reality of his injury. The realization rips through my heart that Tachico may not want to stay in his body once he wakes to its new reality.

His soul was able to reclaim the lost arm, to make peace with the loss. But the physical arm is still gone. What if Tachico enjoys the sensation of being reembodied and reconnected to himself in the other realm so much that he decides to let go of this world rather than inhabit an incomplete body?

To wake, he must make the choice to wake. He can also choose not to.

Now I recognize the pain my mother feels. We came to this ritual with the intention of saving Tachico, reuniting the broken parts of his soul to bring him out of his coma. To rescue him from the place of unknowing, of being neither here nor there, not dead but not completely alive. To bring him back to the people who love him so we can help him recover.

When Waqar first instructed me to get Tachico's arm back, I had not thought it possible. How does one retrieve something from the bottom of the sea, especially something that would be eaten and was surely already picked clean? How could anyone find one set of bones among others? Yet, amazingly, in the world beyond the veil, I found much more than I could ever have imagined. Tachico had, indeed, awakened there. He had been whole there, his body complete.

Only now do I realize that he might not want to let go of that wholeness to come back into this one. My heart becomes a heavy

CALL OF THE OWL WOMAN

stone pulling me into a swirl of dread. I had not considered that he could regret his return. What if my hope of saving Tachico from death, of bringing him back to our family, does not turn out to be what he himself wants?

I watch the long rays of the setting sun paint shadows across his face. His breathing keeps getting deeper, coming easy and slow. My own breath hesitates, hovers, wondering if I can accept letting Tachico choose if what he chooses is not what I hope.

Mother is reciting the closing prayers, welcoming Tachico's soul back into his body. The people surrounding him place their hands on him, anchoring all that we have experienced here. She thanks all who came to share this ritual.

His eyes are still closed.

Tears sting my cheeks. I had been prepared for the possibility of not being able to find his soul and bring it back, but I hadn't considered the possibility that Tachico might not want to stay. That his body and soul could be reunited and he could still die. The ritual may have brought him out of the in-between, but we do not know how much the loss of his arm might cripple his spirit.

I place my hand on the stump below Tachico's elbow. In my mind I am in the other world, where the arm is intact. My hand trails down to where his missing hand would be. I lift it up and place it over his heart. "Keep it here," I whisper. "And here." I put my hand over his forehead and press lightly. He is so calm, so quiet, so still not here. I stroke his arm tenderly, careful to avoid the new tattoo. The shape is perfectly placed, its tail curling above the elbow, spine nestled along the curve, and the embrace of Monkey's arms just above the remaining stump. Monkey's face will be there whenever Tachico looks down.

Mother watches me. "Like Monkey," she says, "we are always with him."

Like Chochi, I think. I notice that the little monkey is not in his usual spot next to Tachico. "Have you seen Chochi?"

Ceremony

"He was just here." Mother looks around. When she turns back to me, her face freezes. Her eyes harden at the sight of something behind me.

I turn to look.

The crowd that had surrounded the clearing is closing in on us slowly. At the front is Achiq, walking beside Pikaq with his arm on Pikaq's shoulder. Both are watching me, almost smiling. Then I see what Achiq is carrying. The ceramic orca that Pikaq had forced me to hold. The one he called a shark. The one that triggered my vision of the ancient temple. It's as if I can feel the ceramic in my own hands right now. I try to shake off the creepy feeling and focus on what Pikaq is carrying.

Two monkeys.

Chochi and the little monkey that had led Chochi to Pikaq when we met the caravan.

chapter 24

Return

Achiq looms above me, poised like a hungry vulture. He places the ceramic orca on the ground before my mother. "I bring a gift for your son's tomb." He looks down smugly, almost purring with satisfaction that Tachico is still in a coma. I try to resist the urge to rip the eyes out of his evil face.

"His monkey can go with him," Pikaq says, gripping both monkeys by the scruffs of their necks. His own monkey trembles but does not resist, while Chochi squawks and squirms angrily. He hisses and twists upward, baring his teeth.

Achiq takes out his knife. "It is not too early to begin the consecration. First the pet and then the boy." He grabs Chochi, who wraps his tail around Achiq's arm. Achiq holds him out at arm's length and laughs. "The little ones always think they are tough. They waste all their energy trying to fight those more powerful and then have nothing left."

I stand to face the priest, but Father steps between us. Achiq addresses my parents. "Like you two," he says. "You refuse to give the gods what they ask of you, what it is your duty to give, what they have already chosen. You robbed them of their

Return

offering. The gods had gratefully received the spirit of the water-guardian's son, but you let a stranger steal that spirit's vessel. You must return the body to the gods to make the sacrifice complete!"

He turns to the crowd, calling out for all to hear, "These people are blind to the gods' will! If the gods did not desire Tachico for sacrifice, they would have returned his spirit to his body. You are not blind! You can see as well as I that Tachico's body breathes, but there is no life in him. His spirit has been taken—let his body follow!" His followers cheer their agreement.

Achiq turns back to my father and threatens quietly, "If you do not do this, they will all blame you for what plagues us. In order to ease their rage against your family, you will have to join your son as a sacrificial offering."

I am about to protest when Chochi twists his neck around far enough to strike. Like a viper, his teeth sink into Achiq's arm. The priest lets go. Aware that everyone is watching, he tries to hide the pain and contain his rage. Chochi scrambles into my arms. From there, he leaps down and crawls onto Tachico's chest, turning to hiss defiantly at Achiq.

Achiq hisses back through gritted teeth. "I will make a stew of you, little monster!"

As I reach to pull Chochi to safety, I see Tachico's mouth twitch. He groans. His eyes blink open and he looks around, confused. The moment he sees Achiq, his voice comes out in a raspy growl. "Not with my monkey, you won't."

Every eye turns to Tachico. Before Achiq can react, I shout as loudly as I can, "Tachico is awake! He is back!"

I waste no time. "You heard our honored priest!" I want the whole world to hear. "You heard him challenge the gods to show their will! You heard him say that the gods would return Tachico's spirit to his body if they did not desire his sacrifice. In the name of the temple, Achiq called on them to show their will! Today

235

CALL OF THE OWL WOMAN

they have done so! Let everyone know that Tachico is awake! The gods want Tachico to live!"

A murmur of awe rolls through the crowd. Chanki is visible among a group of Achiq's followers. I shout in their direction. "They sent Orca to save Tachico from the shark! They brought the sailor to take him to shore! They guided our healers to care for his wounds. Tachico is awake! We are blessed!"

Mother calls out, "We are blessed!"

The whole family chimes in, and soon everyone is chanting with us, even those who came with Achiq. "We are blessed!"

The hatred on Achiq's face is palpable. If I don't think of a way to help him save face quickly, we will feel the fullness of his wrath all too soon. I must give him a way out, make it at least look like we are all in agreement. I pray for words as his eyes burn into me with rage. He signals his guards to come forward and raises his arm. As he opens his mouth, I know he is capable of commanding them to execute us before anyone can stop them.

I think of how Kuyllay always reminded us to be grateful, even in the worst situation.

Before Achiq can say anything, I shout, "We must create something to show our gratitude!" I lift my hand next to his. "Like the days of old, let us honor the gods with a new line in the desert! A new path that we may walk and dance in celebration, a path to remember this miracle! A path in the likeness of Orca that future generations may walk and sing! Sing of the orca who saved the boy and sing of the sailor who brought him home!"

In a lower voice, I tell Achiq, "If you lead the clearing of the path and its consecration, they will soon forget that you challenged the gods and ignored their answer. If you leave my family alone, we won't have to remind them."

I'm not sure who is more stunned by my words, Achiq or my parents. Achiq glares at me, but he grasps the significance of this moment. Of how quickly a crowd can turn.

Return

He hesitates, inhales, and then raises both hands. "Praise to Orca! An Orca Path for the solstice!" He turns slowly, repeating it in each direction, gesturing for all to join the chant. Yantu's drum takes up the beat. He catches my eye and smiles.

"An Orca path for the solstice! Blessed be Orca!"

The crowd sings out enthusiastically, "Blessed be Orca!"

My parents hug me.

"Kuyllay would be so proud. I wish she were here," Mother sighs.

She is, I want to say. But instead, I just grin.

chapter 25

Forward

I study my walking stick, my staff, as I prepare to carve some new designs. It has been almost two moons since the solstice gathering on the plains. People came from all over for the celebration of the new line. It was the first time since the drought began that the priests finally shared some of the emergency stores.

Father and Otocco are helping neighbors repair roofs and walls. Tachico has been getting stronger with each day and is now off with Mochico and Ecco collecting clay for a new batch of pots. Keyka is attending a birth with Quri's help and does not need me for anything that can't wait. This is the first time since the earthquake that I have had time to spend in Kuyllay's Grove.

I was surprised that there was so little damage inside the hut. At home, shelves collapsed and hanging pots fell and broke. Only a few of the pots that I took home from the grove survived the quake, yet the ones I left here are still intact. I guess it turned out to be a good thing that I went to Yuraq Orqo before we finished collecting them. It's nice to be back. I may start spending more time here.

A chunk of guarango resin is softening in the bowl over the fire so I can add some new things to my staff. As soon as the resin

Forward

is pliable, I spread some into the fresh gash and press a line of tiny purple shells into the soft resin. I scrape off the excess before it hardens and hold up my staff to study my work. The new cut follows the lines in the wood, spiraling around it like a vine, colored purple with the broken pieces from Tachico's collection of shells he gathered at the sacred cove.

The early days after Tachico regained consciousness were difficult. He was confused, thinking he was still at the cove, and kept asking why all of us had come. With so little strength, he began to despair whenever he tried to sit up on his own. The realization that his lower arm was gone was such a shock that I feared his soul would fragment again. He refused to look at what was left of his throwing arm and preferred to keep it in a sling out of sight.

When Mother hugged him to her and praised his bravery, he just stared past her. She told him, "You escaped a shark, you survived the ocean, and you came back to us, our courageous Tachico."

"Not all of me," he replied flatly.

He was even sharp with me. When I first tried to help him sit and eat, he sputtered, "I am not a child to be babied."

"Even warriors must eat," I coaxed.

"I am not a warrior. I fought no battles. Stop trying to make me feel better."

"Being attacked by a shark—how is that not a battle?"

"Because I don't remember fighting back." He turned his face to the wall.

I put the bowl aside. His eyes did not leave the wall as he spoke. "The last thing I remember was collecting things on the beach," he said, concentrating hard, trying to conjure the memory. "Achiq gave me a bag to put them in." He turned to me anxiously. "Did Father bring it back?"

I tried to soothe him. "I will ask."

"I don't remember where I left it!" He started to get frantic.

"We'll find it," I said. "I'll go look. But first a little water at least?"

CALL OF THE OWL WOMAN

He finally accepted the cup and drank deeply. When he gave the cup back to me, he turned away. "Please?" he said to the wall, so mournfully it broke my heart. "Look for my bag."

"Yes, right away. But please let me put this on your lips first? Otherwise, it will be very painful if you ever decide to smile again."

"I can do it myself."

I slid the ointment onto his finger and watched him dab gingerly at his lips. "Good," I told him. "I'll go look for your bag."

"Maybe you can find me another hand while you're at it," he said sourly before twisting into the blanket and curling into himself with his back to me.

When I returned with the bag of shells and a wide, flat basket to spread out his treasures, he seemed to brighten just a little. Among the loose rocks and shells were several wrapped bundles. He slapped my hand away when I tried to open one. It was difficult to untie with one hand, but he glared at me if I tried to help. When he finally succeeded in opening the first bundle, he pulled out a large purple sea urchin, dry and hollow but with its spines still attached. Another bundle held a smaller sun-bleached pinkish sphere, rubbed clean of its spines. He ran his fingers over the fragile shell before placing it in the basket. He moved stiffly, trying to conceal his pain. When the last bundle came open, Tachico stared at it for a long time. The shell was broken. "This was the prettiest of all the urchins," he said, holding up a curved fragment. "But it's no good now." He threw it to the ground and picked up the bundle, ready to destroy everything.

I intercepted, unable to stop myself. I held the pieces up to admire them. "What amazing shades of orange and purple! It's like a sunset. If you're just going to throw them away, can I have some for my walking stick?" He looked at me dubiously. I added, "They would look beautiful. And remind me of you."

Forward

"Why? Because they're broken?" he snapped sourly.

"No," I replied, trying to hide my own sadness, wondering if my once cheerful little brother would ever return. "Because I love you," I said, "and you're the one who found them and brought them back."

Just as I was becoming convinced that Tachico would remain as lost in his waking despair as he had been in his coma, Mochico turned the tide. That sailor has become more of a blessing than I ever imagined. He made Tachico a spear thrower in the Moche style and taught Tachico how to use it. Now, he can launch his spear farther than he ever did with the hand he lost. Mochico has been able to rally him in a way the rest of us could not. Tachico is now pushing himself to run and climb again, to retrain his body. Whatever may come, I'm confident now that our family can handle it.

Tachico's colorful shell fragments curve like footsteps up my staff. I add more resin to the heat before carving a small hole into a nook near the top of the stick. I fill the hole with the warm resin and press a small green rock into place, a gift from Waqar. It is pleasing to the touch, speckled like a bird egg and smoothed by the sea. I hold it in place until the resin cools enough to secure it, then hold it out to observe the effect. It stares back like a jaguar eye watching from the shadows. "I shall call you 'Eye of the Desert,'" I tell it, admiring its sheen. "Path-finder and trail-maker, companion for journeys of every sort." My next journey will be to Palpa after the new moon to dance for the equinox ceremony with Yantu as my drummer. I am counting the days.

Each time I add something to my walking stick, which also serves as my ceremonial staff, I rub oil into the wood and revisit the places and people that have become part of it. Now it seems to want feathers. I find a clutch of downy tufts in one of Kuyllay's jars and string them with some beads. I glance toward the garden, glad that the owl cloak and tunic are well hidden with the mask.

CALL OF THE OWL WOMAN

I don't know why I have such an impulse to protect it, or what I might possibly need to protect it from, but it feels good to know that I am the only one who knows it is there.

The last of the fire crumbles into ash while I finish my *muña* drink, enjoying its warmth against my hands, savoring the earthy aroma. I smother the fire with a layer of dirt, then sit against the tree to add a bit more polish to my staff. Sunlight filters through the twisted branches and skitters across the ground. I press my spine into the bark, enjoying the tree's kinship as I inhale the sharp scent and visualize its strength flowing through me and into my staff. "You and this place shall be with me and within me always," I say aloud to the tree. I imagine its roots stretching to the distant water below and can almost feel the water's slow pulse upward through the tree's core. I love this great fabric of sand and sun, water and loam, the tireless labor of earthworms and beetles. *That is our miracle*, I muse, *that we can transform and remake. A broken branch becomes a walking stick. The earth takes things old and rotten and turns them into rich new soil. We do not live merely to survive but to create, to build, to transform.*

The wood absorbs the oil thirstily, deepening its color and taking on a mild sheen. The surface comes to life, catching the light and giving it back again. I get the same satisfaction from polishing wood as I do from burnishing ceramics, watching them leap to another level of beauty as the color deepens and jumps to life. I love the way masks and ornaments gleam in the firelight or catch the sun. How far we can see, or be seen, across the plains at night depends not only on the fire but also on the surfaces that reflect it. Light in the darkness is so magical it makes the moth not care what might happen as it flies toward the flame.

I hold my staff up to catch the sun and lean my head back to feel its warmth, but I am seized with a sudden desire to climb the tree. I tuck my staff into a wrinkle in the trunk and choose a route to the high branches. The tree, weighted by its own immensity,

Forward

stretches nearly parallel to the ground for a good distance before its limbs twist back up toward the sky. I work my way up to a nice perch and nestle into a pocket where several branches crisscross. In this place, in this moment, the world feels good. I sink into the tree, into its comforting aromas. Lulled by the golden haze and birdsong, I slide into welcome dreams of a certain drummer, of creatures I have never seen, and of a giant owl who wraps me in her wings.

Glossary

Acari Valley: the Acari River is south of Nasca
Aja Valley: the Aja River runs past Patya's home
Amaru: snake; spirit of the underworld
apacheta: mound of rocks used to connect earth and heaven and consecrate space
Apu: mountain spirit or essence; sacred powerful being, as Apu Illakata
ayllu: clan or kinship-based group
ayni: reciprocity, balance, harmony, communal work, mutual aid

Cahuachi: ceremonial complex along the Nasca River destroyed circa 400 CE
Cerro Blanco: modern name for Yuraq Orqo (mountain/dune sacred to the Nasca)
-cha: diminutive like the Spanish "-ita" (Rosa, Rosita, Rosa-cha)
charqui: dried llama meat
chicha: fermented beverage made of corn
Coropuna: one of the great Apu mountains of the Andes
Council: decision-making groups in each village area, also regional

Estaqueria (modern): Takarpu K'iti, or place of stakes; ceremonial center after Cahuachi

Grand Temple of Cahuachi: destroyed around 400 CE but still used for burials

Great Spirit: general term for the cosmic energy, divine connection

guanaco: camelid; larger undomesticated cousin of the llama

guarango/huarango: hardwood with nutritious fruit; similar to *algarrobo* in the north

huaico: flash flood or mudslide

Illakata: a large mountain close to Nasca

Iphiño: river valley between Nasca and Palpa (modern: Ingenio Valley)

knowing: intuition or psychic insight

kuntur: condor

Lord of Winds: the spirit of Wayra

Mama Cocha: goddess of the sea

Mama K'illa: the Moon

mesa: altar; collection of sacred objects to connect with energies natural and divine

mullu: a rocky oyster from northern waters valued for offerings and jewelry; *Spondylus*

Muña: elite burial ground near Palpa

pacay fruit: a large pod filled with smooth black seeds encased in sweet fuzz

Pachamama: Mother Earth

Palpa Valley: a wider valley to the north, also featuring geoglyphs and petroglyphs

Paracas: bay north of Palpa; home to Paracas culture preceding Nasca; literally translates to "rains of sand"

puquios: subterranean aqueducts connected by spiral openings

pututu: conch shell; blown for ceremonial use or communicating across distance

Glossary

q'enti: hummingbird

quwi: guinea pig; small rodent used for divination and healing as well as eating

roundhead: someone whose head was not elongated by binding as a child

sacred cove: traditional ritual center overlooked by three caves

shaman: one who intercedes between worlds for understanding and healing

Silver Owl Woman: mythic goddess-like shaman dancer

spirit-talker: one who can hear or communicate with beings in the unseen world

Starwatchers: those who study the movement of stars and planets

Takarpu K'iti: place of stakes; ceremonial center after Cahuachi (modern: Estaqueria)

Tayta Inti: Father Sun

temple priests: guardians of rituals and community ceremonies to keep order

tinkuy: joining of energies, as of two rivers merging

umanqa: mummified head with carrying cord; skin removed then refitted over empty skull

wachuma: a cactus "plant teacher" with visionary properties used in ceremony

wanqor wood: a fragrant resinous soft, easily carved wood; palo santo

Warpa: people of the inland mountains

water-guardians: those charged with the care of canals and water resources

Wayra: wind

Wiracocha: Andean creator god; Lord of Wind and Storm

CALL OF THE OWL WOMAN

Wiracocha Brotherhood: secretive tradition of religious nature

yaku: having to do with water

yanantin: the pairing or relationship of opposites, as with light/dark or male/female

Yuraq Orqo: now known as Cerro Blanco, the dune-topped mountain sacred to the Nasca

Acknowledgments

The spark for Patya's story began during a road trip with my teenage daughter across the northern United States. She was missing her native Peru and asked me to write my next book about a girl in ancient Nasca so that we could explore the mysteries of that culture—the giant lines etched across the desert, the curious images painted on beautiful ceramics, and the water systems that helped them flourish in a land without rain. She also wanted to include the challenge of learning to understand people of a different culture, so we added a young man from the northern Moche region.

When we moved back to Lima, I set out to learn as much as I could about how the Nasca lived. Since there was no written language in South America at the time, I relied on archaeologists, anthropologists, and other scientists to help me understand the Nasca world through what they left behind. Several elements jumped out right away: the importance of the orca (killer whale), the ritual use of severed heads, the visionary use of a particular cactus, and the use of the landscape in art and ceremony. With so many theories among scientists and historians, as well as among fans of mystery, mysticism, and otherworldly magic, I wanted to weave together the basic threads and let the reader imagine the rest.

The explanation behind the mummified heads that were common in ancient offerings and sacred places is still a source of debate among experts. Some suggest that they were trophies taken from enemies, some point to evidence that they were used to honor ancestors, and others note how they served as ritual "power objects." The usual terms of "severed head" or "trophy head" seemed limiting, so I invented the term "umanqa" ("*uma*" means head in Quechua).

I did not use Spanish place names or terms but opted to borrow from Quechua, the language that was dominant in the region before the Spaniards arrived, when Cerro Blanco was still known as Yuraq Orqo. In contemporary Peru, the geographical town and region of Nazca are spelled with a "z," but references to the culture and the people use an "s." For consistency in the novel, all spellings use the "s." The letter "z" is not used in the Quechua alphabet.

The books and articles of Anthony F. Aveni, Johny Isla, Tony Morrison, Donald Proulx, Maria Reiche, Marcus Reindel, Helaine Silverman, and Kevin Vaughn were invaluable for learning about the culture and setting. I am especially grateful to the following people for their writings as well as for the conversations and correspondence with them that deepened my understanding of the Nasca world: teacher and historian Josue Lancho Rojas, archaeologist Giuseppe Orefici, archaeoastronomer Clive Ruggles, archaeobotanist David Beresford-Jones, Oliver Whaley of Kew Gardens, physical anthropologists Elsa Tomasto Cagigao and Kathleen Forgey, dowser and researcher David Johnson, and botanical illustrator Olivia Sejura Watkins, a passionate advocate for preserving Nasca's cultural history.

To better understand the cosmovision and earth-honoring traditions of the Andean region, I explored contemporary healing and shamanic traditions and their ancient roots. It was a privilege to learn from gifted healers and teachers. I am grateful to don Oscar Miro-Quesada Solevo for a profound initiation into Andean shamanic traditions in the lineage of his mentors, don Celso Rojas Palomino of Salas and don Benito Corihuamán Vargas of Wasao, and for his celebration of universal wisdom and cross-cultural shamanism. I am thankful for the teachings and

Acknowledgments

support of Ysabel Chinguel Machado and Olinda Pintado Sidia, *curanderas* from Chiclayo and Huancabamba whose roots in the Moche traditions of Peru's northern coast were featured in *The Gift of Life* by anthropologist Bonnie Glass-Coffin, and to Bonnie, whose insight and encouragement buoyed my own work.

Patya's story would not have come into being without the support of countless allies along the way, beginning with my family. Daughter Cristina lit the spark, and she and her brothers helped keep the fire burning. Nicolas and I joined a traditional *chaccu* roundup for an annual winter solstice shearing of wild *vicuñas*, running through the high plateau above Nasca. He and his brother Carlos not only offered encouragement but envisioned how Patya's challenges could be translated into D&D scenarios and video games. My husband Milo has been Patya's biggest fan, my beacon and support, a tireless proofreader, and fellow traveler on the journey from idea to reality, including a magical moonlit night at the top of Yuraq Orqo.

My Lima writers group (the Tertulia) were gifted midwives throughout Patya's development, like fairy godmothers sharing their magic and blessings through countless drafts and revisions: Carla Barnes, Lauris Burns, Rose Boehm, Charlotte Chase, Sara Fajardo, Jessica Federle, Alison Light, and Dina Towbin—Mil gracias, amigas! Special thanks to Linda Paz Soldan for reading the massive very first draft and asking all the right questions, to Anna Mullen for her perceptive insights, to Lisa "Eagle Eye" Sacio for her many readings and feedback (in both languages!), to my SCBWI mentor Sheba Karim for new tools and perspectives, to Nancy Villalobos for her insights and enthusiasm in the final stages, and to the vibrant author community and support staff at She Writes and SparkPress. Endless gratitude to all those who helped bring this book into the world.

About the Author

Photo credit to Kim Stephenson

k. m. huber (she/her) grew up in the Pacific Northwest, climbing trees, wandering in the mountains, wondering about the world, and writing poems. Unforeseen winds carried her to a new life in New York City, chance introduced her to her future husband, and before long another wind carried them together to the stark desert coast of his homeland, Peru. She fell under the enchantment of mystical Andean peaks, magical valleys, timeless tales, and colorful traditions.

Huber worked with educational organizations, coordinated cultural programs, and explored Peru for over a decade. She dove into research about the Nasca, interviewed experts, walked its landscapes, climbed sacred hills, met some thousand-year-old guarango trees, and collaborated with award-winning filmmaker Delia Ackerman on a documentary about deforestation in the Ica region, both ancient and current.

Huber's writing can be found in *Vice-Versa*, *Earth Island Journal*, *Post Road*, *Rougarou*, *The MacGuffin*, and Latin America Press, among others. Her fiction includes *Patya y los Misterios de Nasca* (La Nave, Peru 2023), and she is currently finishing a sequel that takes Patya to Bolivia's fabled Tiwanaku. After twenty years in Peru, Huber now resides in Maryville, Tennessee with her husband, enjoys living close to mountains again, and still Zooms regularly with her beloved "Lima Tertulia" writers group.

Looking for your next great read?

We can help!

Visit www.gosparkpress.com/next-read
or scan the QR code below for a list
of our recommended titles.

SparkPress is an independent boutique publisher delivering high-quality, entertaining, and engaging content that enhances readers' lives, with a special focus on commercial and genre fiction.